ANNA AUGUSTINE

A *Love* LIKE *Ours*

AN HEIRS OF ALLURA COLLECTION
BY ANNA AUGUSTINE

A *Love* LIKE *Ours*

ANNA AUGUSTINE

This book is for all those looking for love.

God's love is waiting for you. I pray, like Paul,
that you have the strength to comprehend how very
great it is. It is better than all we can ask or imagine.

*"So that Christ may dwell in your hearts through
faith—that you, being rooted and grounded in love, may
have strength to comprehend with all the saints what is
the breadth and length and height and depth, and to
know the love of Christ that surpasses knowledge,
that you may be filled with all the fullness of God."*

Ephesians 3:17-19 ESV

ANNA AUGUSTINE

The Princes of Allura Family Tree
King Willhelm the First
Crowned in 1385
b. 1362. - d.1410
Queen Sophia
b. 1364. - d.1387
Queen Rosa
b. 1365. - d.1406
Queen Lidia
b. 1365. - d.1388
Benjamin
m. 1410
Aurora
b. 1386
b. 1388
Nicholas
m. 1410
Della
b.1388
b.1391
Collins
m. 1410
Sage
b. 1390
b. 1392
Willhelm
b. 1412
Silas
b. 1415
Nettie
b. 1420
Louis
b. 1411
Avyanna
b. 1413
Marcus
b. 1415
Brylee
b. 1413
Thaddeus
b. 1415

ANNA AUGUSTINE

FALLING *For* YOU

THADDEUS AND AMIRAH'S STORY

ANNA AUGUSTINE

"For the Lord sees not as man sees: man looks on the outward appearance, but the Lord looks on the heart."

1 Samuel 16:7

1

THADDEUS

ALLURA-1435

The ballroom was a swirling color of chaos that evening as I sat on the dais. I watched as my cousin, Avyanna, swung by in the arms of a dashing young man. I laid my hand on the armrest of my chair, feeling the vibrations of pounding feet and strumming instruments. The musicians' faces were alive as the tune I couldn't hear poured from the tools of their trade.

I smiled. Even if I wouldn't be dancing that evening, the joy of those who were enthused me.

A tap on my shoulder made me turn to meet my father's gaze.

"Are you enjoying the ball?" I read on his lips.

My fingers stryesd to my throat as I said, "It's been fun. Though I still miss hearing the music."

"Have you tried to dance with one of your cousins?" Father gripped my shoulder, a small frown tugging on his lips.

I shrugged. "They are having fun with the other lords. I don't want to pull them away from that."

I couldn't make myself look at my father to read what he wanted to tell me. Ever since that fateful winter ten years ago, I knew I had been a burden. Nothing him, Mother, or Brylee said would change that fact.

Father stepped in front of me, forcing me to look at him. "I'm sure your mother would love to dance with you."

I shook my head, my joy in the vibrations no longer making me smile. "It's fine, Father."

"Thaddeus." He glared at me, running a hand through greying blond hair. "Please don't be stubborn."

"I'm not being stubborn," I scoffed. "I'm being realistic. No one wants to dance with a man who can't lead."

"Is it so bad to let someone lead you?" Father sighed, his shoulders slumping.

"I don't want to have this conversation again, Father."

He may have said something else, but I was already off the dais, moving through a crowd that was silent to me. It was suffocating, and I hurried out the doors of the ballroom.

I leaned my face against the glass windowpane, trying to cool my heated cheeks. I hated that I could no longer hear. It had been ten years. Ten years since the accident that had stolen sound from me. Ten years of pitying glances along with the occasional disgusted one mingled in. Ten years of being a worthless son and brother.

Someone tapped my shoulder. I turned, seeing my cousin, Avyanna, at my elbow.

"Why are you hiding?"

"Me? Hiding?" I laughed harshly. "Why would I be hiding?"

She flinched, and I swallowed the anger simmering in my gut.

"Sorry, Avy."

"Don't apologize, Thaddeus." She laid her small hand on mine, and I glanced down at it before meeting her gaze. Smiling, she cocked her head to the side. "I have a question for you."

"What?"

"Well, I was invited to a party hosted by Lady Pruella of Marchingville. She wants to host some of the young lords and ladies to help secure matches for them."

"Oh no!" I held up a hand, shaking my head. "No, Avy. That's just—that's not a good idea."

"Why not?" She stomped her foot, scowling at me. She looked so much like Aunt Della in that moment that I couldn't help smirking. "Look, I'm two years older than you, but Mother says that I need one of you men to come with me. And it's only for two weeks, Thaddeus."

"It's almost as if she doesn't trust you." I leaned my shoulder between the two windows and continued to smile at her. "This doesn't have anything to do with you kissing Prince Lachlan when he was here, does it?"

Avyanna's lips curled in a frown, but she stammered, "Why…why would it?"

"Mhm."

My cousin glared at me again. "You're the only one available, Thad. Willhelm is busy with his duties as Crown Prince—whatever those are—Silas and Marcus are training new recruits, and—"

"And Louis hates parties more than me." I sighed.

"Yes." Avyanna grabbed my hand. "Please, Thad. I really want to go."

I stared at her for a long moment. "You will owe me."

"Yes!" She nodded furiously. "Yes, I promise."

"And you won't leave me alone at those ridiculous balls?"

She hesitated. "I'll do my best."

I paused for a long moment, watching as Avyanna clamped her lower lip between her teeth. She shifted from one foot to the other. It was fun to watch her squirm with impatience.

"Fine. I'll go."

She clapped her hands before flinging her arms around my neck. I could feel her chest vibrating as she squealed. She stepped back, her lip between her teeth again as she smiled. "Thank you, Thaddeus. I'll never forget this!"

She practically danced away, her green skirt swirling around her ankles like grass blowing in a breeze.

I sighed, turning from the windows. I needed an escape, and there was only one thing that helped me do that.

My hands physically ached as I strode down the hall and out the door, glancing around before ducking into one of the garden sheds. I squeezed around some water barrels, pulling out a box with a half-whittled chuck of wood and my carving knife inside. Settling onto an old seed bag, I smiled at the feel of the lumber and knife in my hands. They were like an extension of my limbs. Carving the wood, smoothing the edges, molding and creating…it was a way for me to express myself in a way that no one else could.

With painstaking precision, I began to shape the wood more and more, forming the figure of my cousin, her dress swirling as she danced among the royals of the courts.

I swallowed, looking into my box. I had ten such figures, all of my family. Mother and Father gazing happily at each other, much like the portrait that depicted their wedding day. My sister, Brylee, laughing at something some suave courtier said. My Aunt Rory and Uncle Benjamin, the King and Queen of Allura, kissing like I'd seen them do once when I had been hidden away in the library.

I sighed, staring down at the carving of Avyanna. No one understood. I could no longer hear, and yet they expected me to continue in the court. To pretend like I couldn't read the disgust on everyone's faces when they looked at me. Few people realized I could read their lips, a trick I'd picked up when I'd been learning to talk without hearing myself. My family had mastered the art of facing me when they spoke so I could be part of the conversations, but others were not as considerate.

I tightened my grip on the knife, swallowing the lump in my throat. sRevulsion, disdain, and ridicule were what I had agreed to endure for two weeks with Avyanna.

It was going to be the longest two weeks of my life.

2

AMIRAH

MARCHINGVILLE

"Mother, look!"

I winced at the high-pitched squeal of my sister, Sophie.

She held up a letter. "Princess Avyanna has agreed to come to our ball!"

"Ah, that is marvelous!" My mother, Pruella, grinned. "Does she say which of her family is escorting her?"

I raised my brow, intrigued at this sudden interest in the royal family.

"Um…" Sophie scanned the letter, her smile slipping as she read. "Her cousin, Thaddeus."

"The deaf one?" My mother's smile faltered as well. "Why him?"

"She said that he is the only one who is available." Sophie pouted, but it didn't last long. "Well, he's better than nothing!"

"You will not try to garner the attention of some…some less than!" Mother huffed. "Honestly, have I taught you nothing?"

"He is simply deaf," I interjected. "That doesn't make him a less than, Mother."

She glared at me with her shining green eyes, much like a hawk stalking its prey. "When I ask for your opinion, Amirah, then you may give it."

I dropped my gaze back to my sampler, pressing my lips into a tight line.

It had always been that way. I had been Father's favorite while Sophie was Mother's. When Father had died, I had discovered the truth—the horrid truth they had hidden from me my entire life. It was why my mother had grown even colder towards me.

"We will just have to make the best of it." Mother sniffed. "If he's handsome enough it doesn't matter, for all the royals are wealthy. Riches make the heart grow fonder.”

I raised my eyebrows at that but said nothing.

“But what if *I* don’t like him?” Sophie’s pretty little pout formed again.

“It does not matter! For you will be a princess!” Mother laughed.

I stood. “Excuse me, I think I hear Cook calling me.”

Mother shooed me away with a wave of her hand and I breathed a sigh of relief when I reached the kitchen, slumping against the wall.

Cook raised her eyebrows. “They’re a bit much today, are they not?”

I laughed humorlessly. “You could say that.”

Cook frowned with pity at me. “You’ll just have to find a young man of your own at this ball, m’lady.”

“Or simply get Sophie married to one.”

“So that you can be a wedding present to her? I think not! We’ll get you married in these next two weeks, we will!”

"You really don't think Mother would make me Sophie's servant, do you? And I'll find my own husband, thank you very much."

"I wouldn't put anything past her, m'lady." Cook shared a look with our housekeeper as she shoved a leftover sweet roll from breakfast into my hands. "If she asks, you're busy."

"Thank you." I kissed the older woman on the cheek.

She blushed, shooing me out of the kitchen with her apron. I paused on the kitchen stoop, breathing in a great lungful of the flowers in the garden before skipping down the steps to go study the blossoms.

After a few minutes in the garden, my hand itched to pick up my tools and get to work. I stepped into the barn, my sanctuary. The sounds of the animals were a soothing balm for my soul. Tomorrow my home would be filled with strangers, yet here in the barn I would always find a respite from the storms of life.

"Good morning, Abner." I kissed my father's old stallion on the nose. He was one of the few animals Mother hadn't sold after Father's death. Whenever she tried, he'd disappear for hours at a time so prospective buyers wouldn't be able to look at him.

I scrambled up into the loft, opening the doors that pointed toward the countryside of Marchingville.

Situated on a hill, our home looked out over the town to the west, and the hills and valleys in the east. Tugging my shawl closer, I finished the sweet roll while staring at the canvas I had been working on the previous day. I tilted my head back and forth, no longer certain what I had been trying to capture. With a shrug, I bent to pick up my pad of parchments and a charcoal stick instead.

Leaning over the pages, I began to sketch the flowers I'd seen in the garden. The tension in my shoulders eased down my arm, through the stick, and onto the parchment. I smiled, deciding that my apprehension about men, mothers, and meddling maids could wait a few hours. For now, I was going to simply enjoy my art in solitude.

3

THADDEUS

"Are you certain this is wise, Thaddeus?" Mother worried her hands, watching me as I turned back to packing my trunk in my particular way. I occasionally glanced up to catch her words. "I'm sure Avy could—"

"I told her I'd go with her, Mother. I'm not breaking my word now. Keeping my word is what you and Father taught me, after all."

It was a low blow, I knew. Yes, my parents had taught me to follow through on commitments, but it wasn't their fault that keeping that one when I was ten had caused me to lose the use of my ears.

Mother's eyes filled with tears as she plopped onto the edge of my bed, still facing me. "I just wish it wasn't simply you and Avyanna going. She's not the most considerate with your feelings."

But she's the only one who doesn't stifle me. I swallowed, folding another shirt just so. "I'll be fine."

"When did you grow up, Thad?"

Tears were trailing down Mother's cheeks and I stopped packing to sit at her side. I gently wrapped my arms around her shoulders, the sweet apple blossom scent that I associated with her enveloping me. "You raised me well."

She trembled but pulled back to face me. "I remember the day I found out I was expecting you. I was so scared, yet you came into this world absolutely perfect. After almost losing Brylee, I was so thankful."

I had heard this story before, yet I never tired of it. It was nice to think that I was someone's answered prayer, someone's miracle.

"And you've grown into such a handsome, kind, and gentle young man." She laid a hand on my cheek. "You will make someone a wonderful husband."

I smothered my retort, forcing a smile onto my face as Mother pecked me on the cheek. I wasn't planning on subjecting a bride to the same looks of disdain I suffered. No one deserved that, let alone a woman.

Mother smoothed out my bedspread as I stood and closed the trunk lid.

"We shall see," I replied, swallowing the lump in my throat. Had I dreamed of love? Of course. But did I think I could obtain it?

I blinked as the red of Mother's skirt filled my downturned gaze as she stepped to my side and tipped my chin up. "You doubt your value. You must stop that, Thaddeus."

"I'm broken."

"You are not broken, my son." She shook her head. "Someday a young lady is going to look at you and see all the things that your father and I do. How strong and brave you are, how kind and loyal. But they will never be able to love you if you don't let down your guard. Don't be so afraid of getting hurt that you risk the loss of love."

I blinked, turning away from her gaze. "If you say so."

She pressed a kiss against my temple, the way she used to when I was a lad. I watched as she stood to her feet. "I'll let you rest. I'm praying for you, Thaddeus."

"Thank you, Mother."

The door clicked closed, and I flopped onto my back, staring up at the ceiling. Prayers had done little in the last ten years. I had petitioned God over and over to give me back my hearing. And in some ways, I supposed He had. He'd helped me learn to speak again, how to feel my own vocal cords to know what volume I was talking at. He had helped me to read lips so that I could once again communicate with those around me.

But I wanted to truly *hear* again. Hear my sister laugh, the birds sing, my mother and father's voices. A tear trailed down my cheek. It was time to grow up.

You have to grow accustomed to always being the person that is pitied, that's looked down on, I thought as I wiped at my tears angrily, *and you have to grow accustomed to being alone.*

The next day, we bumped along in the carriage as it rolled down the cobblestone road. I craned my neck as I stared at the manor house of Marchingville. It was practically in shambles on the outside. Shingles hung from the roof, the shutters on a few windows completely missing. Ivy clung to half of the house while the other half was a dingy shade of grey.

Avyanna bounced in her seat, dragging my wide-eyed gaze away from the dilapidated house. "I still cannot believe Mother let me come. I'm certain the only reason she allowed it is because you're coming too."

"Have you seen that house?" I asked. "I hope the inside is in better condition, otherwise I might turn tail and run back home."

Avyanna leaned across me, one of her red curls tickling my chin as she glanced up at the manor. She pursed her lips, shrugging a shoulder nonchalantly. "It's not *that* horrible. It has…character."

I shook my head, turning back to look out the window. *Leave it to Avy to find the silver lining.*

We pulled through the gate, and I jumped as Avyanna grabbed my arm.

"Sorry." She winced. "The gate was really squeaky."

I patted her hand. "Does that make this house a little bit more horrible now?"

She rolled her eyes in response, a stray hair fluttering against her forehead as she huffed a breath.

We stepped from the carriage, Avy's hand holding onto my arm. I couldn't help but notice the overgrown shrubs, the weeds intermingling with the flowers, and the cracks in the stone steps as I escorted Avyanna up to the doors. I frowned. If Lady Marchingville could barely keep the grounds up, I was quite concerned about the interior of the manor.

I had no need to fear. My mouth fell open before I could stop myself as Avyanna and I stepped into the foyer. It was plain to see where all their money had gone.

Avyanna tugged on my sleeve. "I've never seen so much…gold."

She had voiced the words that were stuck in my throat. Gold filigree paper coated every wall, with a large golden chandelier hanging down from the ceiling. A staircase painted in the same color hugged a curved wall, with white accents on the newel posts. The floor was a white marble with gold veins running through it. Gold vases and picture frames completed the travesty, leaving me overwhelmed by the glow.

Avyanna pulled on my arm again, turning me toward a woman who was already speaking.

"…Welcome! I am Lady Pruella of Marchingville and am so very glad to have you here." The lady was dressed to match the room. A gown that had enough fabric to clothe three women seemed to cascade off of her. Her hair was pulled atop her head, held in place with sparkling golden combs that bobbed up and down as her red lips moved in a flurry of words.

I stopped trying to read. If she said anything of importance, Avyanna could handle it. My eyes, instead, were drawn to the two younger ladies who stood behind our golden host.

The first was dressed much like Lady Marchingville. A gold gown accentuated her curves and was cut low. A large golden necklace hung around her neck and combs that matched her mother's kept her honey brown hair up off of her long neck. When she noticed me staring, she began to bat her lashes. I resisted the urge to roll my eyes, turning my attention to the second young lady.

She was more modestly dressed. In a simple gown of red, with no sparkling jewels or fancy hair, she was equally elegant. Her auburn hair was braided over her shoulder and she tugged at the end once. When she noticed me staring, she smiled kindly and folded her hands behind her back.

Another pull on my arm made me glance down at my cousin. "Lady Marchingville asked if you had a pleasant trip."

Heat bloomed in my cheeks, but I forced a nod. "It was quite pleasant."

The look was unmistakable. A slight flinch at the way my words sounded. The clenching of her jaw as she tried to hold her smile in place. The nod of acknowledgement before turning back to the person who could hear her.

I looked away, my shoulders stiffening in anger. The two young ladies were staring at me again. The first's nose was scrunched up as if she had smelled something unpleasant. When she met my gaze, she turned it up before stepping over to join her mother in the conversation she was having with Avyanna.

The second young lady, however, had her head cocked to one side as she stepped forward, curtsying before me.

"I know this is not a proper introduction, but my name is Lady Amirah of Marchingville. I'm sorry for the way my mother and sister are treating you, your highness."

I glanced at her mother and sister, but they seemed unaware of our conversation. I looked back at Lady Amirah, brows lowered. "You're not speaking aloud, are you?" I asked in a whisper, and she smiled with a nod.

"I figured you were reading the lips of Princess Avyanna. I've heard about people who can do that. I find it fascinating."

"You're not bothered by the fact that I cannot hear?"

She shrugged. "Why should I be? It's not your fault that you cannot hear. I don't understand why people treat you differently. I like how Princess Avyanna talks to you."

She spoke rapidly, like Lady Marchingville had. Her lips were almost too fast to keep up with and I blinked, holding up a hand. "Please, slow down."

"I'm sorry." Lady Amirah laughed. "I tend to talk rather quickly when I get excited."

"I can tell." A smile tugged on my lips.

Her head jerked, and she looked around me. "My mother said that the maid will show you and Princess Avyanna to your chambers now."

"I hope they're not colored the same as down here," I murmured.

Lady Amirah grinned a little bigger, her eyes flicking to her mother, who must have heard me as well. Lady Marchingville's brows were lowered, but I simply smiled, despite Avyanna's cheeks turning a bright red. She tugged me after a woman dressed in black.

"Thank you for hosting us, Lady Marchingville," I called out as I took the stairs as quickly as possible.

4

AMIRAH

"Well, I never!" Mother huffed as Prince Thaddeus followed his cousin up the staircase to the guest wing. "How rude to comment on our decorations."

I glanced around the blinding foyer. I couldn't say I faulted our prince in the slightest.

"He's not worth the bother, Mother. I'm going to look at one of the richer lords coming tonight. Prince Thaddeus is—" Sophie scrunched her nose, and I resisted the urge to roll my eyes.

"Agreed." Mother nodded. "I could not believe the way his voice sounded!"

She shivered as if she had encountered a snake or a bug over a young man whose only fault was losing his hearing. It made me see red, and I could no longer hold my tongue.

"Mother!" I shook my head. "He's still a human and has feelings like the rest of us."

She sniffed, glaring down her sharp nose at me, but didn't reply. I crossed my arms, glaring right back.

After a long moment, Mother's icy tone filled the foyer, "You can leave, Amirah."

"With pleasure." I huffed, turning and marching up the stairs to my living quarters. I leaned against the wall. Pressing my hands against my flaming cheeks, I took a few moments to catch my breath, collecting my emotions and locking them far down in my chest.

Feeling much calmer, I straightened, smoothing a hand over my skirt. If Mother could justify shaming one of the princes of Allura simply because he could not hear, then her opinion truly didn't matter. I'd learned early in life that it was impossible to please her fully. The only one who could do that was Sophie.

Our dining room was crowded that evening.

All our guests had arrived that afternoon, but I had escaped the rest of the foyer greetings, hiding away in the barn until it was time to ready Sophie for dinner.

I now wished I had refused to come down for the meal.

There were dozens of young men and women, laughing as they sipped wine from their goblets and conversed with those around them. I stood against the wall, my hands clutched behind me, trying desperately to fade into the background. Sophie and Mother were both flouncing from group to group, smiling and flirting unabashedly.

Heat crawled up my neck as I watched my sister drop her handkerchief, bending over so the gentleman across from her got an eyeful of her charms.

I pressed a hand against my cheek, edging around the dining room to step out onto our small terrace. I was thankful for the cool evening breeze that blew over me.

I miss you, Father. I thought, pressing a fist against the underside of my ribs, wishing the ache would go away. He hadn't been gone long, six months was all. But everything had changed. Mother had never loved him, I had decided. Everything that had been a reminder of him she had destroyed. The only reason the barn still stood was because it was tucked away at the back of the property where her friends couldn't see it.

"Good evening, Lady Amirah." I spun around, a breath of relief escaping me when I saw Prince Thaddeus stepping onto the terrace. A smirk tugged on the left side of his mouth. "Did I startle you?"

"Yes, slightly." I smiled back. "Are you not enjoying the dinner?"

"No." He raised a brow at me. "Crowds are not my favorite things."

"They are not mine, either."

We lapsed into silence. Crickets chirped merrily as the sun's final rays glowed through the trees around the manor house. I sighed, glancing behind me at the party. I could see Mother and Sophie were still flirting, and it left a sour taste on my tongue.

"Is something the matter?" Thaddeous asked.

I blinked, surprised by his question. His light brown eyes studied me, the rounded syllables of his words soft as he watched my lips.

"I do not care for how my family is behaving," I admitted. "But they do not care to hear anything about it from me."

"Are you not their sister and daughter? I would think they would value your opinion."

"You would think that, yes." I stiffened, unable to make my gaze meet his. "But they do not. Few do."

He touched my elbow and I glanced up. His head was cocked, a lock of his light brown hair falling across his forehead. "I wanted to thank you for the kind words you gave me earlier. Not many people take the time to converse with me. I…" He dropped his gaze. "I make people uncomfortable."

"Then they are the problem." I shook my head, anger flaring in my stomach again at the injustice of it all. "You are a person worthy of respect and admiration. No matter your differences."

"I thank you for that, m'lady." The left side of his mouth quirked up again for a moment before flattening out in a straight line. "I wish more people felt as you do."

"Your cousin is kind, I think."

"Yes." He glanced into the dining room. "She doesn't treat me like a china doll."

"Do others in your family do that?"

"Not intentionally." He shrugged, turning to lean his back against the railing. "I think they worry about me. Ever since the accident, they tend to hover about."

The rumor was that he had lost his hearing during an accident, but there were few details. And I disliked listening to rumors. The look on the prince's face, however, made me swallow my curiosity. I would wait until he was ready to tell me.

"I think I will like spending time with you, your highness." I smiled up at him. "And I promise, I will not treat you differently because of your past. I know what that's like."

I know what that is like all too well.

5

THADDEUS

I wondered at Amirah's declaration, but simply nodded. "I look forward to getting to know you better as well, m'lady."

She smiled, a dimple appearing in her cheek. She had a nice smile, a quiet and calming presence despite her rapid speech. It was peaceful to be standing at her side in the cool evening, watching the chaos of the dinner inside the manor house.

A breeze blew around us, chasing a piece of Amirah's reddish-brown hair into her eyes. She reached up, tucking it behind her ear as she turned back to me.

"Are you hungry yet?" She gestured toward the dining room. "It should be about time for the meal."

I straightened, glancing toward the dining room. My hand twitched at my side, wishing for my sword. It always made me feel stronger, more in control.

A hand landed on my arm. I glanced down at Amirah again, hating the smirk on her face.

"Please don't look at me like that," I said.

"Like what?" She raised a brow, the smirk still on her face. "I find it amusing that you're looking at the dining room like it is a prison cell."

"When you are unable to hear, it is like that."

"I suppose it would be." She tipped her face to the sky, thinking for a moment before she looked back down to ask, "What is it like, being unable to hear?"

No one had ever asked me that question before, and I was uncertain of how to describe it. I crossed my arms, taking a long moment to think before answering.

"Like watching a scene from a window," I said. "Imagine two people in a courtyard, and you're up in a window." I gestured above us, where the bedchambers were. "You can see them, see what they're doing, but because you're looking through a pane, and are so far above them, you're unable to distinguish what is being said or what sounds are playing around them. It is isolating and lonely."

I bit my tongue, the last part choking me. I hadn't meant to say that, at least not to her. But Amirah touched my arm again, making me look at her. The smirk was gone, a look of compassion and anger on her face.

"I am sorry that people make you feel even more isolated than you are, my prince," she said.

I opened my mouth to reply, but someone in the doorway caught her attention. I turned to look, seeing Lady Pruella glaring at Amirah. She said something, but with the darkness around us on the terrace and the light from behind her, Lady Pruella's face was shrouded in shadow.

I glanced at Amirah, seeing her face pale. Fire flashed in her eyes, however, and she straightened her shoulders. "We were just conversing, Mother."

Lady Pruella stepped close enough that I could now see her face. She was perfectly calm, but a look lay in her eye that I had seen only once before—from the stable manager at the castle. That man had beaten one of the stable boys, and Uncle Benjamin had him arrested for abuse.

I turned toward Amirah, unsure of what she wanted me to do. She glanced between her mother and me, probably wondering how much I had caught.

"Would you do me the honor of sitting with me at dinner, Lady Amirah?" I blurted out.

I could sense her mother pause. Out of the corner of my eye, I noticed her fists clench at her side. A small sliver of satisfaction shot through me as I turned an inquisitive eye on Amirah.

"Yes, my prince." She smiled up at me, causing a warm feeling to bloom in my chest. "I would like that very much."

I offered her my arm, nodding my head toward Lady Pruella as we glided past. She scowled, and I resisted the urge to shudder at her cold, calculating eyes.

"How was your first night here?" Avyanna tucked her bare feet up under her as she sat on the settee before the massive fireplace in my room. She still had on her dinner dress but was pulling hundreds of pins from her curly red hair.

I rubbed the back of my neck as I watched my cousin. Instead of answering her, I asked, "How does your head not hurt?"

"It does." She raised a brow at me. "And you are avoiding my question. How was dinner?"

"It was fine." I stood to pace.

In truth, dinner had been better than fine. I conversed with Amirah most of the evening. Everyone flatly ignored us, so it was only us talking. I had gotten better at reading her lips, despite how quickly they moved as she talked and laughed.

And I laughed a lot with Amirah, something that had not happened in a very long time. She managed to draw out the part of me I buried long ago—a little boy who talked nonstop to his family, the servants, and anyone else who would listen.

"You seemed to get along quite well with Lady Pruella's eldest daughter." Avyanna ran a hand through her loose curls, her mouth tipping up in a smile. "She seems to enjoy your company as well."

"Is that so hard to believe?" I snapped, roughing a hand over my face at the shocked look my cousin sent me. "Forgive me, Avy. I did not mean to be cross. It has simply been a long, tiring day."

Avyanna stepped across the carpet, glancing up at me. In one hand she clutched her shoes and in the other her pins. She laid her fisted hand against my chest. "Do not close yourself off."

"Mother talked to you, didn't she?" I growled.

"No, we just know you too well." Avy laughed. "Amirah is a nice girl. She treats you like a normal person."

"But I'm not normal."

"Yet you speak, you fight, you love." She sighed at the questioning look I sent her. "No. You're not normal. You, my cousin, are extraordinary. And I hope you don't let anyone treat you as anything less than that."

With a kiss on my cheek and a pat on my chest, Avyanna waltzed out of the room.

I groaned, flopping onto my stomach on the bed. Why did everyone keep telling me to stop closing myself off? It was easier that way. Letting others love me hurt them.

The love of my parents had caused dark circles and grey hairs to appear on them. They had endured many sleepless nights as I had cried out from nightmares. I still had them sometimes. It seemed the cruel lot of my family—nightmares over things we could not control.

I sighed, rolling onto my back. Amirah's face flashed across my thoughts, smiling at me like she had at dinner.

You were never part of my plans, and yet here we are. I sighed, rolling onto my side as I hugged my pillow to my stomach. *What am I going to do with you?* I wondered, as my eyes slipped closed in slumber.

6

AMIRAH

I stared at myself in my mirror the next morning, sliding my hand over my light pink gown, a small smile on my face. Dinner the night before had been wonderful. Everyone but Thaddeus ignored me, and I found that I preferred it that way. I no longer cared that Mother and Sophie garnered all the attention. I liked Prince Thaddeus and the easy way we conversed and laughed as we ate.

He did not know the truth, though. Few people did. If Thaddeus knew the truth, I was certain he would push me away just as my mother had.

I straightened, exhaling the anger and fear as I forced a smile onto my face. Father's final words floated through my head, fueling my determination.

Love, Amirah. Be brave and love those that disdain you for who you are. Then you will truly be the noble lady you were born to be.

With that thought, I stepped out of my bedchamber and glided down the hall to the dining room. A few of the guests were already there, breaking their fast and talking softly amongst one another. I filled my plate before finding a seat apart from the crowd, my eye on the door.

Prince Thaddeus soon stepped through, Princess Avyanna by his side. His eyes scanned the crowd, a stern look on his face until his gaze collided with mine. The corner of his mouth ticked up and he guided his cousin through the room to my side.

"Good morning, Prince Thaddeus." I inclined my head toward him. "And to you as well, Princess Avyanna. Did you sleep well last night?"

"Yes." Avyanna smiled. "It is quite a lovely suite of rooms you have given us."

"The finest we have." My gaze flicked to Thaddeus's brown eyes. I cleared my throat. "Are you not hungry?"

"Yes, I am famished." Avyanna smiled up at Thaddeus, tugging on his arm until he tore his gaze away from me and to her. "Will you fetch us two plates?"

He sighed before nodding and striding away. Avyanna smiled after him before slipping into a seat beside me.

"He's quite smitten with you, you know."

My mouth fell open at her blunt statement. "Pardon me?"

"My cousin." She motioned with her head in the direction of Thaddeus. "I have never seen him so drawn to anyone. He usually keeps a wide breadth from others. His way of protecting them or some such nonsense." A servant stopped at our table and poured a cup of tea for the princess before moving on to the next guest. Avyanna took a small sip before raising her brow at me. "I hope you're not making a fool of him, Lady Amirah."

"I—" I couldn't make my lips move. I forced myself to inhale, shaking my head. "No, my lady. I have no intention of hurting him. He seemed lonely and uncomfortable yesterday, and he was the one to seek me out last evening. I'm not trying to hurt anyone."

Avyanna smiled, taking another sip of her drink. She stared at me, and I forced myself to meet her gaze without squirming. Thaddeus returned, handing Avyanna a plate before claiming the seat beside her.

"What were you talking about?" he asked, scooping a bite of eggs into his mouth as he eyed his cousin.

"You," Avyanna stated plainly, causing Thaddeus to choke on his food.

"What?" he managed, after swallowing a gulp of coffee that a servant had hurriedly poured for him. A few heads turned, and a blush climbed into his cheeks. "Why?"

Avyanna shrugged, glancing at me from the corner of her eye. I knew my cheeks were flaming, and I popped a piece of sausage into my mouth to give my trembling hands something to do. Thaddeus' gaze snagged mine, a shiver working through me at the intensity of it. He didn't say a word, however, he went back to working on his plate of food in moody silence.

Avyanna seemed oblivious to it, chattering away without pause. "Your house is bigger than it appears on the outside." She gestured with her hand. "Has this always been your dining room? Or did it used to be the ballroom?"

I swallowed a sip of tea. "It used to be the ballroom, but Mother had a larger one added onto the back of the house and converted this into our dining room for parties like this."

Thaddeus was staring at me again and I bit back my words, turning my gaze back to Avyanna as she prattled on.

"I thought so. The high ceilings and pillars there," she continued, gesturing with her spoon at the marble columns along the walls, "make it feel more ballroom-like."

I nodded, but kept my lips clamped closed. The clacking of heels against the floor had me stiffening even before Mother's smooth, overly calm voice drifted over to me.

"Amirah, dear. I would like to speak with you. Now, if you please."

I stood slowly, placing my napkin on the table, before turning to follow Mother to the side of the dining room. Her cheeks were tinged pink, whether from her anger or her too tight dress, I didn't know.

"How dare you?" she hissed, making sure to keep her voice low so that the other guests could not hear. "Thaddeus should be dining with your sister, since that is the only way for her to be introduced to Crown Prince Willhelm!"

"They came and sat beside me, Mother." I took a steadying breath. "I cannot control what the prince and princess decide to do, just like I could not stop Prince Thaddeus from choosing me as his dinner partner last night."

"You are worthless, Amirah," she scoffed. Her eyes drifted up and down my slight frame with disgust. "You are a symbol of everything that was wrong in my life and you are certainly not worthy of a prince, even a deaf one."

"One thing, at least, that I do deserve is my title of *lady*," I snapped. "I treat people with love and kindness. That, Mother, is something you know nothing about!"

I had gone too far. Mother's eyes flashed as she raised her hand and smacked me soundly across the cheek. Stars danced before my eyes and I blinked back tears.

There had been plenty of times I had not deserved the abuse she so readily dished out. Yet this time, I knew I did.

7

THADDEUS

I watched as Lady Marchingville's hand flew out toward Amirah, smacking her soundly against the cheek. I didn't need to hear the smack to know it was a hard blow. Amirah's head whipped to the side and she stumbled a few paces to the right, her shoulders hunched.

I stood from my seat, causing some of the guests around me to turn their heads. Avyanna reached for me but I ignored her as I strode across the dining room with determination burning in my chest. Reaching her side, I pulled Amirah behind me and leveled a glare at her mother without saying a word. I didn't have to. Lady Marchingville's face paled, but she threw back her shoulders, her green eyes gleaming like a snake's.

"She disrespected me," she said.

"So you slapped her?" I hoped my tone was low, threatening.

Her face paled another shade. "I'm her mother. I can discipline her how I see fit."

Amirah must have said something, for Lady Marchingville's complexion turned from pale to red. "You would defend *him* before your own family?"

I sensed heads turning from the long tables. I wanted to bolt, to be anywhere but at the center of attention, but Amirah needed help. We needed to get out of the dining room.

"We're going to take a turn about the garden since we disgust you so." Turning, I gripped Amirah's elbow. "Excuse us, m'lady."

Not waiting to see Lady Marchingville's response, I tucked Amirah's hand into the crook of my arm and ushered her out of the dining room and into the gardens.

I looked down at Amirah, wincing at the bright red mark forming on her cheek. She kept her gaze on the ground for a long moment before turning toward me. Her eyes were suspiciously bright, but I bit my tongue to keep from commenting.

"Thank you." Her lip trembled, and I was struck by how perfect her they were. I closed my eyes, trying to gather my rather traitorous thoughts.

"Of course," I choked out, prying my eyes open to read her response. "No one should treat another person the way she just treated you."

"It's not the first time. And it won't be the last." She shrugged, tugging me toward an old barn near the back of the house. "Come, this will be a safe place to hide until she calms."

"Do you often have to hide from her?" I asked as I helped her roll the door open.

"More often than I care to admit." Amirah crossed her arms across her chest. "I did deserve it this time, though."

"You're her daughter." I clenched my jaw. "I hate to imagine how she treats those not related to her."

I could sense her stiffening as we stepped into the barn, but ignored it. The smell of hay and horses calmed me, taking me back to my tiny shed that was my own hideaway.

Amirah placed a hand on my arm, and I turned to face her.

"I come here to think. It's quiet." She smiled, stepping up to an old stallion in one of the stalls, his nose bumping her in the shoulder. I followed her, scratching the horse behind the ears as I watched Amirah's face.

"I used to come here with my father. He loved the animals and the manual labor of caring for them." She smiled up at me. "He also let me help, something few daughters of lords can claim."

I smiled at her. "Hard work doesn't scare you?"

"No, it's…refreshing." She rubbed the horse's forehead. "Abner is the only animal left that my father cared for. Mother sold all of them a week after Father's passing."

"I'm sorry." I reached out, touching her elbow. "That must have been painful for you."

"It was." Her gaze met mine. "When Father died, I lost my best friend. When Mother would bring buyers here to sell off the livestock, I'd hide away with Abner in the fields so she couldn't sell him."

"I cannot imagine losing a parent."

She gave Abner one last pat before stepping away. "It's hard. Especially—" She hesitated before shrugging off her comment, then motioned for me to follow her as she grabbed hold of a ladder and scaled it with ease. I followed, sneezing once as I crawled into a loft. The ceiling was low, causing me to have to stoop in order to walk.

Amirah smiled at me as she stepped over to another set of doors. She lifted a latch and pushed on them, swinging them out and open.

I sucked in a breath of awe. The rolling hills were dotted with wild flowers, creating a kaleidoscope of colors in the morning sun.

I sighed, my gaze flicking to Amirah. "It makes me feel small."

Amirah nodded. "I love it up here."

She lowered herself to the ground, her legs hanging over the edge of the window. I took a half step back before sitting cross-legged, a foot from the gaping hole. Amirah raised a brow but turned so that I could see her face.

"What do you do for fun, Prince Thaddeus?"

"Please, call me Thad." I turned to look out over the hills again. "I read and…" I swallowed, my eyes flicking to the side to gauge her reaction, unsure if she would laugh at my secret pastime. "I carve."

She cocked her head. "What do you carve?"

"Figurines, mostly." I picked up a piece of hay, slowly snapping it bit by bit until there was nothing but chaff on the barn floor. "I have a box of them back home."

"Do you not give them away?"

I shook my head. "They're personal. No one knows I do them."

"Is art not meant to be shared?" Her gaze landed on a wood box in the corner. "I want to show you something."

She stood, much too close to the gaping drop, before moving over to pull the box up beside me. Lifting the lid, she hesitated a moment. "Now, these are hidden because"—she closed her eyes—"if my mother found them, she'd burn them."

"Why?"

"She doesn't like my art." Amirah shifted through the parchments until she held one out to me. "This is my father, Lord Derek of Marchingville."

I gazed down at it. Atop of a horse that looked like a younger version of Abner, sat a tall, lean man. He had a large beard, but that didn't hide the brilliant smile that curved his lips up. His eyes sparkled, like he knew a secret that no one else did, and I found myself smiling at the portrait.

"I think I would have liked your father," I stated, handing the picture back to her. "You are a good artist, Lady Amirah."

"Please, call me Amirah." She turned back to the box, but kept her face tipped so I could see it. "And I thank you. I've been practicing more these past few months."

Because she needs to escape. I swallowed, gazing down at my hands clenched in my lap. I knew that feeling well.

Another parchment was handed to me and I turned to see Amirah's explanation.

"This is a sketch of the city," she said. It was detailed, showing the shadows as the sun shone down on Marchingville. Flower boxes, cobblestones, a cloud of dust from a passing horse. Amirah had left nothing out.

"This is amazing." I couldn't tear my eyes away. "The details, Amirah. How?"

"It's like I can see it in my mind." She shrugged. "If I don't get it onto the paper it just swirls around and around until I do."

I understood that. "You drew this from memory?"

"Yes. I remember things clearly. It is as if they are sketched into my mind."

"It's lovely," I stated, handing the parchment back to her.

"I have a whole box of them."

"I'd love to see them," I said, "but we may be missed if we stay away much longer."

She nodded, rising to her feet and placing the lid back on the crate. "You may come up here whenever you like. I may be able to acquire some wood and a knife if you want to carve while you're here."

"Thank you." I blinked up at her. "That is too kind."

"No, my prince. I understand the urge to create all too well." She held out her hand to help me to my feet, and I let her. But once my feet were under me, I found that I did not wish to release her small hand from mine.

"Thank you for rescuing me from Mother, Thaddeus." Amirah gazed up at me, squeezing my hand.

"It was my pleasure, Amirah."

We stood like that for another second before I dropped her hand and took a step back.

"We should return before people begin to talk," I said.

She nodded and I turned to scramble down the ladder. My heart was throbbing, making my chest ache at the force.

What is wrong with me?

8

AMIRAH

I watched Thaddeus climb down the ladder, pressing the hand he had held against my cheek. I didn't want him to let go. I glanced at my box in the corner. He was the first person I had ever shown my art to besides my father.

Pressing my fist against the underside of my ribs, I took a steadying breath before turning and climbing down the ladder. I landed beside Thaddeus, who was leaning against one of the stalls waiting for me.

He smiled as he offered me his arm, but it looked strained. I took it, patting Abner on the nose as we passed his stall. The house was almost in sight before Thaddeus pulled me to a stop and turned me to face him.

"Thank you for showing me your secret place, Amirah." One side of his mouth quirked up in that distracting way it had done last night. "I'm thankful to know I have a place I can go if I need to be alone."

"It's my pleasure, truly, Thaddeus." The way he said *alone* sent a pang of sadness through me, but I forced a smile to my lips.

He stared at me for another long moment before patting my hand and stepping away. "Well, have a nice day."

Then with a sharp turn on his heel, he hurried off down the path.

"What in the world just happened?" I muttered, pressing my fingers to my forehead as I slowly shook my head.

"That's my cousin for you." I leapt, turning to see Avyanna sailing down the terrace steps and up to my side. "He is often abrupt when he is uncomfortable, my lady."

"Please, Amirah is fine." She tugged me toward our hedge maze. "Princess Avyanna—"

"If I am to call you Amirah, then call me Avyanna or Avy." She smiled, tucking one of her curls behind her ear. "Now, what do you want to know about Thad?"

I cleared my throat as she glanced at me with skepticism. "Nothing, m'lady."

"Nothing at all?"

"If he does not wish to tell me about himself, then I do not wish to know. He will reveal to me what he wants to."

Avyanna scoffed. "No, he will not."

"I'm sorry, Avyanna, but why do you think that?" I asked as we began to walk along the hedged path.

She sighed, dropping my arm and clutching her hands behind her back. She tipped her face up to the sun, a thoughtful expression pinching her features.

"When the accident happened, I was twelve years old. Thad had been the lighthearted one in our family. The first to laugh and the last to stop." She smiled, fondness in her eyes. "He had always been my closest cousin. When he lost his hearing, we all were devastated, but he took it especially hard. He shut out all of us. He feels that he is not worth loving or caring about, simply because he cannot hear."

"How…?" I glared at the satisfied look that crossed Avyanna's face at my question. "I know there was an accident, but what exactly caused him to lose his hearing?"

Avyanna sighed, her smirk disappearing. "He was ten and had promised some of his friends to go skating. He didn't truly want to, but his mother—Princess Sage—insisted that he keep his word."

I nodded, showing her that I was listening.

"The ice—" Avyanna's voice cut off for a moment. "It wasn't thick enough. One of the boys—Gerek—fell through. Thad, being his protective self, dove in to save him. He was half frozen when he arrived back home, and he became deathly ill." She shivered, as if the icy water was covering her. "Thaddeus got a severe ear infection in both ears. His fever raged and I remember tending him as he cried out Gerek's name. It was horrible. The healer is still amazed that he survived. However, the damage had already been done to his ears. He has not been able to hear a thing since."

"How horrid." It hurt to swallow as tears filled my eyes.

Avyanna paused, then said, "He told me a few years ago that the last thing he remembers hearing is the crack of the ice and his friend's screams."

"Poor Thaddeus." I wiped at a tear on my cheek, crossing my arms as I tried to stuff my emotions back down.

When I returned my attention to the princess, she was staring at me hard, eyes narrowed. "He needs someone like you, Amirah."

I started. "Like me? I am no one special, my lady. I am not even—" I bit my tongue. "I'm not worthy of him."

"And he thinks himself unworthy of anyone." She stepped in front of me. "Honestly, what is it with my family and being so headstrong and stubborn?" Avyanna planted her fists on her hips before taking a deep breath. "Amirah, you're going to win my cousin's heart."

"That is a horrible idea, Avyanna."

"Is it because of your mother? I happened to notice that my cousin jumped to your aid this morning."

I blushed. "He was quite kind."

"Yes, he is loyal and noble to a fault." She reached out and squeezed my hands in hers. "And I feel that you are much the same."

I opened and closed my mouth twice before I could find the words. "I do not want to *earn* his affections."

"Amirah, truly, he likes you. And I have never seen him show an interest in anyone before." She pulled her lower lip between her teeth.

I shook my head, tipping it back to look at the clouds floating lazily in the sky.

God? What do you want me to do?

A peace settled around me, removing the fear that clutched at my throat. I sighed deeply. Father had taught me to love even those who disdained me for who I was. What would it hurt to try to love a prince who felt that he did not deserve love either?

"All right." I pulled my gaze down to meet Avyanna's sparkling hazel eyes. "What do you want me to do?"

9

THADDEUS

It had been three days since I'd escaped into the barn with Amirah. Three days of hiding there and in my room. She'd been true to her word, smuggling a box of small wood pieces and a knife up to the loft. I had started another figurine, but it looked too much like Amirah for me to finish.

I'd been avoiding her, scared of my own feelings. I was not going to subject her to more hate, more disdain. She deserved a man who could sweep her away from her current situation.

Despite my avoidance, Amirah had formed a fast friendship with Avyanna. They often disappeared together for hours.

Not that I was watching for Amirah. No, I was looking out for my cousin, protecting her like I had promised Aunt Della.

I hacked at a new piece of wood, anger swirling in my gut at my inability to stifle my emotions. I glanced at the box in the corner, where Amirah had her art hidden. Setting aside the wood block, I crawled over to it and reverently lifted the lid, sorting through the art.

A picture of a daisy. A small sketch of a barn cat. I shifted some more, amazed at every piece I looked at, until I pulled out a yellowed piece of parchment near the bottom of the box. It was folded into fourths and I gently opened it.

It showed a man, standing in a doorway. He was shrugging into his coat, as if he was leaving the room behind him. A woman laid crumpled in a heap, her arms wrapped around her middle. Both of their faces were shrouded in shadow, but a sadness tugged at me as I stared at it. My eyes landed on a note scrawled across the bottom of the page:

Am I more than my father's mistake?

My gaze snapped back up to the picture and then back the note. I clenched my teeth, quickly folding the picture back up and shoving it into the box. I slammed the lid down, knowing that I had crossed a line, invaded her privacy.

I picked up my wood, staring out over the fields as I held both it and my knife tightly. My heart ached, and I couldn't seem to forget what I had seen and read. Glancing down at the wood, I began to pour the heat rushing through me into it. I let the knife glide, shaping and forming as I went.

This time, I let the figure look like Amirah without hesitation. I carved a dazzling dress, one that I had seen Avyanna in before. I let Amirah's hair hang around her shoulders, a circlet on top of her head, a smile on her face, and her eyes closed as she swayed to some mystery tune.

I swallowed, staring down at it. Amirah wasn't a mistake. She deserved to be here, whether her father had meant for her to be born or not.

Is that why her mother treats her so poorly? Because Amirah isn't her daughter by blood? The whole thing left a sour taste on my tongue.

A hand landed on my shoulder and I startled, the knife falling to the ground. I glanced up to see Amirah. She had on a light purple dress, and as she knelt beside me, it billowed around her.

"Are you all right?" Her brown eyes, soft as chocolate in the sunshine, studied my face. "You appear upset."

I swallowed, wanting to pull her into my arms and tell her exactly why I was upset. But instead I squashed those desires, scooping up the knife and dropping my gaze back to the carving in my hand.

"I am fine." My throat felt tight as Amirah inched closer to me. "Truly."

She reached over and plucked the figurine out of my hand. My cheeks flamed and I turned to look out over the fields again. What would she think about the figurine? It looked so much like her. Would she be offended? Angry? *Oh please, God, don't let her cry!*

Amirah placed a hand on my shoulder, and I steeled myself as I turned to meet her gaze.

"Is this me?" A small smile played on her lips.

"Yes." I cleared my throat. "Do you…do you mind it?"

"No." She shook her head, smiling in earnest now. "I love it! Although"—she trailed her finger over the dress—"I've never owned a gown this lovely."

"You deserve a whole closetful."

"No, I have no need for a closet full of dresses." She blushed. "I have nowhere to wear them to. I'd rather have good, sensible dresses, and one or two to wear to the occasional party."

"Truly?" I cocked my head at her.

"I would not say that if I did not mean it, Thaddeus."

I pointed to the figurine. "I would like to see you look so happy, m'lady."

"It has been a long while since I was truly happy." She held up the figurine. "May I keep this?"

My chest tightened and I found myself nodding. "If you wish."

She tucked the figure into her pocket. "You should carve a Noah's Ark!"

I raised a brow. "All the animals and a boat?"

Amirah nodded enthusiastically. "Yes! And the top could come off and you could put all the little animals into the boat."

I couldn't help the smile that tugged on my lips. "I could attempt that. What animals would you like?"

Amirah reached over to her box, pulling out a piece of parchment. I held my breath, hoping that she wouldn't notice that I had looked through her art. But she wasn't paying any attention to the sketches.

"I will write them down." Amirah's charcoal stick moved across the parchment. I watched her, my smile never wavering. Her eyes sparkled and her lips pursed as she thought. A finger twirled the ends of her hair. I was captivated—completely and totally captivated.

10

AMIRAH

"This is quite the list." Thaddeus's eyes scanned the parchment I had thrust at him. "I'm not sure I have the tools to make the boat."

"What would you need?" I asked.

Thaddeus shrugged. "I normally rummage around our stables for tools. My family…" He cleared his throat, shifting as he glanced out the loft doors. "They don't know that I carve."

"I think they would admire your work." I reached into my pocket and pulled out the delicate figure. I smiled down at it, tracing the circlet and the swishing skirt, heat blooming in my cheeks. "I do."

"I'm glad you like it, Amirah." Hearing my name from his lips was not helping my emotional state. I peeked through my lashes at Thaddeus as his gaze dropped back to the paper. "I'll start on these animals. If I cannot get the boat done before I leave, I'll send it to you."

At the thought of him leaving, I stiffened, tugging my knees up to my chest and resting my chin on them. I turned to look out the loft doors, blinking to keep my tears at bay.

"Is something the matter?" Thaddeus's quiet voice asked, and I shivered at the butterflies that began to zip around my stomach.

I turned my face so that he could see my lips, but kept my eyes fixed on the horizon as I said, "I finally have a friend. And I suppose that I forgot you're leaving at the end of next week."

He raised his fist and rubbed at his chest as if it ached as much as my own. I turned my head away again, not trusting my tears.

"I…I looked at your art."

My gaze snapped back to him, my eyes widening. "You what?"

He shifted, slowly folding the parchment and placing it in his box of wood. "I thought you should know."

"What did you look at?"

"I…" He visibly gulped and I buried my face in my hands, knowing exactly which picture he had seen.

"I'll go," I whispered, ducking my head as a tear snaked down my cheek.

"Amirah, wait."

I paused at the ladder, feeling Thaddeus's hand on my wrist. He turned me around, placing his large, callused hands on my shoulders. His brown eyes flicked back and forth between my own. "You are not worthless."

"You feel pity for me." I reached up to brush another tear. "That's why I don't tell anyone. Because then they pity me, and I *hate* that they feel sorry for me."

Thaddeus shook his head. "No, I do not pity you."

"What do you feel then?" I scoffed, crossing my arms, glaring at his chest.

"Sadness." He squeezed my shoulders. "No one should feel like they're less than."

"But you do." I took a half step closer, resting my hand on his chest. His heart was pounding as he stared at me, his hands trembling on my shoulders. "Why? Why do you feel like you're less than?"

"Because I am." He gestured with one hand at his ears. "I lost my hearing. And for what? I couldn't even save him."

"He...died?" My breath caught. That was something Avyanna had not mentioned.

Thaddeus nodded once, the trembling in his hands increasing. "It would have been one thing if he lived. Sacrificing my hearing for a life would have been worth it. But he drowned."

"You tried, though." I grabbed his hand, stepping even closer to him. I had to crane my neck back to meet his gaze, and he was hunched, the ceiling too low for him to stand straight. "You tried to help, Thaddeus. That makes you a better man than most."

"Then you're the only one to think that." A tear trailed down his cheek.

"Why are you so stubborn?"

He sniffed, a small smirk pulling on the corner of his mouth. "It's a family trait."

"So I've heard." I wanted him to pull me close. It felt good, standing near him. He smelled like the wood I had given him, like pine and cedar.

He stared down at me for a long moment before stepping back to his box and sinking down beside it. "I'm sorry I looked at it. But I thought you should know that I think you are beyond worthy."

"You are worthy too, Thaddeus." I sat across from him.

"How can you say that?"

I reached out and grasped his hand again. "Because I see the man you are. You're loyal and brave and kind and humorous. You tried to save your friend. You stand up to my mother." I swallowed the lump in my throat as he pulled his hand free from mine. "You know my secret and yet you find me acceptable."

His eyes blazed at my comment. "You are more than acceptable, Amirah."

The intensity of his words rendered me speechless for a moment. "If you say so, my prince."

Thaddeus's brows furrowed in confusion as I stood and walked to the ladder. Without a word to him, I scrambled down to the barn floor, stepping over to Abner. I wrapped my arms around the horse's neck, sighing deeply. "Why does life have to be so complicated?"

<hr>

"Perfect!"

Avyanna stepped back from where she'd been styling my hair. It had been two days since my uncomfortable conversation with Thaddeus in the barn. He had not said anything to his cousin about my past. That I was an illegitimate daughter, whose adoptive mother had been happy to love her for the first three years of her life, until that mother had a child of her own. After that, I became the reminder that her husband had been with someone else. The crowning humiliation was that he had loved me and spent more time with me than her and Sophie.

"What do you think, Amirah?"

I shook the thoughts from my mind, gazing into the mirror. Avyanna had pulled half my hair on top of my head, twisting and braiding it into a crown. Wispy trails hung around my ears and forehead, giving me what Avy promised was an ethereal look.

"I…" I swallowed. "I feel like a princess."

"Well, that's what we're aiming for, is it not?" She laughed, hugging me from behind.

I stood, stepping away from her. "Avy, I don't feel right about doing this to Thaddeus. It's not fair."

"Why do you think that?" She crossed her arms. "He likes you, Amirah. And you care about him, too."

"But what…what if we both get hurt?" My chest tightened at that thought, and I stepped over to the window.

"No one will be hurt." She snorted. "He'll eventually come around. I promise."

I shook my head. "No. I can't use tonight to…to win his hand! I want to simply enjoy my evening. Dance some dances with the young men and…have a good time."

Avyanna sighed. "All right. If that's truly what you want."

That had been too easy. I blinked as she smiled sadly at me, a strange gleam in her eye. Avyanna turned to pull a stunning blue gown from the wardrobe. Sparkles danced across it in the candlelight as she held the gown out to me.

"Even if you are not going to try and win Thaddeus," she said, "you can still look like a princess tonight."

I shook my head. "If Mother sees—"

"It's a gift" —she draped it over the bed— "from me to you. I will be severely put out if you do not take it."

"Are you certain?" I swallowed, reaching out to run my hand over the faux jewels sewn across the bodice.

"Yes." Avyanna tugged me into a hug. "Very certain."

11

THADDEUS

I am going to kill Avyanna.

Tugging at my coat sleeve, I tried to sink into the wallpaper of the massive ballroom. Conversations flowed around me as the guests of Lady Pruella drank champagne and laughed, shamelessly flirting.

I imagined how loud it must be. Part of me wished I could have a headache from hearing the noise. Another part of me was thankful for the overwhelming quiet.

I blinked as Sophie, Amirah's sister, stepped up, batting her eyelashes at me. "Why are you standing here, all alone?"

Taking a sip of champagne from the flute I had grabbed off a passing servant's tray, I shrugged.

Sophie glanced around. "Where is Amirah?"

Again I shrugged, my thoughts unwillingly going to the barn and our last conversation. I had not handled it well at all. While I now knew the truth about Amirah, something told me that there was more to her story than simply feeling displaced by her mother.

Sophie grabbed my hand, tugging me toward the dance floor. I didn't need to see what she was saying to know what she wanted.

I pulled my hand from her and she raised a brow at me. "Well?" she asked.

"No." I shook my head, turning and pushing through the crowd of people. I did not care what Sophie thought of me; there was no way I could dance with her. No way at all.

I breathed a sigh of relief as I sagged against the golden foyer wall, rubbing a hand against my forehead. Where was my cousin? She had promised to not leave me alone this evening, yet she was nowhere in sight.

A flash of blue made me look up.

Amirah. But she looked more stunning than she ever had. Half of her hair was twisted into a crown on top of her head, loose strands curling around her temples and ears. A choker of pearls hung about her neck. Her gown was a pale blue, making her brown eyes sparkle in the candlelight. The neckline showed the pale skin of her shoulders, the bodice hugging her waist and revealed how tiny of a woman she was.

Behind Amirah stood my cousin, smirking at me as I stepped up to the stairs.

"Amirah," I breathed, still in shock.

She startled, raising a gloved hand to her cheek. "Is it too much? Avyanna said it wasn't, but I'm not sure. I feel like a china doll, and I truly am not comfortable and—"

I raised my hand, cutting her off. "May I have this dance?"

I kept the smile on my face, all the while wondering why I had said it. I didn't dance. I *couldn't* dance—at least not well.

But Amirah's smile was worth it. She ducked her head, a pretty red blooming against her pale cheek.

"Yes." She looked up at me. "I would like that very much."

Avyanna placed a hand on Amirah's shoulder, edging past us in her purple gown. "Enjoy yourselves. I'm going to try to secure a dance of my own." She winked—though whether it was at me or Amirah, I could not tell—before gliding through the ballroom doors.

"I must warn you," I admitted as I tucked Amirah's hand under my arm, "I am not a very good dancer."

"You cannot hear the music." She cocked her head at me. "Would you like me to lead?"

I felt a slight heat in my cheeks. "If that would be acceptable to you."

"No!" Her eyes lit up, sparkling more than the jewels on her gown. "I know how we can manage!"

She pulled me onto the ballroom floor, cocking her head to one side again as she listened to whatever tune the minstrels were playing.

"One, two, three. One, two, three." Amirah began to count, dancing up on tiptoes. Keeping her gaze on me, she counted as she went. Soon, I fell into the rhythm with her, even daring to spin her under my arm once or twice.

As the couples around us stopped their waltzing, Amirah stepped back, grinning brilliantly as she squeezed my hand.

"That was extraordinary," I whispered, leaning down so she could hear.

"You're extraordinary, my prince." Her smile made my tongue stick to the roof of my mouth. "Thank you for dancing with me."

I could dance with you forever.

I shook my head as another young man stepped up to ask for a dance with Amirah. A surge of heat flamed in my chest as Amirah curtsied, took the young man's hand in her own, and followed him to the dance floor.

My skin crawled as I watched her with the man, smiling her unknowingly beguiling smile in his direction. Her mouth widened, and I knew she was laughing. He dipped her and spun her with elegance and ease. I bit my tongue, turning away.

Avyanna marched up to me, a scowl on her face. "Why is Amirah dancing with someone else?" She planted her fists on her hips. "And why are you standing here instead of rescuing her?"

"Rescuing her?" I shook my head. "Avy, she accepted his offer to dance!"

"Men," Avyanna mumbled, her glare deepening at my raised brow. "She likes you, you dimwit!"

"What?" I glanced at the swirling blue figure on the dance floor before gaping at my cousin. "How do you know?"

"Because I do!" She huffed a loose curl off of her forehead. "Now, what are you going to do?"

"Nothing." I shook my head, crossing my arms over my chest. "She deserves better than me."

"You are a prince of Allura!" Avyanna stomped her foot, causing a few heads to turn towards her. "For heaven's sake, Thaddeus! Stop feeling sorry for yourself and go after her!"

"Shh!" I hissed, glancing around at the people around us. "All right! All right! What do you think I should do?"

"Oh, I have a plan." Avyanna smirked, holding a finger up in the air. "But are you willing to listen?"

I glanced over at Amirah, who was now dancing with a third partner and then turned back to my cousin, my jaw clenched tightly. "Yes. I want to show Amirah I'm worthy of her."

Avyanna sighed but didn't argue. "Here is what you need to do."

This is a horrid idea, I thought, forcing my panic down as I stepped up to a group of young people talking to Amirah. She was smiling politely, her hands folded behind her back.

Taking a deep breath, I laid a hand on her elbow. "May I have another dance?"

At the sound of my voice, the group turned surprised faces my way. I swallowed, my throat tight. But Amirah smiled up at me, her eyes sparkling with…

I blinked, realizing I had not been paying any attention to what she was saying.

Amirah's smile grew. "You were not paying attention, were you?"

I glanced back at the people who were all gaping at us and shook my head. My dry mouth made it impossible to form words.

"I said I would love to dance with you again, my prince." She winked, and I felt some of the tension ease from my shoulders. "I am glad you asked."

I offered her my arm, nodding at the whispering guests. Glancing around, I caught sight of Avyanna. She motioned in the direction she wanted me to go. Placing one hand in Amirah's and the other on her waist, I let my gaze wander over her face. She smiled, listening to the rhythm of the music before beginning her counts.

It was another waltz, and I let myself grin, following the counts Amirah was making as I spun her toward the terrace doors. Avyanna had worked her magic, clearing a path for us to dance out into the star-studded night. We slowed, dancing in a swaying motion and staring at one another.

"You are easy to dance with," I whispered, pain tightening my chest. How could I do this to her? I had known her for two weeks, not long enough to know whether she would grow to resent me, to hate my deafness. I squeezed my eyes shut. Why would she want more ridicule, more judgment?

Amirah's cool fingers pressed against my cheek and I pried my eyes open.

"What's wrong?" Her eyes flicked back and forth. "Are you hurt?"

Yes, but not physically.

I shook my head. "I am just speechless by how beautiful and happy you look this evening."

She pressed her lips into a thin line, dropping her eyes to look at the ground. "If I am happy, Thaddeus, it is not because of the attention or the fine clothes."

"Why are you happy?"

She stepped a little closer, her brown eyes studying me again. "Because I get to dance with you."

"Have you not noticed the looks we've been getting?" I stared down at her, not fully trusting the words she spoke.

"I don't care about the looks. I like being with you because you are real, Thaddeus." She shook her head, a small smile on her lips. "You showed me your struggles and your art, something you have not shown many others. You're kind. You understand hardships and reach out to those who are different, because you understand."

I let my hands drop to her waist, feeling myself tremble. It was suddenly hard to breathe, whether from fear or exhilaration, I did not know.

"Excuse me, for one moment." I choked out. Then I hurried down the terrace steps and into the garden.

12

AMIRAH

I crossed my arms as I watched Thaddeus run away yet again. A tear trailed down my cheek, and I angrily wiped at it as I walked into the shadows on the far side of the terrace, trying to compose myself.

It was fine if he did not care about me that way. I had only known the man a little over two weeks, after all. But I wanted to know him better. Wanted to smile more, like I did when spending time with him. He hadn't thought me disgusting but special.

A small sob escaped my lips and I sucked in a sharp breath, bracing my arms against the banister as I gulped in another deep lungful of the cool night air. Closing my eyes, turned my face to the stars.

"Tears are not becoming to you, daughter."

I flinched, turning to see Mother gliding out of the shadows.

"Then you can leave," I said, closing my eyes again.

"It's not I who will be leaving."

I heard a twig snap. My eyes flew open as a solid thud sounded behind me. A meaty hand clamped over my nose and mouth, a sickly-sweet smell invading my senses. I tried to struggle, but an arm wrapped around my torso, rendering me immobile. My head swam, my vision blurred.

The last thing I remembered seeing were the cold eyes of my mother before I was falling, falling, falling into blackness.

The sound of creaking wheels was the first thing I was aware of as my spinning head tried to focus. My stomach lurched, and I wasn't sure whether it was from the rattling cart or the drug that had rendered me unconscious. A smelly gag was in my mouth, choking me.

I tried to twist my wrists to shake off the bindings holding my hands behind my back, but it was no use. I couldn't feel my fingers, the cords were tied too tightly.

I tried to calm myself, but my chest was heaving as I attempted to push myself up. A tarpaulin covered me, trapping me in the cart. I wiggled around, trying to breathe, trying to escape, trying to not cry.

Where was I? What was happening? What was the last thing I remembered?

Thaddeus. I remember Thaddeus walking away.

That thought did nothing to keep the tears at bay, and they slid down my cheeks unhindered. I let myself cry. When my tears at dried up at last, I sucked in as deep a breath as I was able. I kept tugging at my wrists, even as I felt blood trickling over my numb hands. The memories of the rough grip, the drug, my mother.

Does Thaddeus even know what happened? Is he going to think I walked away too?

The thought made my muscles tighten as I continued to twist at my bindings. No, I was not going to let him think that. I was going to come back to him. These men, whoever they were, were not going to take me away from my happiness. I was going to fight.

The wagon lurched to a stop, and I let my resolve grow as the tarpaulin was thrown off, the light blinding me. Rough hands hauled me to my feet, and lightheadedness made my knees give way for a moment.

"All 'ight, girl." I blinked as a man with a gap-toothed sneer glared down at me. "We's givin' you five minutes to relieve yourself."

Another man with thinning black hair bent over as he untied my legs and then my wrists. "No funny business."

I nodded. It was not hard to appear terrified, for I was. Everything trembled as I stepped into the woods.

A cool summer breeze with the promise of rain blew against my bare arms as I leaned against a tree. I glanced over my shoulder, seeing the two men drinking from a waterskin.

It was time. I turned and ran back the way the wagon had come from, dodging around trees and bushes. Rocks cut through my thin slippers, and my hair snagged on gnarled branches. I felt thorns slice into my arms, but didn't stop.

I found a stream, and ran through it to the other side. The cold water seeped through my shoes, but I did not pause, running in time to my thundering heart. A tear trickled down my cheek, but I could not waste time on them. Those men…I could not imagine what they were planning on doing to me.

Realization struck me then. My mother had sold me. My *mother*. I had known she hated me, hated to even look at me. I was a reminder of the sham her marriage had been. But sell me?

I gulped a breath of air, taking a slight pause to lean against a tree and listen. A shout echoed over to me, the angry cry of my captors. I wiped at my cheek with the back of my hand, a momentary pang of disappointment shooting through me as I looked down at my torn and dirty ball gown.

But I buried my emotions. Each minute was precious, and I couldn't spend it wallowing. I had five minutes to get ahead, five minutes to try to grasp my freedom.

Five minutes to try to return to Thaddeus.

13

THADDEUS

I paced at the entrance of the hedge maze, trying to compose myself. But every time I thought about Amirah, I could hear the memories of the screams. The cracking of the ice. My failures taunted me.

I cannot fail her like I failed Gerek, I thought, pressing my fist to my lips. *I cannot bear it.*

But that horrible day still haunted me. Even thinking about loving someone, of being responsible for their welfare, of their protection, sent me spiraling. It was bad enough that Avyanna looked up to me, cared about me.

But when Amirah's eyes sparkled with admiration and hope, it petrified me. Love was terrifying, for what if I failed at loving her like I had failed at saving Gerek?

God, why are you doing this to me? I am not made to be a husband, to be responsible for another's welfare. But ... she looks at me and I'm undone. I cannot bear the thought of leaving her at the end of the week, yet I must. Because I am not worthy of her.

I redeem you.

I blinked, looking around for the voice that I had clearly heard.

Heard? I choked on my intake of air, my legs trembling as I dropped to my knees. *Lord?*

I redeem you.

But I am unworthy.

I have called you by name; you are Mine. I make you worthy. And Amirah, she chooses you.

Why? I buried my face in my hands. *Why would she want me?*

The voice wrapped around me like an embrace, peace blanketing me as more tears slid down my cheeks.

She wants you for the same reason I do, My son. Because We love you.

Amirah...loves me?

94

A warm chuckle, like honey on the tongue, filled my mind. Its sweet sound dried my tears, calming my chaotic thoughts.

Yes, child. Avyanna and Amirah tried to tell you, but you would not listen. Are you willing to release your guilt? To move into the light of love and to live each day without regret? To see that, because you are in Me, you are able to love with abandon?

I opened my eyes, whispering, "Yes," into the dark of night and smiling at the weight that rose off my shoulders. I stood to my feet, a giddy feeling stirring within me. I practically ran back to the ball, to the terrace, to Amirah.

I skidded to a sudden stop, confusion flowing through me. Lady Pruella stood above me on the steps, her hand planted on her hip as she glared at me. "She's gone, Prince Thaddeus."

Something prickled along my skin as I stared at the woman. I took a step closer to her, the light of the ball falling across me even as the shadows seemed to pulse around her. Her shoulders were thrown back, her lips pressed into a thin line.

"What do you mean she's gone?" I asked.

"She left," the woman sneered. "Take my advice, you are better off without her. She brings nothing but heartbreak wherever she goes."

"I will be the one to decide that, Lady Pruella," I said, and her eyes widened a fraction. "Where is she?"

She shrugged. "I know not."

I was up the steps faster than I thought possible, gripping her arms tightly as I glared down at her. I lowered my face. "Might I remind you that I am your prince. You best tell me what I wish to know, or it will not go well for you. Now, Lady Marchingville, where is Amirah?"

Fear filled the woman's eyes and she stammered, "I—I sold her to the slavers of Taletha."

I could feel the ache in my chest, the suffocating fear of losing someone else I loved. I gasped, pressing a fist against my chest and squeezing my eyes shut. I still had one hand clamped around Lady Pruella's bicep and I wasn't planning on letting go.

Dragging a ragged breath into my lungs, the peace I had felt moments ago surrounded me again, the gentle voice whispering in my ear.

Trust Me, My son.

With a nod, I straightened, dragging Lady Pruella into the ballroom. Heads turned, staring wide-eyed at me as I hauled our host toward Avayanna.

Avyanna's mouth hung open, stiffening as her gaze flicked from me to Lady Marchingville. "What in the world are you doing?"

"She sold Amirah." I could feel my voice cut out, the lump in my throat growing. "That is against Alluran law."

"You sold your own daughter?" Avyanna's glare was dangerous as she turned it onto Lady Pruella.

"She is not my daughter!" the woman spat. "She's the daughter of a servant that my husband loved more than me! She was never my daughter, and never will be. I hope she dies the same way her worthless mother did."

"I'm going after her." I tightened my grip, causing Lady Pruella to flinch. "You had better hope for your own sake that she is whole and healthy."

"You're going?" Avyanna laid a hand on my shoulder. "Are you sure that's wise?"

She was thinking of the past, of my sanity. And it would have been valid ten minutes before.

"I must." I shook my head. "Avyanna, Amirah's in trouble."

Avyanna smiled, gesturing to Lady Pruella. "I'll see to her."

My cousin turned, ordering one of the male guests to take the enraged woman from me. I didn't wait to see if they had everything in hand before bounding up the stairs to grab my cloak and my sword.

Please, Lord, protect her. I gasped as I flew down the road on my horse. *Keep Amirah safe.*

14

AMIRAH

My bleeding hands smeared against the rocks and leaves that littered the forest floor. Exhaustion weighed on my shoulders, and I shivered violently despite the sun that had now risen high overhead.

I had long since lost my captors. At least, I thought I had. I tripped over another log and crumpled into a heap, hugging my hands to my chest to try to hold in any warmth I could generate. The wind whistled, seeping straight through my thin dress.

I let a few tears slide down my cheeks. I didn't even know where I was or how I was going to get home. A sob broke free and I pressed the back of my hands against my lips.

"No. No crying." I stubbornly pushed myself up, wincing as the rocks cut into my bare feet. I had lost my shoes ages ago. I glanced around, noticing the thinning of the trees to my left.

A road?

Moving as quickly as I could toward it, I gasped, my legs burning from holding me up, my hands and feet throbbing from the cuts and bruises. I dashed at my forehead, sweat trickling down my temple, but it was stickier than normal.

Blood? I reached up again, feeling a scratch I couldn't remember getting.

"I will make it," I whispered. I only had to think about Thaddeus. It would be all right. Even if he did not love me, I had hope that someone, someday, would be as good and kind and loyal as him.

Trees lined each side of it as it stretched forever in each direction as I stepped out onto the road. I looked back the way I had come. Much to my relief, the road was empty. With a straightening of my shoulders, I turned and headed forward. After only a few minutes, I began to limp. My tired legs and feet protested each movement, my head screaming from lack of food and water. I hadn't had a chance to eat dinner before Mother sold me, and the sun was reaching its apex in the blue sky.

I was so tired. So very tired. My eyes slipped closed and I shook myself. I needed to lie down, if only for a small while.

Finding a bush along the side of the road, I crawled under it. Hugging my arms around my middle, I let my weary eyes slide shut.

The pounding of hooves startled me awake. I froze, not daring to move until the sound dimmed. Crawling out of my hiding spot, I watched the figure ride away, relief making my shoulders sag as another round of tears filled my eyes.

I must keep going. I rallied myself, pushing myself wearily to my feet and stumbling along the road. Part of me wondered about the horseman. Could that have been someone who would have helped me? He could just as easily have been someone who would hurt me.

I shuddered, watching the sun begin to lower behind the treetops. One foot, one foot in front of the other. I stumbled again, falling, my forehead smacking onto the hard-packed road.

"God?" I screamed, forgetting my need for stealth. "Why? Where are You? I know I'm unloved, a shame to my family. But why did You leave, too?"

I curled onto my side, hugging my knees to my chest. "I'm so tired. I'm so cold. I cannot go on anymore."

Everything hurt. My head pounded like a smithy's hammer on an anvil; my skin burned from the scratches, and my chest ached from fear and loneliness.

"I cannot go on."

Darkness ebbed into my vision, my body shook, and then everything faded to black.

15

THADDEUS

I pulled up on the reins, studying the empty wagon along the side of the road. A sheet was in the back, some rope thrown on top of it. I reached down, snagging it. Dried blood caked the fibers and my stomach lurched as I gazed around. The road was empty.

Did she escape? Oh, please God, help her be all right.

I glanced down the road, and then back the way I had ridden. Which way should I go? Even if she cried out, I couldn't hear her. I had to trust the Lord to guide me.

I do. I trust You.

A motion caught my eye and I vaulted off my horse and into the underbrush. A solid fist flew toward my face and I ducked, throwing a punch of my own into a man's stomach. He doubled over and I brought my knee up into his jaw. My attacker sprawled onto the ground, but I hauled him to his feet, adrenaline and anger giving me a strength I didn't know I had.

"Where is Amirah?" I ground out.

"I don't know!" The man's head lolled to one side. "I swear it, sire. She escaped. Me and Richard, we's been lookin' for her."

"Which way did she go?"

He pointed back the way I had come and I growled. Dragging the thug behind me, I bound him with the blood-soaked ropes and sat him in the bed of the wagon. I tried to remain calm as I lashed my horse to the back of the wagon before turning it toward Marchingville once more. An urgency tugged at me. Where was Amirah?

The ache in my chest intensified. Would I never get to tell her that I loved her? That I wanted to be worthy of her love, and that I was willing to fight for her?

It cannot be too late. A flash of blue caught my eye and I pulled up on the reins, leaping to the ground and to the edge of the forest. A bush had snagged a piece of pale blue fabric, though spots were stained with brown and red. I ran a finger over it, remembering the feeling of

Amirah's dress against my hand as we had danced. Had that only been a dozen hours ago?

I straightened, gazing around. She must have come this way, heading back to Marchingville. A fresh burst of determination flared in me, and I whistled to the horses. The wagon flew down the road, bouncing and shaking precariously over the ruts and dips in the road. I would find her. She would be fine; she had to be.

A flash of color up ahead made my heart skip a beat, the crumpled form of a woman taking shape as I drew near. I held my breath, leaping over the side once more and rushing to the body in the middle of the road.

"Amirah?" I dropped to my knees and smoothed a hand against her forehead. Dried blood flaked off a gash that ran down her temple. "Oh love, what did they do to you?"

She didn't stir, her skin as cold as ice. I leaned my hand against her lips, feeling a faint rush of air against my fingers. I scooped her slim frame into my arms, tightening my cloak around us both. A moan vibrated in her chest as she curled into a ball against me. I glared at the man in the wagon bed.

"You will pay for this," I said.

"It was a fair trade." He spat to the side. "She didn't 'ave to run."

I settled onto the wagon seat, picking up the reins with one hand and clicking my tongue to get the horses moving, albeit much slower than last time. I glanced down at the girl in my arms, relief, anger, and fear warring in my heart. Amirah was alive, but a mess. Her dress was torn, most of the jewels gone. Her hair was wild, sticks and twigs caught in the auburn tresses. Scratches covered her arms, with blood trailing down them. I swallowed the lump that formed in my throat.

"No." Her chapped lips formed the word before her whole body began to tremble and thrash. "No!"

Her eyes flew open, her wild gaze landing on me. She paused her struggle and stared at me in a daze. "Are you a dream?"

"No. I'm here and you're safe."

Amirah smiled. "If you are a dream, you're the most wonderful dream ever."

"I want you to rest. We'll be back to Marchingville soon."

"Thank you for being here." Her eyes fluttered shut, her breathing leveling out.

I tightened my arm around her. "Always, Amirah. I'll never leave you again."

Amirah slept most of the ride home, waking only when I roused her to sip from a waterskin. She was shivering, moaning and crying out, causing me to wonder whether she was cold or fear-ridden. The man in the back of our wagon never tried to escape. I wondered if he knew what his punishment would be for buying another human. My uncle did not take kindly to the slave trade in Allura.

We pulled up to the Manor House and I carefully climbed down, brushing past the servants as I carried Amirah.

"Take this man to the sheriff and call for the healer!" I barked, striding up the steps and into the garish foyer.

Avyanna came flying down the steps, her gaze sweeping over Amirah and me before motioning for me to follow her. She opened the door to her bedchamber. "Lay her on the bed," she commanded, pouring water from a pitcher on a stand and soaking a handkerchief.

"What happened to her?" she asked, her eyes on Amirah as she spoke.

"I found her on the side of the road. She escaped from the men who had her, running through the woods.

I must have ridden right past her before I caught one of the men and doubled back."

"You found her though." Avyanna's eyes met mine as she wet the handkerchief again. "That's what's important. She's safe, Thad, and she's home."

I nodded, sinking down into a chair that I had pulled to the edge of the bed.

"She's safe." I laid my hand over Amirah's, rubbing the back of it with my thumb. "There's so much I must tell you, Amirah. Please, love. Wake up."

"*Love*?" Avyanna's grin was brighter than the sun. "Truly?"

"I wouldn't go thundering into the unknown for just anyone, Avy." I glared at her, but the corner of my mouth turned up slightly.

"Oh, yes you would!" she countered, moving to wipe down Amirah's arms. "But never mind that. Would you check her feet, please?"

"Her feet?"

Avyanna raised a brow. "You didn't notice her feet earlier?"

My gaze flicked over her dress, noticing that it was more than just muddy.

"Is that…?" My stomach rolled.

Blood soaked the dress, covered the front. I turned her hand over, the sticky sensation on my fingers tightening my chest.

I stood, moving to her feet and gently tugging up the hem of her dress to her ankles. Her feet were black and blue. Scrapes and oozing blood were all over the bottom and top of them, bits of rock and dirt clinging to the shredded skin.

I buried my face in my hands, turning away as my stomach lurched. I breathed through my nose, trying to calm my rage.

"I'm going to kill them. How dare they do that to her?" I ground my teeth together, turning back to Avyanna. She was staring at me, her expression unreadable.

"What?" I asked.

"I've never seen you like this." She turned back to Amairh's hand, gently dabbing out the rocks and grime. "I'm not sure I like it, Thaddeus."

"They did this to her." I fell back into the chair, my hands trembling.

"And you think that revenge won't hurt her? Or you? Revenge is never the answer, cousin. Justice is fine.

The slave traders will be dealt with. By Uncle Benjamin."

"I hate that she's hurt."

"I know." Avyanna squeezed my hand. "But I know I would rather have the man I love by my side when I awake from a living nightmare, than to have him out punishing those who did it to me."

I nodded mutely, helping Avyanna wrap Amirah's bleeding hands until the healer could arrive to properly look over the wounds.

An hour later, the healer had come and gone. and still Amirah slept. I dozed in the chair by her side, all the while praying that God would let her wake.

16

AMIRAH

The low murmur of voices was the first thing I heard, along with the feeling of a hand rubbing over my own. A warm blanket covered me, but the cold had seeped into my very bones, making me shiver. The conversation paused and I felt the bed shift.

"Amirah?"

This has to be a dream.

My eyes felt gritty, my mouth dry. A tear slid down my cheek as I forced my eyes open, the light making everything a blinding haze. I blinked a few more times, focusing on the beautiful face of the man in front of me.

"Oh, Thaddeus." With trembling fingers, I reached up and laid my hand against his cheek.

My throat burned and my chest felt tight as I coughed. A mug was pressed to my lips, and I gulped the cool water. Thaddeus had claimed my fingers in his, gently rubbing his thumb over the back of them.

"Are you a dream?" I whispered when I could breathe once more.

"No. I'm here." His warm tone was comforting, and I wanted to pull him closer. But I was exhausted, too tired to even move. My eyes slid closed again, a sigh slipping out.

Lips pressed against my forehead, the heady smell of cedar filling my nose. "She's feeling warm, Avyanna."

A murmured response I couldn't understand floated around me as hard cough shook my frame. Another sip of water, a cool cloth laid against my forehead, and then I was drifting through the endless blackness once more.

They were chasing me. Grabbing at me, tearing at my hair and my arms. A hand clamped over my face, cutting off my voice, my screams. I thrashed about, trying to free myself. A cry tore from my mouth as I pushed away, running through the woods.

"Amirah." A gentle hand shook my shoulder, shattering the nightmare into a thousand shards.

That voice. It wasn't one of my captors. Was it? I sat up, breathing hard as another cough shook my shoulders. My head was spinning. I blinked, the dim light of the fire casting shadows on the walls all around.

"Are you all right?"

I turned toward the voice, my gaze meeting the concerned eyes of Thaddeus. A cry of relief slipped past my lips as I wrapped my arms around his neck. He stiffened, but only for a moment, his arms enfolding me into his embrace as his shoulders relaxed. "Oh, love. What's wrong?"

"I—I was so scared."

I was still hugging him, shaking horribly, and he gently eased me back enough to read my lips.

"Thaddeus. I was terrified." I tugged a blanket around me, letting the tears slide down my cheeks unchecked. "I thought I was going to die."

His jaw popped in and out as he stared at me. "We caught one of the men and your mother."

A pang speared my heart then, and I gasped. "I had forgotten that she…she…" My tears cut off my words and I sagged against his shoulder again. Thaddeus, for his part, sat in silence, rubbing my back as I cried. My heart ached, my body hurt, and I simply wanted to curl into a ball and sleep forever, much like I had on the side of the road.

"It is going to be all right, Amirah."

I shook my head against his shoulder, my throat aching too much to say anything.

"It will be." He eased me back, tipping my chin so I could look him in the eye. "Because we will be together."

"Together?" I sniffed, not understanding him. "But I thought—"

My words were cut off my Thaddeus's lips against my own. His strong arms wrapped about me, tightening protectively as he deepened his kiss. I sighed, my arms sliding around his neck as I kissed him back.

"Thaddeus," I whispered as he leaned back ever so slightly, our noses brushing as he stared at me.

"I…" His words were shaking. "I was so scared when you disappeared. I feared that I would never get to tell you how much I care about you. How much I admire your grace and poise, your smile, and the way you treat me as if I'm not different."

"You aren't," I murmured.

"I am." He smiled down at me. "But I'm learning to see that I have value despite my differences."

I cupped his cheek with my hand. "Yes. You do."

"Amirah, I—"

A knock sounded on the door, drowning out Thaddeus's words. I whispered, "Someone's at the door."

He sighed, easing me back against the pillows before standing to open the door to my room. Avyanna sailed in, followed by a maid. "We're here to help clean Amirah up!"

"How did you know she was awake?" Thaddeus asked with a raised brow.

Avyanna grinned slyly. "I have my ways. Now"—she practically shoved Thaddeus towards the door—"out with you!"

Thaddeus paused in the doorway, his eyes meeting mine. I smiled at him, emotions I had buried long ago swirling through me as I mouthed the words, *I love you.*

Thaddeus's eyes widened, right as Avyanna slammed the door in his face.

Being clean felt wonderful. A warm tub of water was drawn, Avyanna and the maid washing all the dirt and grime off of my body. My cuts stung as they gently cleaned them, but I knew it was better than infection. That thought had me shivering as Avyanna eased me back into bed.

"Did you get chilled?" Avyanna asked, smoothing out the skirt of my fresh gown before covering me with a heavy blanket.

"No." I stared at my freshly bandaged hands. My stomach growled loudly, and my friend raised her brow.

"I think we may need some food."

I grimaced, the thought of food making me want to gag, but nodded.

Avyanna grasped my hand. "Is that truly what you want?"

My head was swimming from everything that had happened in the last twenty-four hours and I bit my lip. "I…I do not know what I want."

"I know what will make you feel better." Avyanna smiled.

I watched her sail gracefully to the door, opening it and motioning for someone on the other side. I leaned back against the pillows, my eyes already half closed as

Thaddeus stepped in. I smiled, some of my swirling thoughts falling into place as he strode across the room and into a chair beside my bed.

He gently took my hand in his again, whispering, "Rest, my love. We'll talk when you wake."

That was all the permission I needed to curl onto my side and slip into a dreamless sleep.

17

THADDEUS

I love you.

My mouth fell open as Avyanna closed the door in my face, my eyes not believing what I had just seen.

She…loves me? I swallowed, rubbing the back of my neck as I leaned against the wall. I had known what the Voice had said but seeing her say it sent hope flaring through me.

The wait was agonizing. I was certain I would wear a tread in the carpet from pacing. Finally, Avyanna gestured me into the room. I hurried in, seeing Amirah's smile as I stepped over to the bed.

Her eyes were already half closed as I sank into the chair and I clasped her hand in mine. I wanted to tell her my feelings, to share everything I had been bottling up for a week. But it would have to wait a few more hours.

"Rest, my love." I ran my thumb in circles over the back of her hand as her eyes slid closed and her breathing leveled out in slumber.

A hand landed on my shoulder, and I glanced up at Avyanna.

"What did she say to you? Before I shooed you out?"

"She said she loved me." I swallowed, my gaze settling on the sleeping woman.

Avyanna's arms wrapped around my shoulders, and I peeled my gaze back to her. "And what are you feeling, cousin?"

"I love her too, Avyanna. I realized it when I was riding down the road. If she hadn't made it…" I sucked in a shaky breath, "I wouldn't have survived."

Avyanna grinned. "Well, it's a good thing you saved her."

"God saved her."

"What are you going to tell your father? He arrives later today, you know."

I shrugged. "I will tell him the truth. About everything."

"What are you hoping will happen with her mother?"

"Whatever Amirah thinks is fair." I settled my gaze back on her.

"Truly?"

"I want Amirah to be happy. Safe. Whatever that looks like."

"Your temper has cooled." Avyanna smiled. "Good."

She sailed out of the room, and I sighed. I wasn't sure what was going to happen, but I did know that I was never leaving Amirah's side ever again.

I woke up with a pain in my neck. I rose, wincing. My head had been laying on the bed, my hand still holding onto Amirah's. Her eyes were open, and she was gazing at me.

"Good morning, sleepy." She smiled, squeezing my hand.

I couldn't seem to move, to speak. In that moment, I knew. I knew I wanted to spend every morning waking up with Amirah at my side. To kiss her good morning and good night and all the times in between. To go through all of life's highs and lows side by side, hand in hand.

"Is something wrong?" She sat up, wincing slightly.

I eased to the edge of the bed, tucking a strand of her hair behind her ear. "Amirah, I—"

The door flung open and I growled as my father strode in, his eyes hard as he gazed between Amirah and myself.

"Hallway. Now."

I stifled a sigh, my eyes gazing over Amirah—who was still smiling despite her wide eyes—before I stood and followed my father.

"What happened?" His hands were planted on his hips, his jaw tight as he studied me.

"I—" I swallowed. "I fell in love, Father."

"Well, that's wonderful, son." He raised his brow, a smirk tugging on his lips. "But I was referring to what happened with the girl and her mother."

"Oh." I reddened as Father laughed and clasped my shoulder.

"While I want to hear all about that," he said, and motioned for me to follow him, "we have other matters to see to first."

We stepped into the dining room, and I started when Uncle Benjamin rose from the table. He glanced at me with his expressionless gaze before turning to Father. "Well?"

"I was waiting until he could explain it to both of us."

Uncle Benjamin nodded, motioning for me to take a seat in the chair on his right. "All right, let's get on with it then."

"What do you want to know, Uncle?" I sat, shifting slightly as Father lowered himself into the seat beside me.

"What happened?"

I recounted everything that I could remember, twisting my fingers in my lap as my uncle stared hard at me.

"And then I brought her back here."

Uncle Benjamin thrummed his fingers on the table, his chin resting on his other hand. "What made you go after her, Thaddeus?"

I cleared my throat. "I…She was in trouble."

"But after the last time," my uncle said, "I thought you would be…cautious. Send someone else."

"I…I wanted to go, sir."

Uncle Benjamin leaned forward. "Why?"

With a hard swallow, I glanced between my father and uncle. "I love Amirah, Uncle."

"Good." A small smile tugged on his lips and he nodded. "Very good."

I raised a brow. "What—?"

"Have you told Amirah that yet, son?" Father asked.

"No." Under my breath, I added, "We keep getting interrupted."

"Well, go on then." Father smiled. "Tell her your feelings, then we'll talk to you both."

I leapt to my feet. "You're certain this can wait?"

"Yes." Uncle Benjamin chuckled with a shake of his head. "Go."

I took the stairs two at a time, pausing outside Amirah's door to level out my breathing before knocking and stepping inside.

18

AMIRAH

Thaddeus looked decidedly rumpled as he pushed into the room. Avyanna, who had claimed Thaddeus's spot after he left with his father, smirked at me before patting her cousin on the shoulder and exiting the room.

"Is everything all right?" I asked as he shifted from foot to foot. "What happened?"

He ran a hand through his hair. "I…I have something I need to say."

I bit back my words, watching as he slowly moved closer to me, his eyes on the ground.

"Did you mean what you said, earlier? Do you…do you love me?" His eyes flicked up to catch my words.

"Yes, Thaddeus. I do."

He raised his gaze fully, smiling as he stated, "I'm glad."

"Are you, truly?"

He leaned closer, his hand running from my shoulder to my hand. "Yes. For I love you, too."

Tears sprung into my eyes, and I leaned my forehead against his. "I have not heard those words in a very long time."

He kissed me then, gentle and slow. My hand settled against his waist, holding him tightly. A tear trailed down my cheek, and I leaned back to wipe it away.

"Are you in pain?" he asked.

The worry in Thaddeus' tone made me smile. "No. I...I am just so happy."

"You have dimples." He returned my smile, his finger trailing down my cheek.

I blushed. "Yes."

"They're stunning. You are stunning, Amirah."

I smiled, but then a different worry slammed into me. "What will your family think when they find out who I am?"

"They will love you as much as I do. My family"—he twisted so that one leg was tucked up underneath him—"we are all imperfect. My Aunt Della is stubborn, much like Avyanna."

I laughed at that.

"My uncle Benjamin has been accused of being too solemn and serious. And the whole country knows that my mother killed a man. So yes, love, they will adore you and embrace you as one of us. All of them will."

"I trust you, Thaddeus." I blinked through tears.

"And even if they don't," he said, a roguish grin I had never seen before blooming on his face and making me giggle, "I'll marry you anyway, if you will have me."

"Marry? Marry you?" I gasped, my hands pressed to my lips.

"If you will have me," he repeated. "I'm not perfect, Amirah. I have my problems and quirks. But if we chose to love one another, despite all of that, I think…maybe we could make a marriage work. If you're willing?"

"Yes! Oh, yes!" I nodded, flinging my arms around him.

He chuckled as he hugged me tighter. "I love you, Amirah."

I pulled back, holding still long enough for him to see the earnestness on my face. "And I love you, Thaddeus. So very much."

19

THADDEUS

I held Amirah up as we slowly walked down to the dining room. Her feet were hurting her, even wrapped in bandages and without shoes pinching them. Halfway down the steps, she paused, leaning against the wall.

"I could always carry you," I offered.

She shook her head emphatically. "No, I will meet your father with dignity and on my own two feet."

I smirked, even though a part of me wanted to hold her in my arms again. "I don't want you to be in pain, love."

"I'm not." The wince as she pushed off the wall betryesd her.

We made it down to the dining room, Amirah only slightly limping as we walked to the table. A tray of cheeses, breads, and meat were placed in front of Father and Uncle. They smiled at Amirah as I settled her into a chair.

"Amirah, it's nice to meet you. Officially." Father winked at her, making a pretty blush bloom on her cheeks. "I am Thad's father, Prince Collins, and this is Benjamin, King of Allura."

Amirah inclined her head.

"We've heard Thaddeus's story." Uncle Benjamin motioned for us to take some food. "Now we would like to hear yours."

Amirah's face paled. "What would you like to know, m'lords?"

"Why did your mother sell you?" Father raised a brow.

I reached over and clutched Amirah's hand in mine. Her other hand was in her lap, trembling as she dropped her gaze to the tabletop.

She closed her eyes. "I am not her daughter."

I watched Father and Uncle Benjamin's expressions. Uncle simply raised one brow, his chin resting on his hand like before. Father's mouth fell open, his eyes flicking from me to Amirah and then back again.

"Tell us the tale, please," Uncle Benjamin said.

"They thought Mother could not have children," she began.

I turned to watch Amirah, wanting to know this story, though I knew that nothing would change how I felt about this amazing woman.

"Father so desperately wanted a child. Mother convinced a few servant women to…to try and have a child with him."

I felt my free fist tighten. I glanced at my father, but his expression was stony.

"It was only one servant, and Father felt so guilty that he told my mother. She told him the truth; she had paid the servant because she wanted children too. She said that if the servant had a child, she would claim the child as hers.

"Well, that servant girl did become pregnant. She had me, dying from complications. Father claimed me as his daughter, and for the first few years of my life, it seemed as if my mother had too. But then—"

She pulled away from me, covering her face with her hands. I moved my hand to her back, rubbing it slowly as I waited for her to continue. I felt her chest expand and she looked up at me.

"But then they had Sophie," she continued. "After that, it was as if I were the interloper, the child born out of desperation. Mother hated the reminder that Father had—" She shook her head, a tear slipping down her cheek. "Father loved me, though. He was a good man, and I…I loved him. But when he died, all the love in my house was gone. I was loathed by my mother and my sister. The servants tried but it just was not the same. I suppose this party gave Mother the final push to do away with me."

"What do you mean?" Father asked, glancing between me and Amirah again.

"She hated the attention both Avyanna and Thaddeus gave me." She tucked a piece of hair behind her ear. "She accused me of not letting Sophie have a chance at meeting the crown prince."

Uncle Benjamin raised a brow at me, and I nodded.

"Well," Father exhaled, "I still cannot imagine *selling* anyone."

Amirah shrugged, her eyes staring down at the table again. An awkward moment of silence settled around us.

I took a deep breath, pushing to my feet as all eyes turned to me. "Father, I would like your blessing on marriage between Amirah and myself."

A grin slowly bloomed across Father's face.

"I never thought I'd see the day." Both of Uncle's brows rose and he smirked.

Heat crawled up my neck, and Amirah's smile only deepened it.

"Do you love my son too, Amirah?" Father asked. When she nodded emphatically, he laughed. "Good. Then, yes, you have my blessing."

I pulled Amirah into my arms, her feet hanging a few inches off of the ground. Completely ignoring propriety, I kissed my wife-to-be quite soundly on the lips. "Thank you for finding me worthy, Amirah."

She smiled, resting her forehead against mine with her arms around my neck, "No, thank you, Thaddeus. Thank you for showing me that I am worthy of love."

EPILOGUE

TWO MONTHS LATER...

"I now pronounce you man and wife."

Collins smiled as the people in the cathedral cheered. Thaddeus smiled down at his new wife, Amirah's love-struck gaze never leaving his. She said something, making his son's smile grow even more before he leaned in and kissed her.

"They look as happy as we did." Sage, his wife, dabbed at her eyes. "And to think I tried to talk him out of going with Avyanna."

Collins laughed, wrapping his arm around her shoulders as Thaddeus and Amirah walked down the aisle hand in hand. "God knows what's better, my dear."

Indeed, He had. Collins smiled as he thought about Thaddeus, the new Lord of Marchingville. Pruella had been found guilty of the illegal sale of a human. At the request of Amirah, Pruella had been exiled rather than put to death, and banished to Ironwolf. The men responsible for purchasing Amirah had been sentenced to ten years in prison, a lenient punishment by Allura standards.

Sage squeezed his hand, her loving gaze settling on his face. "Did you ever think that Thad would find such love?"

"Yes. I knew he would." Collins pressed a kiss to his wife's temple. "He comes from a long line of love, my dear. It's only natural he should fall so hard and so fast."

Sage smiled up at him, a twinkle in her amber eyes. "You've grown wise in your old age, Collins."

With a peck on the lips, Collins intertwined his fingers with Sage's. "I suppose that comes from being in love with you for over twenty years, my love. You make me a better man."

Striding down the aisle, Collins and Sage followed Thaddeus and Amirah back to the castle for the feast, rejoicing that their son—who had once counted himself unworthy—had found a woman who showed him how deserving of love he truly was.

THE END

ANNA AUGUSTINE

LIKE

Never

BEFORE

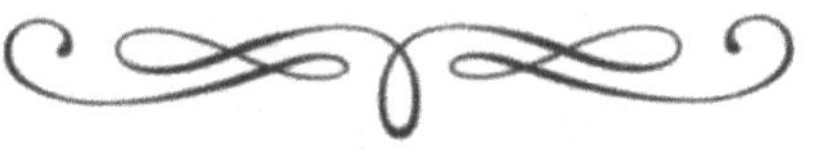

LACHLAN AND BRYLEE'S STORY

"Put on then, as God's chosen ones, holy and beloved, compassionate hearts, kindness, humility, meekness, and patience, bearing with one another and, if one has a complaint against another, forgiving each other; as the Lord has forgiven you, so you also must forgive. And above all these put on love, which binds everything together in perfect harmony."

Colossians 3:12-14 ESV

1

LACHLAN

HILLINGSFARTH-1435

"What do you mean?" I planted my fists on the edge of the desk, glaring at Lord Willoughby as he shakily unrolled and spread a parchment onto my desk. "Allura would never back down from their agreement in that way."

Willoughby swallowed, his thinning grey hair falling across his forehead as he continued to shake. I resisted the urge to roll my eyes. The man thought I was terrifying, a fact I found amusing. I was simply the Prince of Hillingsfarth, barely above him in my title. Yet he trembled like a leaf whenever he was in my presence.

"I—I do not understand it myself, your highness," he said.

I ripped a hand through my black curls. "What exactly happened?"

"They have rescinded their trade agreement, Prince Lachlan. I do not understand it myself," he repeated as he shifted from one foot to the other. "Your father has told me that an ambassador of Findley is coming to try to fix this mess. He said you are to be the representative of Hillingsfarth in this arrangement."

I clenched my teeth together. "Truly?"

"Yes, highness." Willoughby raised his brow. "They are already on their way. And I don't see an alternative."

"I suppose that is better than me going there." I sighed and tore *both* hands through my hair now.

"Well, I will tell your father you are willing. They are expected to arrive in two days' time." Willoughby bowed as he backed up toward the door. He bumped into the doorframe, leaping forward with a strange red tint on his face before turning and scurrying away.

I buried my face in my hands as I sank into my desk chair. I had been to Allura only once, and it had not ended well. My nightmares were haunted by the tearstained face of Princess Brylee and the mistakes I had made. And now I was expected to be courteous and kind with whoever came, to try to smooth things over with a nation whose princess I had gravely hurt. An ambassador who most likely be *her* relative.

I stood, needing to expel the energy coursing through me, and stepped out into the hall, striding quickly through the dimness to the indoor training arena. The wide open, high ceilinged room had weapons along the right side, with tall windows on the left. A few knights sparred in the rings spaced around. Merely stepping through the door relaxed my stance as I prepared my mind for a bout.

My friend, Everett, hurried over, grinning his giant, exuberant smile. "Heard about the ambassador coming. Figured you might want to spar.

"Yes." I let out a small laugh. "I need to do…something."

Everett tossed me a training sword as we stepped into a ring. His grin became wicked now and he eyed me as we slowly circled each other. He shouted, "En garde!" right before he launched himself at me. I easily parried, and our spar was underway. The swords flew as we danced around each other, sweat dripping down our faces as we went. A few of the knights gathered round, eager to watch the two finest swordsmen in Hillingsfarth duel.

The cheers grew as Everett, with a twist of his sword I had not been expecting, yanked my weapon from my hands.

"Plead mercy, m'lord," he panted and stepped onto the hilt of my sword.

Breathing heavily myself, I bowed in exaggeration. "Mercy, good knight."

"Yes, I grant it." He laughed, swiping his sleeve across his brow, and then retrieved my sword. Waving the knights back to their training, he walked over to place the mock weapons in one of the bins along the wall.

"So, how nervous are you?" he asked. "About the ambassador?"

"It should not be that bad." I sighed, rubbing the back of my neck. "As long as it's not Avyanna."

A memory of her I did not wish to relive sprang to mind and I gagged. Avyanna had ruined so much, and my failure to stop her mocked me daily.

"You don't know then?" Everett pulled me to a stop.

"Don't know what?"

"Who the ambassador is." Everett rolled his eyes when I shook my head. "Oh, well Willoughby made a mess of this, he did."

"A mess of what?" I balled my hands into fists. "Everett, who is the ambassador?"

I felt the blood drain from my face as Everett said, "Princess Brylee is the ambassador from Allura."

"No! Absolutely not!" I paced the length of my father's study with agitated steps. "The last time I spoke to her, she said she never wanted to see me again!"

My father stroked at his greying beard, one bushy eyebrow raised as he watched me throw my tantrum. "Are you quite finished, Lachlan?"

I fisted my hands at my side, sucking in a deep breath. I held it for a few seconds before expelling it in a rush. "Yes."

"You know that the easiest way to fix this trade mess is to speak with someone from Allura."

I braced my hand against the wall, sudden nausea making me feel lightheaded. "But why Princess Brylee, Father?"

"It's who they are sending, my boy." He shrugged. "Probably hoping after the mess you made last time that she won't fall for you again." He laughed, like it was a grand joke.

"Well, that's quite likely." I ran a hand through my hair, shame weighing on my shoulders. "As I said, she never wanted to see me again."

Those words had stung, but not as badly as knowing I had deserved them. And losing Brylee…that had been the hardest. I had truly cared about her. Then I had thrown it all away in one moment of stupidity.

Yet some inane part of me wanted to see her. Wanted to soak in her amber eyes and soft smile. Not that there would be many smiles directed my way. I wondered that she was coming at all. *At least it's not Avyanna.* I shivered. That would have been much worse to deal with.

Father sobered at my sullen expression and clamped his big hand on my shoulder, shaking me from my melancholy. "I'm sorry, Lachlan. I know this is hard. You tear yourself up every day over letting her go; I see it plain as the nose on your face."

I rubbed my nose, turning to gaze out over the rolling hills. A few herds of sheep with their shepherds dotted the landscape, like fluffy white clouds against a sky of green. The actual sky was brilliantly blue that day, touching the grass on the horizon without any gray—a rare occurrence.

"Yes," I said. "And I will continue to do so until I make amends."

"Lad, you cannot *do* anything. You simply must ask for her forgiveness."

"You did not see her face that day, Father." I sighed. No, he didn't understood half of it. The half I'd told him. "I am fairly certain that out of everyone I have wronged, Princess Brylee will be the very last to ever forgive me."

2

BRYLEE

ALLURA

I glared at my uncle, King Benjamin of Allura, my arms crossed defiantly. My anger did not bother him, and he simply raised a brow.

"Did you not tell me a few months ago that you would do whatever possible to ensure peace?" he asked, voice low.

I resisted the urge to growl. "Yes, but—"

"This will help." He motioned to his youngest son. "Silas will go with you, but *you* are the ambassador."

I glared at my cousin now. His arms were crossed as he stood beside his father, his face almost as expressionless as Uncle Benjamin's. His blond hair—a strange contrast to the rest of his family's dark coloring—fell in his blue eyes as he raised a brow at me.

"Is that a problem, cousin?" Despite his dispassionate expression, I could very clearly hear the grin in his voice. He knew why this bothered me. Of course he did. Silas seemed to find out everything. He was insufferable that way.

"No, there is no problem," I said through gritted teeth. "I will be the ambassador to Hillingsfarth."

"Good." Uncle Benjamin clapped his hands. "You leave in an hour."

"What?" I glanced between the two men.

Uncle Benjamin nodded, a small smile tugging on his lips. "Yes. Your maid already has your trunk packed."

"Unbelievable!" I muttered under my breath as I turned and practically stomped out of the study.

"Brylee! Wait!"

"What?" I stifled another growl as Silas grabbed my arm.

"I'm sorry." He rubbed the back of his neck. "I tried to get him to send only me, but Avyanna told him you would want to go."

"Avyanna?" I let the growl lose. "Of course she did."

Silas cleared his throat, looking like he wanted to bolt. "I know you two had a tiff. And I suspect it has something to do with Lachlan, but what happened exactly?"

"It's none of your business," I snapped. I was done with meddling, nosy family. I pushed around Silas, wanting only one person at that moment. "I will see you in an hour, Silas."

He did not respond, and I probably would not have replied if he had. I stomped into the family sitting room, thankful to find my mother curled on the settee reading a book.

"Mama."

She looked up, her brows dimpling in worry as she rose and moved to my side. I stepped into her embrace, a tear slipping down my cheek. The anger had melted into fear the moment I had entered the safety of our room.

"What's wrong, Brylee?"

"Uncle Benjamin is sending me to Hillingsfarth." I sniffed.

Mama was the only person I had told about that day, when I had caught the man I fancied kissing my best friend and cousin. I had barely spoken to Avyanna, and I had kept my word and never seen Lachlan again.

"Is that really so bad?" Mama smoothed back my hair from my face. "Maybe you need to see him to move on, my love."

I shook my head. "No. No, I told him I never wanted to see him again and I meant it!"

Mama tilted her head to the side, studying me. "Do you remember the story your father used to tell you? About the forest nymph and the handsome prince?"

I nodded slowly, confused by the change of topic. "The prince was a horrid person, and he was banished to the woods. While there, he met a forest nymph who was very lovely and who valued goodness above all else. The prince wanted to please her, so he tried to be a better person. But he kept failing, over and over."

"Yes. And how did he mend his ways?"

"He went down to the river. There he met a kind man who told him that the only way he could change was to have his horridness washed away. He helped him bathe, and the young prince was made new. He married the forest nymph, carrying her back to his land where he was pardoned by the king and they lived happily ever after."

Mama nodded. "That story is about me and your father."

I stared at her for a long moment. "You're jesting."

"No." Mama laughed, her amber eyes dancing. "Your father created that tale for you and your brother, thinking it was a clever way to teach the lesson he learned while making it fun for you two."

"All that time it was your story." I shook my head in disbelief.

"Yes. But do you see the message of it, Brylee?" Mama clutched my hands in hers. "Forgiveness. I forgave your father of all the horrible things he had done and said. And more importantly, Jesus forgave him too, and made him new."

I swallowed. "You're saying I need to forgive Avyanna and Lachlan."

"That's what I'm saying." She pecked my forehead. "It's not easy, but it is freeing."

"I need to think about this."

"I'll be praying for you." She smiled. "I do not understand why God is sending you now, or what will be waiting for you once you're there. But it will be for your best, love. That I know for certain."

"Pray for strength, Mama." I wiped away a tear.

She pulled me into another hug. "Strength, and peace, and love."

"Love?" I scowled at the word. "No, Mama. Anything but that."

Papa wrapped me tightly in his arms that afternoon as Silas waited for me by the carriage and pressed a kiss to my forehead, all the while glaring at Uncle Benjamin. The look was not lost on me; he was livid that I was being sent to Hillingsfarth.

I squeezed his forearms. "I'll be fine, Papa. Silas is going with me."

"Yes, and if he fails to keep you safe…." He let the threat hang, saying it loud enough for Silas and Uncle to hear.

"She will be fine, Uncle Collins." My cousin smirked and nodded. "I promise."

I huffed a breath. "And it's not like I'm defenseless."

I patted the sword that was strapped to my back. My Aunt Della had made sure I learned the art of swordplay early in my life, adamant that I know about the ways of warfare. Between her and Uncle Nicholas, I had learned to shoot a bow, wield a sword, and throw and fight with daggers. I had even beaten my cousin Marcus in a sword fight a few weeks before, and he served as one of the captains in Allura's army.

"Do you have the dagger Thad gave you last Christmas?" Papa asked, his brows lowering. "I like to think you could take the prince down if he hurts you again."

I smiled at that. "Yes, I have it. But I will be fine, Papa. I was scared about seeing Prince Lachlan again, but I'm not now. Everything that is meant to happen will happen."

He pressed another kiss to my forehead as Silas strode over and pulled me toward the carriage. "But nothing can happen if you do not let us start our journey, Uncle Collins," he said.

"I would not be opposed to that, Silas."

I laughed, but as soon as the carriage door swung closed, I wrapped an arm around my churning stomach.

Silas sprawled onto his back on the seat across from me, bracing himself with one leg propped up on the cushioned seat. He tucked an arm under his head, turning to study me as the carriage began moving. "So how are you truly?"

I shrugged, watching the rolling landscape pass outside the window. "I am nervous. And angry at your father. I don't understand why he thought to send me, even with Avyanna's suggestion."

"Maybe he believes you have what it takes to mend this bridge." Silas shrugged, letting his eyes slide closed.

I scoffed but didn't say anything else. Soon Silas' snores rumbled along with the wheels, his breaths ruffling the hair that had fallen across his face. He looked so young while he slept, even though he was only a year younger than my own twenty-two years. My mind wandered to our growing up years. I remembered the day that Silas climbed up to the top of the old oak tree in the garden to rescue my kitten. He never even hesitated. It's what made him such a great reconnaissance officer for our kingdom. Yet, there was a gentleness beneath him, a tenderness. The way he kissed his mother and smiled at her as if she were worth more than all the jewels in the coffers. If he ever let someone close enough to see, he would make plenty of women swoon.

But of course, he didn't. He was impassive when it came to the ladies of the court. I'd even heard him tell Marcus once that he thought he'd never marry. I shook my head. That I could not imagine. Silas was far too caring to never fall for a woman in need.

I felt my eyelids lower as the warm sun kissed my face, my head leaning against the side of the coach. With a sigh, I let myself doze, waking only when we hit a deep rut in the road.

Silas sat up with a swear, blushing when he saw me. "Sorry."

I shrugged. "Where are we?"

He glanced out the window. "Nearing Marchingville, I think."

A smile twitched my mouth at the thought of seeing my brother. He'd been given the lordship of Marchingville and had married Amirah four months earlier. They had agreed to house us for the evening before we finished our journey on the morrow.

"You're excited," Silas said, leaning back with his arms crossed.

"Yes, I haven't seen Thad in months." I grinned at my cousin. "And Amirah is such a dear."

Silas shrugged. "I admire your connection with Thaddeus. I've never been particularly close to Willhelm and Nettie. Comes with the job, I suppose."

I raised a brow at him. "You've only been a reconnaissance officer for three years."

"I was always closer with my cousins." He smirked, his eyes sliding closed again. "You specifically, Bry."

I laughed as a squeaky gate groaned open and we rolled to a stop in front of a fine manor home. From what Thad had written, they had done extensive work on the house. It was painted a light shade of grey, ivy trailing along the left side. The dark green shutters were thrown open to accept the early autumn air.

The door of the house flung open as Silas helped me out of the coach. Thaddeus, with total abandon, came flying down the steps and scooped me up in his arms, spinning me in a circle.

"You're here!" he cried, planting a kiss on my cheek as he set me back on my feet. "It's so good to see you, sister."

"And you!" I looked up at him, smiling. "Marriage seems to appeal to you."

A faint blush colored his cheeks and he looked over his shoulder at Amirah, who was smiling down at him from the top of the steps. When he turned back, his smile had grown even larger.

"Yes," he said. "It's very good."

Amirah's laugh danced over us as I moved up the steps to greet my sister-in-law, and Thaddeous enveloped Silas in a manly embrace.

"You look very well." Amirah pecked my cheek. "How was your journey thus far?"

"It has been good." I stretched with a groan. "Silas and I slept most of the way."

Amirah smirked as she linked her arm with mine and we moved inside. "How Silas and you manage to sleep on the road, I'll never know."

"Well, we did wake before we reached the gate." I gazed around the foyer, at the red paper and marble flooring with a gold vein running through it. Hand drawn pictures in white frames lined the wall, and a few wooden figurines graced the tables, evidence of my brother and sister-in-law's artistic gifts.

Amirah gestured to the room. "Thaddeus redecorated the foyer for me as a wedding gift. Before, it was rather garish."

I heard the men behind us and turned to grin at my brother. "Was this the hideous gold room you told me about?"

"Yes." He smiled back, nodding. "I greatly improved it."

Amirah stepped up to him, laying her hand against his chest until he gazed lovingly down at her. "You did wonderful, as I have said before. Now, I'm sure Silas and Brylee are hungry and tired."

I stifled a yawn, and Silas smirked at me. "Someone is," he said, "despite the fact that she slept the whole way here."

I shrugged. "Who knows how much rest we'll get in Hillingsfarth?"

At the name, my brother stiffened, gazing at me for a long moment as if he could read what I was feeling just from my face. Maybe he could. Being deaf had made him good at seeing others in ways I still did not understand.

With his eyes still on me, Thaddeus asked, "Amirah, will you show Silas to his room?"

Amirah glanced between us, then motioned for Silas to follow her up the twisting staircase without a comment.

"Why are *you* being sent?" Thaddeus asked once they had gone.

I sighed, turning to face my brother. He was standing ramrod straight, his arms crossed over his chest, looking very much like our father.

"Uncle thinks that I am the best hope for reconciliation." I laid my hand on his arm. "I will be fine, Thad."

He shook his head. "Did you not tell him about the kiss?"

"No." I sighed. "No one was supposed to know about that except Mother. How do *you* know about it?"

"Avyanna."

She *would* tell Thaddeus. For all that Silas and I were close, Thaddeus and Avyanna were much the same. She would have told him, especially when I had stopped talking to her.

"What—what did she say about it?" I choked out, wanting to know but not wanting to hear the truth all at once.

"She said it was a mistake." Thaddeus laid his hand gently on my shoulder.

I laughed bitterly. "Of course she would say that after I stopped speaking to her."

"I think it was more than that, Bry." Thaddeus paused. "But that's something you need to talk to Avyanna about."

I shook my head and did not reply.

Thaddeus sighed. "Let me show you to your room. We want you to have all the rest you can before facing Prince Lachlan."

My stomach twisted at his name, but I took a steadying breath and nodded. All I needed to do was mend our ties with Hillingsfarth and get home as quickly as possible. It would be easy.

There was nothing to worry about. Nothing at all.

3

LACHLAN

I swallowed back bile as the carriage with the royal emblem of Allura rolled through our massive gates and around the first of our three fountains. The time it took for it to roll to a stop at the base of the palace steps was far too much time to think. I clasped my shaking hands behind my back, willing myself to keep breathing. It would be perfect, this greeting. There was no other way for it to go.

Behind my shoulder, Everett shifted. He leaned close to my ear, whispering, "Try not to look like you're going to lose the contents of your stomach, my prince."

I stifled a snort, earning a reprimanding look from my father and I schooled my features back into my royal smile as the carriage halted. One of our footmen opened the door and a prince of Allura—whose name escaped me—leapt out. His silver circlet was pushed back, resting more on the top of his head than his forehead. One of the blond locks fell into his blue eyes as he gazed over us all and I felt analyzed, more like a chess piece than a person.

His assessment must have been favorable for he turned back to the carriage, offering his hand to the woman in the opposite seat. She stepped down and I caught my breath.

Brylee looked lovely. Her pale-yellow gown brought out the faint golden flecks of her eyes, her light brown hair hanging down her back, a golden circlet resting perfectly atop of her forehead. Her lips were pressed into a thin line as she gazed over Father, Everett, and then me. I watched her jaw tighten as she studied me before turning back to Father.

"Thank you for having us, King Benedict," she said. "This is my cousin, Prince Silas, and we both hope that this trip will be beneficial to all concerned."

"Yes, Princess Brylee. That is our hope as well." Father cleared his throat, gesturing to the castle. "May Trinity Palace be as much a home to you as your own."

Her smile faltered, a distraught look crossing her features for only a moment before she inclined her head and bobbed a small curtsy. "Yes. May it be."

When she straightened, her smile was back in place, more strained than before. I could feel Father staring at me, so I stepped forward and bowed. "Brylee, may I—"

I swallowed my words when I saw her hand on her companion's arm. She smiled at me, but it was cold and hard as she motioned to the steps. "Shall we, *Prince* Lachlan?"

Wincing, I nodded and motioned up the steps. "This way, Princess."

Everett raised a brow at me as I turned, and I shook my head ever so slightly. He stepped back, letting me pass. I heard Prince Silas whisper something as I began to step up to the door.

"I hope that you will find Trinity Palace comfortable, m'lady," I said, slowing enough to fall into step beside Brylee. "It is not quite as grand as Findley's palace."

She looked at me out of the corner of her eye. "I am sure it will be as nice as any place that has you within its walls, your highness."

I glanced at Father, but he was far enough ahead to not catch the whispered words.

Brylee followed my gaze before asking, "He does not know?"

"He knows some." I cleared my throat when the words came out an octave higher than normal. "Not the full story. I regret what I did daily and that is punishment enough."

"Well," she said, "I hope to avoid a repeat of our last visit together."

"As I am the spokesman for Hillingsfarth in this endeavor, I too wish for as little conflict as possible."

"You?" Brylee stumbled slightly, and it was only Prince Silas' hold on her hand that kept her from planting her face into the ground. "You are the ambassador's consultant?"

"Yes." I raised a brow at her. "Did you not know?"

"No." She made a grunting sound in her throat and it almost sounded like a growl. "I did not know I was even coming until two days ago."

I glanced at her companion and he shrugged a shoulder. "My father prefers surprising us at times," he said.

"Your father...?" I swallowed. "Is King Benjamin?"

"Yes." Silas inclined his head. "There are a lot of us living within Findley Castle. It is easy to become confused."

"You do not look like the king." I cleared my throat, shifting my feet and feeling the overwhelming urge to flee.

"Yes. It does help at times." Prince Silas flashed a smile and did not elaborate further.

I dared another glance at Brylee. Her jaw had tightened, her gaze straight ahead as she followed my father into the front hall and then up our large, wide staircase to the second level. The plush green carpet muted all our footsteps. Statues of mythical creatures sat between the large white columns and stared us down as we moved to the guest wing.

"One room for Princess Brylee and one for Prince Silas." Father gestured to the doors. "If there is anything you will be needing, don't hesitate to ring the cord by the door. A maid will arrive promptly. Dinner is in three hours, so plenty of time for you to get ready." He had not paused for a breath through the whole speech and was looking a little red in the face by the end.

"Will you be needing an escort?" I asked, clasping my hands behind my back as Silas stepped into his room. "I would be most willing—"

"No." Brylee interrupted again. "We shall find our own way."

I nodded, my eyes flicking down to the ground. I should have expected it, this cold greeting. But the old attraction, the old fire, had sprung to life inside of me the moment she had stepped out of the carriage.

"Well." Father cleared his throat. "Rest well, your highness."

He bowed quickly then fled back the way we had come. I nodded to Brylee before following.

Everett was waiting in the entry as I walked down the steps, his hand resting on the hilt of his sword. Amusement twinkled in his eyes. "That was one of the most awkward meetings I've ever witnessed, if you don't mind me saying. Was it that cold the first time 'round?"

"No, and we both know why it was so cold this time." I glared at him, thankful Father had retreated to his study.

"You still like her, don't you?" Everett's grin faded. When I did not respond, he groaned. "Oh no. You do! You still like her!"

"Yes," I hissed him into silence. "I did not expect this. It has been a year, after all. A blasted awful year, but a year just the same."

"She was colder than a midwinter morning! What are you going to do, Lachlan?" Everett studied me. "You're not going to try to woo her again, are you?"

"Yes, that would work," I said with a harsh laugh, "since she can barely speak civilly to me."

"Well, then maybe some wooing is in order."

I crossed my arms. "Absolutely not."

"Not you." Everett waved a hand at me. "She truly hates you, that much is obvious. No, I was talking about me." He threw back his shoulders, straightening to his full height. He was a good three inches above my six-foot height. Some of the knights had even taken to calling him, *Our Friendly Giant*. They also teased Everett about the women who were constantly batting lashes and giggling when he walked by. Though Everett was aware of his attractiveness, he rarely used it to sway a woman to his side. But if any of the knights could charm Brylee into liking them, it was Everett.

The thought made a surge of heat flare in me. "No. No flirting, Everett."

"And why not?" He flicked a strand of hair off of his forehead.

"Because your prince commands you, that is why!" I swallowed the oath that wanted to fly out. "Truly, Everett, stay away from her."

"Good. Very good." He smirked as he turned on his heel and meandered away.

What is happening to my nice, orderly life? My brow furrowed, and I groaned. Somehow, I doubted that my life would return to normal in the foreseeable future. Not so long as Princess Brylee of Allura was under my roof.

Dinner was a tense affair.

Brylee sat as straight as a rod, picking at her food with her utensils, barely eating anything. Her gown was a beautiful red wine color, bringing out the red tints in her hair and the shimmering brown in her eyes, eyes that kept glaring at me every time they flicked in my direction.

Silas was oblivious to the tension, or so it seemed. He ate his food in moderate silence, answering the few questions Father asked him in short responses. He had on a vest that matched Brylee's dress in color. Under that was a plain white shirt. Black pants and boots completed his style.

I wanted to tug at the collar of my shirt but settled on fidgeting with the napkin in my lap instead. Clearing my throat, I decided to try to speak with the princess again.

"Did you have a nice rest, m'lady?" My voice sounded loud in the nearly silent dining room, echoing off the walls and making our guests jump.

Brylee's scowl deepened for a moment, but she quickly forced a smile. "It was quite pleasant, Prince Lachlan. The room is lovely."

It was the most she had spoken to me since she arrived. I smiled at her, but she dropped her gaze to her plate again.

"I never did get to ask how your journey to Hillingsfarth was." I popped a bite of meat into my mouth, chewing as I waited for a response.

"It was uneventful." Throwing her shoulders back, Brylee met my gaze with a frosty intensity.

Silence settled around us once again. My father coughed, wiping his mouth before pushing to his feet. "Thank you for dining with us, Prince Silas, Princess Brylee."

Both the royals inclined their heads as Father practically ran out the door, leaving me to face the wrath of Brylee alone.

4

BRYLEE

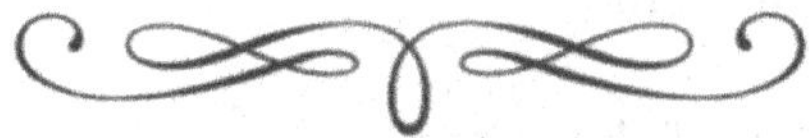

I wanted to cry, and that made me mad. I had no reason to cry, for Lachlan had never been mine. But seeing him—with his kind smile and curly black-brown hair that fell across his eyes—made the wound open up all over again.

He dragged his green eyes back to me and I forced my shoulders to relax. But then he smiled. I twisted my napkin around my fingers, wanting to bolt back to my room. Silas cleared his throat, shifting slightly beside me. Even my normally unshakable cousin could sense the tension radiating off of us.

"Would you like a tour of the castle?" Lachlan finally asked. Silas stood quickly, nodding.

I gritted my teeth and slowly rose. Dropping the napkin onto the table, I glared at Lachlan. "What will we see?"

He shrugged. "Whatever you would like to, m'lady."

"Let us be off!" Silas stated, a forced cheer to his voice that proved he simply wanted out of the dining room and didn't care one bit about the castle. He took off toward the doors. I growled under my breath as Lachlan stepped up to me.

"May I?" he asked.

Did his voice seem strangled? I clenched my hands into fists as he held out his arm, wanting nothing more than to follow after my traitorous cousin. But I forced a breath into my lungs as I laid my hand lightly onto Lachlan's arm, trying in vain to ease the ache in my chest.

"Where are you taking us?" I asked as he began to leisurely stroll down the hall.

"Let's find Prince Silas and decide together."

The sun was just setting over the green hills, painting the sky a brilliant palette of purples, pinks, and reds. The white pillars to our right glowed in the light, warming the hall that was paneled in walnut wood. The carpet muted our footfalls as we reached the spot where Silas was waiting for us.

A large set of double doors stood open and Silas was peering in. I felt Lachlan stiffen ever so slightly by my side, but when I glanced up, a smile was still firmly on his face.

"I see your cousin has found our indoor training arena," he said.

"An indoor training room?" I pulled my hand away, stepping up beside Silas. The room was large, darkening as the sunlight disappeared from the windows on the left side of the room. Four rings were set up around the room. Pillars that matched the ones in the halls supported the roof and weapons lined the right side of the room.

"Yes." Lachlan replied and I glanced back at him. He had his hands clasped behind his back, rocking on his feet. "We train here in the colder months or when it is raining outside."

"I hear it rains a lot here." Silas met his gaze over my head and Lachlan nodded.

"Yes, we have our share of rainy days," he said.

I resisted the urge to sigh. Hillingsfarth was lovely, I begrudgingly admitted. I loved the rain, the clouds, the need to be cozy and content inside. I liked the rolling hills, and the coolness in the air.

This was almost home.

I sucked a sharp breath between my teeth, refusing to think that. It was not my home, and it never would be.

"Do you still train, Princess Brylee?" Lachlan stepped to my side, the three of us now staring into the dim room.

I kept my eyes forward. "Yes. Occasionally."

"More than occasionally," Silas said under his breath with a soft scoff.

"Would you be opposed to a sparring match?" Lachlan turned to me. "Perhaps tomorrow after our business is concluded for the day?"

"A spar with you?" I planted my fists on my hips, turning to face him. "That's hardly a fair match. For you."

"And you would know this how?" A little bit of anger tinted his words, and I couldn't stop the smirk that pulled on the corner of my mouth.

"I know my skill," I said, "and it is better than most."

His brows lowered. "I do not fear skill, m'lady. A match tomorrow between you and me."

Lachlan stared at me, waiting. I continued to smirk at him for a long moment before turning away from the doors and continuing down the hall.

"It's your pride on the line, Lachlan." I said. "Do not blame me when you are made a fool."

Later that evening as I brushed my hair, a knock sounded on the door before Silas poked his head in.

"Good, you're still up." He padded over to me, dropping cross-legged onto the floor. "Do you think it was wise to accept Lachlan's challenge?"

I shrugged one shoulder. "Why not?"

"Because then everyone in Hillingsfarth will know that you are formidable." My cousin raised a brow.

I sighed, setting my brush down on the vanity. "I know you're here to protect me, Silas. But I will be fine. It's Prince Lachlan I'm fighting. He will be fair."

Silas frowned. "He was not very fair before."

My stomach twisted at the words and I pressed a hand against it. "That's the past. It's dead."

As far as my head is concerned. My heart? That's another matter entirely.

"Are you sure, Brylee?" Silas gripped my hands, pulling my gaze to his. "I do not want you to be hurt again. We all thought he was going to propose to you and then he left—"

"I will survive, Silas." I smiled, ignoring the pain that stabbed me. Instead, I ruffled Silas' hair like I had when we were children. "Now, go back to your room. I'm tired."

One side of Silas' smile appeared for a moment before he pushed to his feet and kissed the top of my head. "If he hurts you, he is a dead man."

"I am sure your father would love dealing with the aftermath of that."

"He would go to war for you, Brylee." Silas was quiet for a moment before he snorted. "Any of us would, for that fact. We are family and family comes first."

I was surprised by the tears that sprung into my eyes at that thought. I grabbed Silas' hand, pulling him into an embrace he didn't know what to do with. I released him just as quickly. "Thank you, cousin."

He nodded, hurrying out the door before he had to suffer through another hug.

I climbed into the big bed, pulling the covers up to my neck as I curled onto my side, my feet tucked underneath me. I closed my eyes, but my mind whirled.

Lachlan.

Sparring matches.

Trying to resolve the trade issues.

Lachlan.

Not falling in love again.

I growled, rolling to my other side. *I refused to fall in love. After all, I hate black hair. And green eyes are...are...*

I groaned as I flopped onto my back, smothering my face with my pillow.

They are absolutely wonderful.

5

LACHLAN

If dinner had been tense, breaking our fast the next day was a kettle at the boiling point. Brylee ate this time, but she looked exhausted. I wondered if she had tossed and turned as much as I had the night before.

What had prompted me to challenge her? She already hated me, and this was not the impression I had been hoping to make to our ambassador. I shifted in my seat, my eyes flicking to her once again, surprised to find her staring at me.

"Are you nervous?" she asked, a hint of a smile playing on her lips.

"Why would I be nervous, m'lady?" I smiled back. "I have won our tournaments the last three years."

"I'm impressed." She raised a brow. "I hope you find me a worthy adversary then." Brylee took a bite of her eggs, her eyes never leaving my face, a slightly terrifying gleam in her eye.

"I shall go prepare the necessary papers for you to view," I said. "Meet me in the library in a half hour." I pushed my plate away, scratching at my chin as I rose.

She nodded, the challenge still in her gaze as I turned on my heel and hurried from the dining room. My heart thundered as I leaned against the hallway wall, trying to catch my breath. This was ridiculous. She should not have such power over me, to immobilize me with a single look. I loosened the top button of my shirt, rubbing the back of my neck.

I took a deep breath, pushing off the wall and walking with determination to the library. I quickly sorted out the papers that Brylee needed to view, then crossed my arms on the desk as I reread them.

Allura had stopped shipping the promised fine silks that my people traded the wool from our flocks for. We had not received word as to why; they had simply stopped. I tapped a finger on the paper. It made no sense. We had not left Allura a year ago on the happiest of terms with the royal family, mainly because I had not proposed to Brylee. Yet politically we had had a treaty in place where both benefited immensely. For Allura to cut the ties now, and so abruptly, did not make sense to me at all.

A knock sounded on the door, light and airy, and I pushed to my feet as I called, "Enter."

Brylee sailed in, shoulders thrown back and head held high. She waved me off when I moved to help her into her seat, lowering herself with all the grace of a dancer. Hands clasped firmly in her lap, she leveled her gaze on me.

"So, what papers are you wanting me to review?" she asked.

"This is the trade agreement that King Benjamin and my father arrived at last year." I picked up the top set, reaching over the desk to place them in her outstretched hand.

She read them over slowly, nodding her head as she went. After a long moment, she handed it back to me. "That appears to be a mutually beneficial agreement. You are trading an excess of wool from your many flocks in return for our finer silks and lace."

"Yes." I nodded, impressed with her knowledge of our economy. "But two weeks ago, the wagons meant to deliver our silks and lace never arrived. That is the invoice we received from the border."

Brylee scanned it again, lips pursing ever so slowly. "Well, that is not normal."

"No, I did not think so. Allura would never balk at a trade agreement in such a fashion."

"I thank you for thinking the best of my country."

"I would be amiss to think anything other than the best." I inclined my head. "Your king is good and fair. If there were a problem, I do not doubt that he would be the first to correspond with us."

Brylee did not reply immediately, her eyes scanning my face before dropping back to the paper in her hand.

"I do not know what happened," she said, "but if you would be willing, I shall send a message to the border station and see if they know anything more about this." She angled the paper toward me, pointing to a signature from the station master. "He may know something about the shipment and if it ever passed by. If he doesn't respond in a timely fashion, I shall go myself."

"Not alone." I shook my head. "We could always send your cousin, or one of my guards."

"Why not me?" Her eyes flashed with indignation. "I am not helpless, as you shall soon see."

Our sparring match. The thing that had kept me up most of the night.

"Are you sure you still wish to fight me?" I rested my chin in the palm of my hand.

"Yes. I think I do." Brylee laughed, but it was sharp. "And I shall trounce you, Prince Lachlan."

It was my turn to laugh. "I look forward to seeing you try."

Her face reddened and she shot to her feet. Turning in a flurry of skirts, she strode toward the door. "No, not try. I *shall!*"

I flicked my sword around my wrist, bouncing on the balls of my feet as Everett leaned up against one of the pillars, grinning at me.

"You are truly going to do it then? Fight the ambassador of Allura?"

I sighed, stopping my warmup as I walked over to him. He was to be the judge, for though he was my guard, he was impartial when it came to sparring.

"She did not leave me much of a choice, my friend." I sighed, crossing my arms over my chest.

"She is a fiery one, that's sure and certain." Everett chuckled. "She would fit right in as a Hillingsfarth lass."

I swallowed the lump in my throat. Running a hand through my hair, I only managed to reply with a strangled, "Yes."

The doors opened at the far end of the training room, Brylee turning the head of every knight as she walked toward me. She had on a hunter green tunic with a matching split skirt. Brown leggings peeked out as she strode forward. Her hair was pulled high atop her head. She stopped before Everett and me, hands planted on her hips.

"Princess Brylee, you look lovely." Everett pushed away from the pillar to offer a low bow.

"Thank you, Sir Everett." A bemused smile graced her lips as he straightened.

"Here." I held out my sword. "Does this suffice?"

She took it, the tip touching the floor as she struggled to lift it. I couldn't help the smirk that pulled on my lips as I turned to pick another sword off the wall.

I turned back, gasping as I barely managed to block the blow that Brylee had thrust at me. I ducked, turning to an offense as I spun on my heel and lunged at Brylee, who whirled back around. We parted, stalking around the outer rim of the sparring ring.

"Attacking from behind?" I shifted my grip on my sword. "A sly move, Princess."

"You gave me your sword," she said, "thinking it too heavy for me. Is that not equally as devious?"

I shrugged, seeing an opening and attacking again. Brylee blocked, leaning against my blade until the hilts pushed against one another. Both of us strained, trying to gain an advantage. She was strong. Much stronger than I had expected. When I could not find an opening, I stepped to the side, our swords grating against each other. Brylee stumbled forward. I spun around, but she had already recovered, hefting her sword to block me again.

Back and forth we went, exchanging blow for blow, step for step. When one of us appeared to have an advantage, the other would recover. We were perfectly matched.

The knights had gathered around, interested in watching this woman who was so evenly pitted against their prince. They cheered and jested, some even placed bets. An hour after we had started, Everett shook his head, pushing off the pillar.

"I call a draw."

Brylee growled, a flurry of sword and skirt as she pressed against me. I continued to meet her blow for blow. She paused and I went onto the offense, striking her weapon over and over, pushing her into a retreat.

She growled again as Everett cried out, "Draw!"

"No!" she hollered back, a bead of perspiration trailing down her temple. "No, there must be a winner!"

I was panting as I stepped back. "Can we not agree that we are equals? I underestimated your skill, Princess. You are a fine swordswoman and would likely have won against any other knight you would have faced in our army."

I was impressed by the number of knights who nodded in agreement, unashamedly gawking at the woman in the ring.

"You are willing to admit that?" Brylee huffed a stray hair off her forehead as her eyes flicked to Silas, who had stepped up to Everett's side. "That I am equal to you?"

"Yes." I raised my brow at her. "For you are."

Color rose to Brylee's cheeks that had nothing to do with our exertion. She bowed her head. "You are a formidable opponent, Prince Lachlan. It was…an honor to spar with you."

Everett shouted at the knights to resume their training, a low grumble working its way through them as they moved to obey.

"Where did you learn to fight like that?" I moved forward to take my sword back from Brylee.

"My aunt." She handed me the sword. A zing of electricity worked its way up my arm as our fingers brushed. I stepped up to place the swords back on the weapons wall, trying to catch my breath.

"Is she as impressive at the sword as you?" I asked, clenching my hands behind my back as I turned back to her. "Or is it a skill that you alone possess?"

"We both do, though I wish I could claim I was the only one." She smiled up at me, a real smile that reached her eyes and made them scrunch at the corners.

I smiled back, offering her my arm.

"You're sweaty." She wrinkled her nose at me.

I smirked. "So are you."

"I suppose you are correct." She chuckled, laying her hand on my arm.

"Did my ears deceive me?" I place my free hand over my heart in mock shock. "Did Princess Brylee truly just say that I was correct?"

"Enjoy it, Lachlan." Silas chuckled as he stepped up next to me, clasping my shoulder tightly. "It rarely happens."

I felt Brylee shift, but I kept my gaze on her cousin. "Yes, I shall."

She swatted at me lightly on the arm. "I can admit when someone else is correct!"

"Oh, of course." Silas snorted, crossing his arms and raising a brow at Brylee. "Like the time Marcus fell out of the tree?"

"We've been over this, Silas." She blushed. "I did not push him!"

"You pushed him?" I asked.

"No!" she protested at the same time Silas said, "Yes!"

"Well, I shall endeavor to never climb into a tree with you." I tried to suppress a grin, failing miserably.

Brylee gazed up at me and I felt my chest tighten. It felt so natural to tease and laugh with her, to try to make her smile, to have her hand on my arm.

"Are you all right, Prince Lachlan?" she asked.

"Yes. I'm fine." It came out higher than my normal voice, and I cleared my throat as I moved toward the door, Brylee following beside me. Silas scooted around us, hurrying out the door and down the corridor as we stepped into the hall.

Brylee pulled her arm from mine. "I wish to go wash up, sire."

I nodded, my pulse thundering. As she turned to move down the passageway, I reached out and grabbed her wrist.

"Brylee, I—" I stared into her brown eyes, my words sticking in my throat.

Her gaze flicked back and forth between my eyes as she waited for me to respond. The corners of her mouth twitched, as if they were trying to decide whether or not they wanted to smile.

I licked my lips, taking in a steadying breath before I forced the words out. "I am truly sorry about what happened a year ago."

Her lips dipped into a frown, and she tried to tug her hand out of mine. "Lachlan. Let go."

"I hope that someday you can forgive me." I let out a slow breath, dropping her hand. "I know that I hurt you, and I am truly sorry."

"I…I can't, Lachlan." She crossed her arms over her chest, turning so I could not see her eyes. "Not yet."

I inclined my head. "But can I ask you to…think about it?"

Brylee gazed at me from the corner of her eye, her lips pressed into a thin line. "Yes, that I can do."

"That's all I am asking." I swallowed. "I know it was wrong. And—"

She was already moving down the hall, practically running away. I slumped against the wall, my chest aching worse than before. Why did it matter that one girl disdained me?

Because Everett is right. I'm still in love with her.

6

BRYLEE

I leaned against the door to my bedchamber, tears slipping down my cheeks. He had asked me to forgive him. He'd said he was sorry. I wiped at my tears with my sleeves as my shoulders trembled. Why did that shake me so? It was easier to loathe him when he appeared aloof and arrogant.

I groaned, pushing to my feet and stepping over to the bath I had asked the maids to prepare before I left to go spar. The water was the perfect temperature and I quickly shed my clothes and dipped below the surface. The water filled my ears, muffling the sounds around me. I held my breath, letting my lungs burn for as long as I could bear before breaking the surface with a gasp.

I leaned back, relishing the warm water as my muscles eased from the fight. I had been surprised by

Lachlan's skill and more so at my ability to fend him off and even challenge him. He was a worthy rival. He always had been.

Shaking away thoughts of the Hillingsfarth prince, I grabbed my soap, lathering my hair well before dunking under the water again to scrub it clean. Quickly washing my body, I wrapped a towel around me as I stepped from the tub.

I stared at my reflection in my vanity mirror after I had dressed. My sleepless night showed. I scrubbed a hand over my face to try to make the dark circles disappear. It was pointless; I knew.

I smoothed out my dress, another tear slipping free from my eyes. I wanted to forgive Lachlan, and that scared me. If I forgave him, would I open my heart again? And if that happened, would I get hurt once more?

"No." I tightened my jaw, resting a hand over my churning stomach. "No, I cannot bear that!"

Brushing my hair, I fought to forget about Lachlan. But it was impossible. He was an itch, an itch I could not be free of no matter how much I scratched at it. I twisted my hair into a braid, growling as I did. My thoughts were traitorous, replaying our spar and every moment we brushed hands or pressed up against one another. Placing my circlet on my head, I took a steadying breath and walked to the door.

I stepped into the hall, adopting my poised ambassador face, and turned sharply toward the dining room. Almost as soon as I did so, I stumbled right into a solid form.

A hand darted out and grasped my arms, steadying me as I glanced up. My thanks died on my lips as Lachlan's mouth twitched with a smile.

"You look lovely," he said.

"What are you doing in front of my room?" I hissed, yanking away from him.

"I came to escort you to our noon meal." His green eyes narrowed a fraction of an inch before he smoothed out the front of his dark blue shirt.

I glared at him, walling off my heart again. I could not risk it. It had been stomped on once, and no amount of smiles and laughter could repair the damage done.

Lachlan pressed his lips together, like he was suppressing a sigh, then offered me his arm. I stared at it for a long moment, wondering if there was any polite way to ignore him With a small sigh, I slipped my hand under his arm. Falling into step with me, he led me down the hall.

"I meant what I said earlier."

I jerked, startled by Lachlan's nearly whispered words, and looked up at him. "About?"

"Being sorry." He cleared his throat. "I have never forgotten your face from that day."

I stiffened, pressing my lips together. How did I respond to *that*? Should I say that I remembered his stricken face as well, the look of someone being caught? Or that my heart had splintered in that moment, and had crumbled a little more every day since? Or perhaps that when I was near him now, it was both torture and heaven?

"Here we are." Lachlan halted my wild train of thoughts as we stepped up to the dining room doors.

"I–I don't know what you want me to say in response to your earlier statement." I swallowed, dropping my hands into the folds of my dress to hide their trembles.

"Nothing. You said you could not forgive me yet and I'm not going to push. My only hope is that you can see my repentance."

"Why did you do it?" I whispered, slapping a hand over my mouth as the words slipped out.

"Do you truly want to know?" He studied me.

"No." I shook my head hard, pointing to the dining room as I did so. "Please go. I'll be in in a moment."

Lachlan nodded slowly and then stepped through the doors. I slumped against the wall, burying my face into my hands. Despite all my carefully hidden hurt, all my walls and barricades, Lachlan had smashed through them all with two little words.

I'm sorry.

I did not want him to be sorry. I wanted arrogance and pride, because that meant that I did not have to feel guilty for hating him.

"I don't feel guilty!" I pushed off the wall. "He deserves my anger. I won't forgive him; I can't let myself be hurt again."

Pulling in my emotions, I pressed my lips into a thin line as I stepped into the dining room. Silas was the first person to glance up at me, his brows immediately lowering at the look on my face. I straightened my shoulders and put on my carefully constructed princess mask. That caused the divot on his forehead to lessen slightly, but the tension in his jaw remained.

I sat beside Lachlan, picking up my utensils. My stomach turned as I cut the meat on my plate into tiny bits, pushing it around as I listened to Silas and Lachlan talk about combat. King Benedict wasn't there for this meal, easing some of the tension that had been there the night before, yet I couldn't force a bite into my mouth. The number of glances both Silas and Lachlan sent my way told me they noticed. It didn't matter. If I forced food down my throat, it would end up all over the table.

"Brylee."

I tore my gaze away from my mutilated meat and toward Silas, not able to look him directly in the eye. "Yes?"

"What's wrong?" My cousin drummed his fingers on the table, studying me intently. The usual glimmer in his eyes was gone, replaced with a calculating gaze that was all reconnaissance officer.

"Why does something have to be wrong?" I muttered and felt Lachlan stiffen next to me as I stabbed a bit of meat.

Silas shot a pointed look from me to my plate. "You're glaring at your food like you want to kill it again."

I snorted, unable to stop myself from slamming my utensils onto the table. "Excuse me." Rising to my feet, I sailed out the doors as elegantly as I could. The moment they closed behind me, I hiked up my skirts and broke into a run. I didn't know where I was going, just that I needed out. Out of the Palace of Dothe and out of my own head.

7

LACHLAN

The drumming of Silas' fingers increased as Brylee fled, and I swallowed my nerves as his glare settled on me.

"What did you say to her?" he asked.

I resisted the urge to shift in my seat. Silas was in my land, and though I got the distinct impression there was more to him than met the eye, I was not about to show him he intimidated me.

"I asked her to forgive me," I said.

"Did you, truly?" Silas pressed his fingers flat against the table and raised a brow.

"I wouldn't lie to you, Prince Silas." I cleared my throat. "I have regretted what happened between us since the day it happened."

"What happened, exactly?" Silas crossed his arms and leaned them on the tabletop. "I've heard Avyanna's side, but I'd like to hear yours."

I did shift this time. "Are you certain?"

"Yes." Silas nodded. "I am."

I took a steadying breath, and let my mind wander back to a year ago.

Brylee's smile mirrored my own as I spun her across the dance floor. A pretty color bloomed in her cheeks and I tightened my hold on her waist before I spun her under my arm.

"You're a marvelous dancer, Princess Brylee."

"I am moderate, Prince Lachlan. But I thank you for the compliment."

I smiled again, something in Brylee's warm gaze arresting my attention and making any other words impossible as my tongue stuck to the roof of my mouth. She gazed over my shoulder as we twirled past the dais, waving at her brother, Thaddeus, as he tapped his fingers against the armrest of one of the thrones. He waved back, grinning. I felt my chest tighten as I stared down at her.

"You love your family very much, do you not?"

The music had stopped, and I offered Brylee my arm. She slipped her hand under it quickly, smiling up at me as I guided her to the side of the dance floor.

"Yes," she said. "They are the most important people in the world to me."

My chest tightened even more. I tipped my head to the side, my hair falling into one of my eyes. "It would be hard to leave them?"

She took a deep breath, then shrugged. "It would depend on the reason."

I stared at her, my thoughts whirling. How could I do that to her? Ask her to leave the people who loved her more than anything? I had not had that type of love. My father loved me the best way he knew how, my mother having died giving me life, but I was a constant reminder of all he had lost.

The ballroom had grown hot and I needed a moment to think. I bowed politely to Brylee before striding across the ballroom to stop before my father.

"Father," I said, "may I speak to you for a moment?"

He excused himself and followed me over to a quieter corner of the room.

"I cannot do it." I swallowed. "I know you arranged all this with King Benjamin and Prince Collins, but I cannot do this to Brylee."

"You will not get cold feet now." His bushy red brow lowered. "This will help to strengthen the trade agreement."

"It's not fair to her."

"You care for her?" Father asked. When I nodded, he added, "Then marry her."

I rubbed the back of my neck, glancing over to where Brylee watched the people on the dance floor. I liked her. We had spent almost every day together the past few weeks and I was continually amazed by all her different skills and graces. She was not afraid to say what she was thinking, and she stood up for herself and others without hesitation.

But was that enough to build a marriage on when I was unsure of my ability to love her?

Pushing through the crowd, I ignored my father's call as I stepped out into the cooler hallway. Striding up to the window, I braced a hand against the wall, trying to calm my spinning thoughts.

"Not enjoying the party?"

I jerked as Avyanna slipped under my arm.

"I know what will make it better." Her green eyes glowed in the setting sun as she grabbed a fist full of my shirt and pressed her lips to mine.

Shock was the first emotion to register, rendering immobile. My lips moved on their own, kissing Avyanna back before a startled cry broke through my muddled mind. Panting hard, I stepped away from Avyanna and turned to see the stricken face of Brylee. Her eyes were shining with unshed tears, her shoulders shaking.

"Brylee," I said, "Let me explain. I—"

"No." She shook her head hard. "No, nothing you can say will fix this."

I raised my hand, approaching her like I would a spooked horse. "It's not what it looks like."

"No." Another sob and she stepped back, nearly bumping into a marble pillar. Her eyes met mine and I was struck by the pain there. "Just go."

"Brylee." I held a hand towards her. "Please."

She hesitated, her eyes flicking to my hand before they hardened, cold as ice, and met my gaze once more.

"Go away, Lachlan. I don't want to ever see you again!" She turned and ran down the hall, her sobs floating back to me.

I yanked my crown off of my head and ran a hand through my messy hair before whirling on Avyanna. "You just ruined everything."

Tears pooled in her eyes, her lip quivering. "I didn't think she'd find us."

"I never asked for that!" I waved my hand at the wall. "Why did you do it?"

"You've been spending all your time with Brylee. It was my turn." Her tone turned defensive. "Why do you like her?"

I choked back the curse that sprung to mind and shook my head. "You ruined everything. Brylee's happiness and mine."

"It was only a kiss." Avyanna jutted her chin out.

"To someone who didn't want it." I took a step toward her, anger fueling my words. "Stay away from me and stay away from Brylee. You are a flirt, Avyanna, and that's a dangerous person to be in this world."

Her back bumped against the wall and I grabbed her arms. Her eyes went wide, and she struggled to pull away from me. "Let go of me!"

"If I was less scrupulous, I could harm you." I leaned closer, my voice low and controlled. Dangerous. I had never felt the level of rage that was coursing through me, but I smothered the part of me that wanted to shake Avyanna silly.

I held on a moment longer before I stepped back, glaring at her.

Her whole frame trembled as she turned and hurried off in the opposite direction of Brylee. As the adrenaline fled, I slumped against the wall, sliding down it.

Heat simmered in my chest as I realized that I had lost Brylee and nothing I could say nor do would ever be able to fix it.

"The only one who knows the whole story is Everett." I swallowed. The lump that always appeared when thinking about that night made it hard to spit the words out. "Even my father doesn't know the whole story, only that I decided to not pursue Brylee anymore."

"Has that changed?" Silas steepled his fingers, studying me with his blue eyes.

"I don't know." I raked my hand through my hair. "She deserves someone better than me. Someone who can stand at her side. Fight *with* her."

"You're fighting for her right now, are you not?"

"She doesn't seem pleased with it."

"She is." Silas' mouth quirked upwards into a smile. "It's only that she wasn't expecting what you're showing her."

"What was she expecting? And for that matter, what am I showing her?" I gestured for him to continue.

"You're being humble, Lachlan." Silas' smile grew a little more. "You aren't being prideful, which I think would have made it easier for us to hate you."

"You hated me too?"

He chuckled. "You hurt my cousin."

"I forgot that the cousins of Findley's princes are inseparable. How silly of me."

"You mess with one of us, you mess with all of us." Silas winked, then sobered a bit. "Although I suppose Avyanna did start this whole blasted mess."

"I need to write her a letter, apologizing for my behavior that night." The lump in my throat seemed to grow at that thought.

Silas tipped his head back, a lock of his blond hair brushing his forehead. "You are a complicated fellow, Lachlan of Dothe."

I squeezed my hands together under the table, hoping that that comment was a good thing. Because, despite how much I was trying to ignore it, I was still completely and totally smitten with Brylee, and now her overprotective cousin knew it.

Wonderful. Simply wonderful.

8

BRYLEE

I wandered through the palace garden, the sweet scent of sage dancing on the breeze as it pulled my hair away from my face. I'd had a servant direct me here four days ago after my abrupt exit from the noon meal and retreated here almost every day since.

The calm of the birdsongs and the bleating of the sheep from the other side of the wall eased some of the tension in my shoulders. Papa had often taken me on walks in the Findley gardens when I was little, something that slowly tapered off as I grew older. Uncle Benjamin had formed the reconnaissance department and put Papa over running it. I had forgotten how much peace being in nature brought me.

God, what do you want me to do? Why did you bring me here to face the past? It's in your hands; isn't that good enough?

A sound near the vegetable beds made me pause. I squinted, slipping behind a tall willow tree that bent over a small pond. A man stood in the shadow of the wall, a black cloak over his broad shoulders despite the summer heat.

Another man slipped over from the kitchen door. He was tall and thin, with a balding head. He gripped the man on the shoulder, shaking him slightly as he whispered. I caught a few of the words—*"royals, arrogant, dangerous"*—and something about the meeting sent a shiver down my spine. I sucked in a breath as the man in the cloak turned and stomped toward the pond, skirting the edge and passing right beside my hiding spot.

His face was shadowed by the hood, but I caught sight of dark brown hair and a pointed beard. A sword thumped against his side, and he walked with the stride of a man who knew where he was going.

I rubbed my arms, turning to watch the thin man step back into the palace and then narrowed my eyes, my thoughts going to the missing silks. Could these men have something to do with it? Dothe was not too far from the sea. A person could easily waylay a wagon and smuggle the stolen items to a ship along the coast.

Yet, the words…they didn't fully fit my idea of a smuggling ring. A dark sensation pulsed around me and I shivered, straightening and stepping out from behind the willow tree.

"Well, well, well. What do we have here?"

I stiffened, turning as a heavy hand landed on my shoulder. The man in the cloak stared down at me, his mouth curling into a predatory smile. His eyes gleamed black under his hood.

"I…I was admiring the pond." I gestured to the water. "I thought I saw a frog."

"Are you not Princess Brylee?"

I nodded, and his grip on my shoulder tightened.

"Then why," he asked, "would you be chasing after a frog?"

"I grew up with a brother and four male cousins." I forced a smile, hoping I was not trembling too badly. "One gets used to creatures such as frogs and snakes."

The man continued to study me and I tried to keep my eyes innocent enough.

"Is there a reason you're detaining me, sir?" I asked.

He hesitated a moment longer before dropping his hand and stepping back. "No. Beg pardon, my lady." He bowed stiffly, then turned and walked toward the stables.

I laid a hand against my chest once the man disappeared. Something here was not right. I could go to Silas, but he had little power here. No, there was only one person I could tell who had the power to do something. Someone who would listen because I was the ambassador and he was my consultant.

Straightening my spine, I glided into the castle and back to the study that I had met Lachlan in earlier that morning. Hesitating for only a moment, I knocked on the door.

A muffled, "Enter," sounded and I pushed inside.

Lachlan was leaning an elbow against the deck, his hand tangled in his hair. The other shifted through the papers on his desk. A man stood in front of him, trembling like a dead leaf on a tree branch.

I cleared my throat, both men turning toward me. Lachlan's green eyes widened, and I could not seem to look away from them. They glittered in the lamp light, like emeralds in a dazzling crown. For a moment, I forgot the reason I had come to see him.

Opening my mouth to speak, my gaze flicked to the man standing in front of the desk. He felt strangely familiar. Tall and lean, his trembling hand smoothed a few strands of his thinning hair across the top of his head. His grey eyes, however, studied me sharply, much like Silas when he was sizing a person up. Unlike my cousin, this man's calculating gaze was cold and hard.

"Prince Lachlan," I managed to squeak out, "I have an urgent matter I must speak with you about."

If Lachlan was surprised, he did not show it. "Willoughby, you're dismissed. We'll talk more about this plan of yours later."

"It was a pleasure, Highness. A true pleasure." He bowed, backing up as he did so. He bumped into the door, reaching back to open it. With another swift glance at me, he slipped out the door, shutting it with a soft click.

"Who was that?" I asked. He looked so much like the man in the garden, but I had been too far away to know for certain.

"Lord Willoughby. He is my advisor on trade deals and other such political treaties." Lachlan tapped a stack of papers on the desk to make them all level before spearing me with his gaze. "Now, what did you need?"

I stared at the door a moment more before sinking into a chair.

"I was out in the gardens." I paused, biting my lip as I tried to think of the best way to explain.

"That's what you wanted to tell me?" Lachlan leaned back in his chair, crossing his arms over his chest.

"No!" I sighed, rubbing at my temples. "I was in the garden, down by the pond, and I saw a man."

"A gardener?" He pushed his chair back onto two legs, balancing as he smirked at me.

I shook my head, feeling my cheeks warm, "Will you please shut up for half a moment?"

He snapped his mouth closed with an audible click, but his smirk remained.

"I was in the garden"—I glared at him, daring him to interrupt—"and the man was over by the wall behind the kitchens. He had on a black cloak that hid most of his face. Another man, with a balding head and a thin frame, approached him from the kitchen door and they talked for a few moments before the man in the cloak turned and headed for the stable. I was hiding behind the willow tree when he came up behind me."

Lachlan stiffened, dropping the chair back to four legs as his eyes narrowed to slits. "He didn't hurt you, did he?"

I shook my head. "If he had tried anything, I know enough self-defense."

Lachlan did not relax. "Continue."

"He gripped my shoulder and I pretended like I hadn't noticed him and the bald man."

"What did he look like?" Lachlan picked up a clean piece of parchment and a pen.

"I could not make out much of his features. But he had a pointed beard that was a dark brown, and he had dark eyes. His shoulders were broad, and he was about a head taller than me."

Lachlan wrote furiously, before looking up at me. "Who do you think the other man was?"

I hesitated for only a moment before speaking slowly. "I think it's someone who works here. They seemed comfortable exiting through the back door. And the bit of conversations I heard...I think they are planning something, Lachlan."

"They could be the ones stealing the silks and other shipments from Allura." He tapped his finger at the parchment. "The second man you described...there's only one person I know who fits the description." I could hear Lachlan's teeth grinding.

"It's Lord Willoughby." It was a statement and by the pinched expression on Lachlan's face, I knew that I was right.

"I don't want to believe it, Brylee." Lachlan ripped his hand through his hair. "He's been guiding me in this position since I was fifteen."

Eight years. Eight years of trust and loyalty ripped away so quickly. I swallowed the lump in my throat, understanding the sting of betrayal all too well.

"Are you certain he's the only one who looks like the man I saw?" I asked. "You have no other clerks or servants who match that description?"

"No. If these people are behind the stolen shipments, then Willoughby is the only one who would know when they would be coming in." Lachlan had pulled his hands down over his face. "We try to limit that knowledge for this very reason."

"How do we know that they are not planning something else? What if they are planning an assassination of you or your father?" I shifted, not liking that train of thought. As much as I loathed Lachlan, I did not want to see him dead. "I wasn't close enough to hear them."

Lachlan sighed. "The truth is, until the messenger returns from the waystation at the southern outpost, we don't truly know what is happening."

"I had another thought." I swallowed, hating to add to the weariness on his face.

He glanced at me. "What?"

"What if this isn't about the silks at all." I struggled to draw in a breath as he gazed at me, his eyes stealing the air from my lungs. I slammed my eyes closed, trying to order my thoughts as coherently as I could. "What if they are planning a coup?"

"I suppose anything is possible at this point." Lachlan rubbed the back of his neck, staring down at the woodgrain of his desk.

"I heard the words *'royals'*, *'arrogant'*, and *'dangerous'*. I…"

My voice trailed off as something pulled at my chest. I noticed the circles under Lachlan's eyes, the way his shoulders drooped. He was exhausted.

What was wrong with me? Was I feeling pity for him? I ground my teeth but could not seem to find the anger in me anymore. He apologized. What was left for me to do but forgive?

God, help me to mean it. Help me to forgive him.

"I have done a lot of praying," I said, the words coming out of my mouth before I could think about them.

Lachlan's eyes snapped up to me. He cocked his head to the side, his hair falling across his face like it had that day a year ago when I had danced with him. I swallowed hard.

"Yes?" Lachlan prompted. He clenched his hands together on top of the desk.

Could I do it? Could I let go of a year of hurt and anger and truly mean it? I shifted, dropping my gaze to my own trembling hands in my lap.

"I…I know what I have to do," I whispered. "But it's hard, Lachlan. I was so hurt by what you did."

"I know." He pushed away from the desk and came around to sit in the chair next to mine. "And I am truly sorry."

I stared at his leg that was bouncing up and down then I shook my head. "I do not want to live in the past anymore. I am letting it go. I forgive you, Lachlan. And I will pray every day for God to take and hold onto the hurt that may spring up."

"Thank you, Brylee." He smiled and some of the tension eased from his shoulders.

I smiled back, the weight lifting off my shoulders as well. I no longer had that churning bitterness in my gut, and I could look at Lachlan in the eye and not flinch away.

"Well, I suppose we should figure out what those men are up to." Lachlan's smile faltered. "Do you think it could be an assassination attempt?"

I thought of the man's grip on my shoulder. He had been wary, alert to his surroundings. His light tread had caught me unawares. I swallowed the lump of panic that bloomed in my chest and said, "Yes. At this point, it's as likely as the smuggling ring."

Lachlan sighed. "We only have speculation."

"We know something suspicious is going on. That is reason enough to place an extra guard outside your father's room tonight. And yours as well."

He grimaced. "I think that may be a bit hasty."

"Hasty is not always wrong." I raised my brow and crossed my arms, daring him to disagree.

"If you think it would be wise, then it shall be done." Lachlan's mouth quirked up at the corners again.

I dropped my gaze to my lap, smoothing out my skirt and trying to ignore the way my heart leapt at his smile. "Would you like me to show you where I spotted them?"

Lachlan studied me for a long moment, an emotion I couldn't name flicking across his face before he rose and offered me his hand to assist me to my feet. "I would like that very much," he said, squeezing my cold fingers as he guided me out the door.

9

LACHLAN

She forgave me.

It was still too much to comprehend. I could not seem to tear my gaze away from Brylee as she led to the spot she'd seen the strange men. The sun was setting, the shadows lengthening as we strolled as casually as we could to the wall.

"Here." Brylee pointed to the spot and I knelt to study the ground. The soil was still soft after the last rain, a few half-tracks visible in the waning light.

"Two men," I mumbled, rubbing my neck. "One was fidgety." I pointed to the tracks on the right. "He kept shifting his weight. The other man barely moved. He walked here"—I pointed to one set of tracks—"then he stood and talked to the other man. Then he left."

"That's no new information at all." Brylee growled in the back of her throat.

I suppressed a grin, turning my attention back to the prints. "But this does tell me the man who came out of the kitchen was likely Willoughby." I pointed to one imprint. "That star is the stamp of the royal cobbler. Only a handful of the royal advisors use him, as he's quite expensive." I pressed my lips into a tight line, curling my fingers into fists. "Yet, he's been so loyal. I don't understand why he would do this now."

"Oh, foolish boy."

I leapt to my feet, pushing Brylee behind me as a cloaked figure oozed from the shadows.

Willoughby lowered his hood, a crooked smile twisting his lips. "How naïve and trusting you are," he said. "This is about so much more than you realize."

Brylee's fingers bit into my arm and I felt her press something against my spine. I curled my arm behind my back and clenched the handle of a dagger. Where had she gotten a dagger?

"Are you part of a smuggling ring?" I bit out. "Stealing from the people of Hillingsfarth?"

"You would like to think so, wouldn't you, Lachlan?" He laughed and it sounded too cold, too calculated for the bumbling lord who served my father and me. "It would make this betrayal so much easier. But no, I'm afraid I have loftier goals in mind."

A strangled cry sounded behind me and I wheeled around, dagger flashing, as a second man clamped a hand over Brylee's mouth. A knife of his own glinted in the waning twilight, pressed against Brylee's neck.

"Drop it," he ground out. "Or she dies."

I swallowed the panic in my chest as Brylee stared at me. I had failed her once before and I could not do it again. I dropped the dagger, raising my hands slowly into the air as Willoughby stepped forward and bound them roughly behind my back. The other man threw Brylee away from him before tying her hands together.

"She doesn't need to be taken," I said. "It's me you want."

Willoughby laughed coolly. "Yes, so she can run off and tell that interfering cousin of hers to come save you?"

I bit back the curse that sprung to my lips and glanced at Brylee, who had been hauled to her feet, her dress streaked with mud.

"You know the plan," Willoughby said. "Take them to the room and lock them up. Use whatever means necessary to ensure he cooperates." His eyes glinted. "A pretty thing like that could be fun."

The man gripped my arm and shoved a gag into my mouth before doing the same to Brylee. Keeping to the shadows to avoid the guards, he slipped into the castle. He led us up a back stairwell I did not know existed. Cobwebs clung to the rafters, dust coated everything, and the dank smell of disuse assaulted our noses.

The thug threw Brylee roughly into the room, and her hands scraped against the stone floor as I was shoved in after her.

"One sound from either of you, and the girl dies," the man promised, the door shutting soundly behind him.

I tried to swallow, but my mouth was too dry from the gag. Brylee turned to face me, her big brown eyes wide with fright. She crawled to my side and the smell of her lavender soap filled my senses, calming me slightly as silence enveloped us.

Ducking my head, I pressed my forehead against Brylee's mouth to try to pull the gag out for her. I grimaced, hating that I was invading her personal space, but she seemed to sense what I was doing and followed my lead.

After a few minutes of struggle, she finally spit the gag out, smacking her lips to try to moisten them again.

"Come closer," she whispered, her breath caressing my cheek as her eyes flicked to the door.

I eased forward and she twisted, her face a hair's breadth away from mine. She hesitated for only a moment before catching my gag between her teeth and pulling it out of my mouth. Her nose brushed mine as she eased back.

"Thank you," I whispered, but it sounded scratchy.

She nodded, shivering as she glanced around the empty room. One window sat high above, letting in a bare slit of sunlight. "Where are we?"

"The left tower." I bit back a curse. "We never use it anymore. It's above the knights' rooms."

"You have parts of your castle you don't use?"

"We're not a large country. We don't need as much space as my ancestors originally thought." I squinted up at the window. "Do you think Silas will suspect anything?"

"When we don't come to dinner, he will." She squeezed her eyes closed, a tear trailing down her cheek. "I'm scared."

If my hands had been free, I would have pulled her into my arms. But I had to settle for leaning my forehead against hers.

"We'll be fine, Brylee. We'll fight and escape. Save Dothe together."

"You can't promise me that, Lachlan." She shook her head. "We might very well be tortured or…worse."

"Maybe." Every muscle tensed at the thought of that thug laying a hand on Brylee. "But I will fight as hard as I can before, during, and after that." I closed my eyes. "I should have fought harder for you a year ago. Instead, I let you go."

"I said I didn't want to see you." She gasped a little, another tear trailing down her cheek.

"But I still should have fought." I shook my head. "By leaving, I made you think that I really didn't care about you. But I did, Brylee. I do."

"I…I care about you too."

It was the worst place to confess feelings: in an empty room, hands tied, captured by traitors that wanted me dead. Yet I didn't care. Tipping my head again, I brushed my lips against Brylee's. She returned my kiss eagerly. The smell of lavender swirled around me in the dusty air and the warmth of Brylee's lips on mine made me momentarily forget our predicament.

Dust tickled my nose, causing me to sneeze, breaking our kiss. Brylee giggled and then moaned again. "While I'm glad we now know how much we care for one another, we're still stuck in this room."

"Yes, let's try to untie each other."

We twisted around so that our backs were to one another, working on the ropes with fingers that were long since numb. There was no way to find the knots in Brylee's rope, no matter how hard I tried.

"It's no use," I finally declared, flopping onto my back. "If there was something sharp here..." I trailed off. "You don't happen to have another knife on you, do you?"

"No." She shook her head. "The dagger I had was from Thaddeus. I had it on my calf."

The thought of Brylee toting around weapons on her person caused my heart to flutter.

We sat there for a time, shoulders pressed against each other. Brylee's head landed on my shoulder with a sigh as I continued to try to form a plan.

There was only one option. Hopefully it was the right one.

I shrugged the shoulder Brylee's head was on, whispering, "I have an idea, but I'm not sure you're going to like it."

"Anything is better than being stuck here." She glared at me as she sat up.

"Yes, that's true." I could not stop the small smile that slipped onto my face.

Brylee rolled her eyes, somehow looking dignified despite being covered in dirt and sweat, and having her hands tied behind her.

"All right, here's my plan."

10

BRYLEE

I shook my head, tears pooling as I stared at Lachlan.

"I don't know if I can do that," I whispered, my throat feeling tight.

"You're the fiercest, strongest woman I know." His voice dropped to a whisper as footsteps sounded in the corridor. "I know you can do it."

I thought I might pass out, my gasps coming quickly and erratic. It was one thing to train and fight a friend in a sparring ring. It was very different when it was life or death on the line. "Lachlan, I—"

The door swung open and the man stepped in. His predatory eyes swung over me, a leer curling his lip.

"One minute." He jabbed his finger over his shoulder. "A chamber pot is in the room across the way. And don't even think about trying to run."

I glanced at Lachlan, who had managed to rise to his feet. He nodded at me, a small smile on his lips.

"I wouldn't leave without him," I said as I turned back to the man.

His sneer deepened as he untied my hands and shoved me toward the other door. I stumbled slightly, my legs shaking from lack of use. Leaning against the wall, I tried to pull myself together. Lachlan thought this plan would work, and it had to. Otherwise, we would both be dead, our kingdoms possibly at war with one another.

My throat tightened at that thought and I pushed off the wall and down the stairs. I pictured all the horrible things that could happen to Lachlan, all the pain and torture they could inflict on him. Squeezing my eyes shut, I prayed that the man holding us hostage was smart enough to keep his mouth shut about losing me to Willoughby.

"Get to the bottom of the stairs and find the tapestry depicting a battle."

Lachlan's instructions floated through my mind as I ducked behind the tapestry.

"Behind it is a door. There should be a key. It unlocks both doors in the tunnel."

My hand closed around the key. I shot a prayer of thanks heavenward before unlocking the door and slipping inside.

It was dark, but Lachlan had said it was a straight path all the way to the woods. I hoped he was right as I stumbled down the tunnel. I kept one hand clutched to the key, the other stretched to the wall. It was slick with moisture and a chill worked down my spine.

An eternity seemed to pass as I stumbled down the narrow path, but soon the toe of my slipper stubbed a step. I practically crawled up them, my fingers brushing the damp wood of a door. I located the lock, my teeth clattering together of their own accord. My heart raced as I pushed the door open, wan sunlight brushing my face.

"Once you leave the tunnel, you need to find the river."

I sucked in a breath of fresh air as I tried to find the stream Lachlan had mentioned. A gurgle came from the left and, after making sure the door was hidden in the underbrush once more, I set off toward it.

"Follow it upstream until you reach a hill. Climb to the top of it, and you should see a small cabin in the valley. Go to it and tell the man who answers that you're

a friend of mine and that I'm in trouble. He'll know what to do."

Breathing deeply, I picked up my pace, crashing through the underbrush like a rabbit. A large branch sliced against my forehead, another against my calf. I couldn't seem to feel anything. I kept pushing, kept flying. I had to reach the river and find Lachlan's friend.

Time seemed to crawl, my pace woefully slow in my thin slippers and foggy, fear-riddled mind. My brain repeated my kiss with Lachlan, his smile and certainty as he told me his plan. I could not let him down. I would not. If I wanted to explore this new future, then I had to keep going. Giving up was not an option.

I yelped as I splashed into the stream, the cold shocking some clarity into me. My legs ached, my head pounded, and I drank a few handfuls of the cool, clear water to soothe my parched throat.

It was a strong current, bubbling over rocks and fallen tree limbs in a trickling form of music. Wiping my wet hands off on my skirt, I turned upstream, splashing a bit more against the flow to the other side. It was then I realized how much my legs were trembling, but I pushed on. For Lachlan. For Hillingsfarth. For myself.

The wind rustled through the trees as I stepped out of the water and squished along the side of the river. Shivering, I hugged my arms around my middle as the river water dripped down my legs and off my sodden skirts. Another gust of wind set my teeth chattering once more.

Thankfully, the trees were thinning as the sun began to rise into the sky. I nearly stumbled as the ground began to rise upwards.

The hill.

A tear of relief snaked down my cheek and I wiped at it.

"No crying, Brylee," I reprimanded as I struggled up the steep incline. "You are stronger than that. You're a fighter, a warrior. Aunt Della taught you to be brave. You don't need a man to save you. In fact, you're going to save him!"

That line of thought had me surging upward, breaking through the trees with a gasp of surprise. I tipped forward, catching myself as I toppled to the ground. My hands and knees throbbed as I sat up and took a moment to catch my breath.

The hill rolled gently downward, surrounded on all sides by slopes that bellowed out lazily to meet the ever-darkening azure sky. Sheep bleated as a few lonely shepherds guided them away from the shelters that broke up the green. It was calm and serene, and I found myself relaxing for the first time since the whole ordeal started.

My gaze snagged onto a cabin that sat about three hundred yards away, smoke trailing up from the chimney. It was the only structure on the whole plain that looked like a house. It had to be the location that Lachlan told me about.

Pushing to my feet, I forced my legs to run down the hill and up to the door, ignoring my exhausted body. I thumped up the steps, practically sagging against the doorframe as I knocked.

The sound of tromping feet echoed in the room before the grinding of three locks greeted me. The door opened an inch, a light green eye peering out.

"What do you want?" a voice asked.

"My name is Brylee." I cleared my throat, the greeting confusing me. "I was sent by Prince Lachlan of Hillingsfarth. The kingdom as well as the prince are in danger. He said he needs your help."

The man swore, flinging the door open wide. His eyes studied me, scanning over my muddy and wet dress, my wild hair, and my scratched and bruised face. He ran a hand through his blond hair, another curse slipping past his lips.

"You need food," he said. "We'll ride back after you've eaten."

Grabbing my wrist, the strange man all but hauled me to the table. The cabin was small, the kitchen and sitting-room one open space. A fireplace sat in the middle, a door on either side of it. Above that, a loft with barrels and other provisions sat. It was quaint and cozy.

Muttering under his breath, the man pulled out a loaf of bread and a block of cheese. Hacking off a generous portion of both, he handed them to me before turning a chair around and straddling it, resting his chin against the back.

"Now, what happened?" he asked. "Why is Lachlan in danger?"

I studied him for a long moment as I finished chewing a bite of cheese. He looked to be about thirty, but the beard covering his face made it hard to tell. His light green eyes were alert. He was dressed the part of a shepherd, but something in his gaze was much like Silas', calculating and methodical. This was not a man used to herding sheep, no matter how reclusive he appeared.

"Who are you?" I asked, ignoring the question he had posed to me as I straightened.

"My name is Terrin." His light green eyes studied me again. "You are no common lady, are you? You are a warrior."

I could not help the snort that slipped out of me.

If he had only seen me, running like a scared animal through the woods, he wouldn't say that.

Taking another bite of bread, I chewed slowly to avoid any more questions.

"Why is Lachlan in danger?" Terrin repeated.

"He and I were captured by a man Lachlan trusted. He had us tied up and thrown into a tower in the castle. Lachlan told me how to escape and told me to get you to rescue him."

"Who would dare touch the crown prince?" Terrin leapt to his feet. He grabbed at his side, as if he expected a sword to be resting there. His brows furrowed and he muttered something under his breath again as he stomped through the door that sat on the right side of the fireplace.

A loud splintering sound made me jump, and I nearly choked on the bread I had started to swallow. A curse echoed out to me and then a loud, "My apologies, m'lady."

I smirked when Terrin stomped back out to me, a sword strapped around his waist and daggers across his chest. He grabbed a green cloak off of a hook on the wall and threw it over his shoulders.

"I don't suppose I can convince you to stay here?" He raised a brow at me when I shook my head. "I thought as much. Finish eating while I saddle my mare. It may be hard for her to carry two of us, but she is a fast beast. We should be able to reach Hillingsfarth in time."

"Should." The word turned my stomach sour as Terrin slammed the door. What would happen if we were too late? Had I forgiven Lachlan, mended the bridge I had thought burned, only to lose him all over again?

Leaning my head against my hands, I ignored the dried blood that flaked from the gash on my forehead.

"Dear God, please protect him. Help us to reach Hillingsfarth quickly and rescue Lachlan, safe and sound."

11

LACHLAN

I winced as the door to my prison slammed closed, my captor done with another round of beatings. After Brylee had escaped, our guard—whose name I had learned was Davian—had taken his anger out on me, and bruises now covered my chest and stomach. I was fairly certain I had a cracked rib, every breath causing a wave of pain to cloud my vision.

Brylee.

Her face appeared in my mind's eye. Her smirky smile, her amber eyes, the joy that poured from her as naturally as breathing. She was strong and courageous, bold in a way few women were. She was not intimidated by me. She stood toe to toe with me, never backing down. She was my equal in every way, and I wanted her to be my partner in life.

If I make it out of here alive, I am going to spend every minute of every day showing her how much I need her. How much I value her. I made a good mess of it the first time around, but this time I swear, I'll show her how priceless she is. Oh God, please let me live.

The door opened again, and I closed my eyes with a groan. *Already?*

"Lachlan? Saints above, you look awful."

I cracked open an eye to see a blessedly familiar face.

"Everett?"

"And Silas. Don't forget Silas." Brylee's cousin grinned down at me, but a divot of worry marred in his forehead.

"We're getting you out of here." Everett withdrew a knife, sawing at my bonds.

"How did you know where I was?" I asked, my lips cracked and bleeding from lack of water. Silas pressed a canteen to my lips and I greedily gulped it down.

Everett hauled me to my feet. "Willoughby's begun his coup. And he may think I'm a loyal traitor." He winked. "I suppose I'll let him go on thinking that."

I shook my head as they helped me out the door. Davian was bound and gagged, glaring dangerously at my friends as they helped me down the stairs to the door I had guided Brylee through hours before.

"Take care of him," Everett ordered Silas.

Silas glared at him. "He may be your crown prince, but if he dies on my watch, I will be plunging both our kingdoms into war."

"And we can't have that, sure and certain." Everett winked at me before stepping back into the hall, letting the door close behind him.

"Where is my cousin?" Silas asked as he and I began stumbling through the tunnel.

"Escaped," I gasped, every word and movement spearing pain through my chest. "I sent her to get a retired knight."

"Oh?" Silas asked.

I nodded. "Terrin. He lives as a shepherd after he and my father had a disagreement."

We reached the far door and Silas withdrew a key. Where he had gotten it, I did not know nor care. I sagged against the wall, wrapping an arm gingerly across my chest as Silas pushed the door open. He offered his hand and helped pull me out.

Instantly, we were surrounded. Silas held his hands up and after a moment a guard stepped forward. "You got them, Prince Silas?"

"One of them," Silas said. "Apparently Princess Brylee has already escaped." His tone was skeptical as he eyed me.

"She did, Silas," I said. "She—"

A horse whinnied as a rider charged toward us. His sword was drawn, and his eyes flashed as he crashed through the underbrush.

"Terrin!" I called out, ignoring the twinge in my side as I leapt toward the man, stopping him from cleaving some heads off of shoulders.

"Lachlan?" He pulled up, his eyes flicking around like a cornered animal.

"Yes! Yes, it's me. I called for you."

"You must have been truly desperate to come to me." Terrin swung off his mare and strode up to me.

"Yes. We were." I relaxed, lowering my hands.

Following him to his horse, he gave me the half smile I remembered so well. "Brylee is a remarkable woman," he said. "She seems like the kind of woman you would pursue."

Heat flamed my cheeks and I felt Silas stiffen beside me. I managed to shrug, instantly regretting it as my lungs spasmed again.

"She's a warrior." Terrin chuckled. "You can see it in her eyes, her stance. She'll fight for Hillingsfarth. For you, my prince."

"*My prince?*" I raised a brow. "It's been a while since you've called me that."

Terrin scratched at his beard. "It may have not been a wise choice to leave the way I did."

"No, it wasn't." I clasped his shoulder. "Whatever wrong you suffered under my father's hand, Terrin, I apologize for them. I will do my best to see that you are repaid for the service you've rendered to the crown."

He glanced at me, but before he could respond, Silas stepped forward.

"Where is my cousin?" he asked.

I nearly smacked myself as I glanced around. Brylee was nowhere to be seen. Terrin cleared his throat, shifting from foot to foot. "She's going in."

"What?" I felt my legs buckle, and it was only Silas gripping my arm that kept me on my feet. "Why would she do that?"

"She said they were planning a coup. She wanted to go in and get you, Prince Silas, and the king out."

"Of all the stubborn, foolhardy ideas!" Silas swore. "The king is out already. He's over at the camp planning an attack."

"Then let us join him," Terrin said. "The best plan now is to get in and help the princess."

I nodded, swaying once again.

Terrin motioned at me. "You need to rest."

"Later." I pushed away Silas' hand. "Right now, we must help Brylee."

12

BRYLEE

The gates were open. I slowed as I neared the edge of the woods, scanning the wall for the taletell sign that all was peaceful—the pacing of guards on the battlement. But nothing moved.

I swallowed, sliding the bow Terrin had given me off my shoulders. Grabbing an arrow, I notched it, drawing back and letting it fly over the battlement. Through the open gate, I watched as it plunged into the courtyard. A swarm of soldiers darted out of the gate. They scanned the tree line, looking for the lone bowman.

I crouched lower, wondering what on earth I was going to do now. Were King Benedict and Silas already dead? Lachlan? Without them, how would I flee to Allura? Would Father and Uncle Benjamin ever find out what happened if I were caught?

I wiggled further back into the woods, standing to pace. Pacing helped me think. But my thoughts were spiraling, anger and fear making me irrational. I wanted nothing more than to charge down the hill and into the courtyard, my sword drawn to enact my revenge against Willoughby for what he'd done to me, Lachlan, and everyone else.

"Brylee."

A hand clamped around my arm. I turned, whipping out the dagger Terrin had given me to press against the chest of the man behind me.

Silas leapt back, hands raised, relief flashing across his face. "Thank God. I thought you were down there already."

Relief of my own crashed through me and I threw my arms around my cousin. Swallowing tears, I let myself cling to Silas for a long moment. He hugged me back, nearly cutting off my air from the pressure.

"What happened, Brylee?" he asked, easing me back. I realized then that we were not alone. King Benedict stood at Silas' side, his sword drawn and brows lowered.

"Is Lachlan with you?" I asked, trying to breathe deeply.

"Yes. Everett and I rescued him." Silas ran a hand through his hair. "Terrin is with us too. He's eating, but he hasn't told us how you found him."

I quickly filled them in on everything that had happened. Their expressions grew grave, their stances stiff as they glanced at each other.

"This is worse than I feared," King Benedict growled, roughing a hand through his hair like his son often did. "How soon until your father arrives, Prince Silas?"

"It all depends on how swiftly he mobilized his men. We only sent the message yesterday. It's a day's hard ride to Findley and then they have to move men across the border." Silas shook his head. "It will take time."

"There is one option." I shifted, and they all looked at me. "They wouldn't expect me to return. Not after escaping."

"Absolutely not!" Silas shook his head vehemently. "I didn't like it when Terrin told me that's what you had planned the first time. I'm in charge of protecting you, Brylee. I'm not going to let you waltz back into a besieged castle and put yourself in danger for—"

"For the kingdom of the man I love." I swallowed, shaking my head. "Silas, I want to do this. For Lachlan and Hillingsfarth."

"Love?" Silas blinked, his mouth opening and closing in surprise. "Did you say…love?"

"Yes, love." I rolled my eyes. "A lot happened in the past day and a half."

"Obviously." Silas rubbed the back of his neck. "But I'm still not risking you for one blasted man."

I glared at my cousin. "I can get in and stop Willoughby. Without him leading, the traitors will give up. He's out for King Benedict and Lachlan. He wants them dead, not me."

"He wants the royals dead." Silas pointed down the hill. "I barely got out. It was only because of Everett. Willoughby will kill you just as quickly as he would Lachlan and Benedict."

"But he won't expect me to fight back. I can stop him, Silas. Please?"

Silas' jaw worked as he stared me down. I met his gaze unflinchingly. Finally, Silas threw up his hands. "I give up," he declared. "If you want to risk your life, I suppose I can suffer the wrath of Uncle Collins." He pointed his finger at me. "Just remember that if you die, I'm dead too."

"Thank you, Silas." I wrapped him in my arms again. Straightening, I turned to King Benedict. "Now," I said, "I just need some more daggers."

I stumbled up to the gate, something that was not all that hard to do. My feet did hurt, my dress was torn, and my hair was in total disarray.

"Help!" I cried as the men hurriedly surrounded me. "Help! Prince Lachlan has been kidnapped!"

A few of the knights raised their brows in surprise. Others looked at me like I was out of my mind. Did they know he was no longer their prisoner?

I did not hold back the tears, letting them slide down my cheeks to sell my part. "Hurry! They're taking him out to kill him. I barely escaped."

One of the knights stepped forward, his brows pinched. "Let me take her to Lord Willoughby. She's clearly unwell."

"I'm fine!" I persisted, letting a laugh escape my lips to sell my unstable act. "But I would like to see Lord Willoughby. Or King Benedict. Where's my cousin Silas? He may be able to find Lachlan."

No one answered me, a few nervously looking at the man who offered to take me to Willoughby. I swallowed the smirk that wanted to creep onto my lips. I was a better actress than I had thought.

"Allow me, Princess Brylee." He held out his arm and gestured my way. Something about him was vaguely familiar.

I slipped my hand onto his, allowing him to lead me inside. I stumbled and staggered, acting exhausted and spent—which was not far from the truth.

The knight opened the door to the study that I had worked in with Lachlan a few days before. Willoughby sat behind the desk, fingers steepled as he stared off into space. He blinked as the knight closed the door, standing in front of it with his arms crossed over his broad chest.

"Ah, Princess Brylee." Willoughby's smile was chilling as he rose. "You've somehow escaped."

"It wasn't too terribly hard." I straightened, wiping away the remainder of the tears as I glared at Willoughby. "Your buffoon of a thug was easy to outmaneuver."

He hummed a dismissal. "And yet you came back."

"Where is Lachlan?" I demanded, sticking to the script that Silas and I had prepared. "And the king and my cousin? What have you done with them?"

"They're dead, Princess," he hissed.

That was not the answer I had been expecting, but the surprise was authentic as Willoughby laughed. I fell hard onto one of the chairs in front of the desk.

"No, you're lying," I protested. "They can't be dead."

"Oh, but they are." He pointed to the knight at the door. "Sir Everett took care of the matter himself."

Everett. Of course. My eyes flicked to him, and he offered a slight incline of his head. He was on my side, and had helped Lachlan and Silas escape. Taking a steadying breath, I turned back to Willoughby, pretending with every fiber of my being that I was distraught.

"No, no." I buried my face into my hands. "They can't be."

"Hm." Willoughby hummed again, his long fingers pulling a twig out of my hair. "But there is no reason for you to have to join them in death, Princess. Marry me."

"What?" I jerked back.

He studied me like a wolf stalking its prey, and a chill snaked down my spine. I reached into my skirt, my hand clamping around the dagger hidden there.

"Yes," he said. "You'd make a fine queen."

"After you locked me and the prince of Hillingsfarth in a tower, slyesd the king and my cousin, laughed at their deaths…you truly expect me to want to marry *you*?" I stood, backing up as he continued to stalk closer. "You're insane."

Willoughby sneered, reaching out to slap me. I grabbed his wrist, glaring at him as his eyes widened.

"I'm not as helpless as you thought, am I?" I sneered at him now, whipping out my dagger and pressing the tip into his neck. "You *will* release this castle back to the rightful heir of Hillingsfarth."

Willoughby scoffed. "And why, Princess, do you think I'll do that?"

I pressed harder, twisting his arm up behind his back. Kicking the back of his legs, I forced him to drop to his knees. "If you don't, I will kill you."

Everett's eyes widen in my periphery, but I kept my gaze firmly on the man in my grasp. He began to shake, but it wasn't in fear.

"Never!" he spat, and I pressed the knife firmly under his chin.

"Sir Everett," I ordered, "escort this man to the dungeon. He's to be tried for his crimes by King Benedict of Hillingsfarth, who is very much alive and waiting for my signal."

Willoughby jerked, but I yanked up on his arm, stopping any further attempts at escape.

"It would be my pleasure, m'lady." Everett bowed, winking at me as he hauled Willoughby to his feet.

The moment the door closed, I sank into a chair, my body convulsing in relief. I'd done it. It had almost been simple. I buried my face in my hands, wanting nothing more than to rest. But the question remained looping through my mind: Why had it been so easy to stop him?

13

LACHLAN

I gasped as a knight wrapped bandages around my torso. Silas sat across from me, a cup of coffee in his hands as he watched the man tie off the bandages.

"That will have to do for now, your highness." He wrinkled his nose. "You need to bathe."

"Yes, thank you for that." I rolled my eyes as he sniffed in disgust and hurried off to his tent.

Silas eyed me across the fire. Taking a sip of his drink, he cleared his throat. "She said she loves you."

"Pardon?" I shook my head.

"Brylee. She said she loved you. You're not planning on hurting her again, are you?"

"I didn't intend to hurt her the first time." I sighed in frustration. "I told you that."

"Yes, but you did hurt her, just the same." Silas tipped his head to the side. "So?"

"No. I don't. I plan on…" I swallowed the lump in my throat as desire welled up in me. Brylee was so much better than me. Stronger, bolder. She was everything I had ever looked for. I had walked away once, and I was not going to make that mistake again.

"I want to marry her, Silas," I said. "She's everything I could ever want, my equal in many ways, and surpassing me in many more. She stands up to me, something most women I know don't do. They just see me as a prince. Brylee treats me like Terrin and Everett do. Like a normal man."

"She likes the normal man version better." Silas smirked. "So do I, for that matter."

"Yes, me too." I met his gaze. "For the record, I love Brylee for the woman she is. Not for her title or connection to the Allura crown."

Silas lapsed into silence once again as he studied me. I had the distinct feeling that he was calculating the truth of my statements before he nodded. "Well, you can tell Uncle Collins that."

"What?"

"Yes, he and my father are on their way here. We sent a messenger when we realized what Willoughby was doing."

Now I was nervous for a whole other reason than my near-death experience.

"Sires." Terrin stepped forward from out of the trees. "The flag has been raised. Brylee has done it. She's stopped Willoughby."

I let Silas help me down, gingerly wrapping my arm around my chest as Brylee came flying down the steps. She pulled up short before crashing into me, worry making lines appear on her forehead when she saw me cradling my ribs.

"I'm all right." I held my hand out to her. "Stop looking at me that way."

"You look horrible." She took my hand in hers, weaving her fingers in between mine. The lines on her face didn't lessen. "What happened?"

"He'll live," Terrin stated, hauling a guard Father had captured past us. "Takes more than a cracked rib to knock down Prince Lachlan."

I chuckled but stopped as my breath was stolen. That only made Brylee's brows lower further and her hand tightened around mine.

"Papa is on his way." Brylee glanced down at her dress. "He could be here any moment."

"Do you want to go get cleaned up, Brylee?"

"I—" Her voice cut out, and I turned her toward me. Her amber eyes were glassy, and she was breathing in and out in measured counts.

"Are *you* all right?" I reached up, ignoring the pain for a moment to brush a strand of her tangled hair behind her ear. "You ran through a tunnel and the forest and then came all the way back here to foil a coup. Any one of those is a lot for a person, let alone all three."

"I will be fine, Lachlan." She leaned her forehead against my shoulder. "I am not sure what to feel at the moment."

"I'll have a maid bring up a bath to your room. That will help you feel better." I squeezed her hand.

She glanced up at me. "What would make me feel better is having a healer look at you."

"I'm fine. A knight with a bit of healing experience wrapped my ribs." I started to shake my head, groaning when she poked at my chest. "Stop that! I'm fine."

"Liar. You need a real healer to look at them. A healer for you, and a bath for me."

"I was told earlier that I could use a bath as well." I laughed as she wrinkled her nose in agreement.

"I'm glad you're all right, Lachlan." The worry and weariness still lingered in her eyes.

"I'm glad you made it out in one piece," I said. "We need to talk about you running in here to stop Willoughby."

"I did what needed to be done." She stiffened, glancing around the courtyard. "Everett was a help in stopping Willoughby. Though he didn't put up much of a fight. I'm fearful that some of your knights are on his side."

My brows lowered and I nodded. "We'll figure that out later. Right now—"

"A bath and a healer," she finished.

"Yes. And you might want a healer looking at your scratch, too."

Brylee reached up, wincing when she touched the wound on her forehead. "I forgot about that."

"Yes." Neither of us made a move to enter the castle, and I found my eyes drawn to her lips. "Brylee, I—"

She pressed her fingers against my mouth. "We will talk later."

"But I need to say—"

Her hand slipped behind my neck, gently pulling my head down. "You want to do this now? When we both smell like farmers, are covered in leaves, twigs, and blood, and you have a cracked rib?"

"I've waited a year for this," I whispered, leaning my forehead against hers and closing my eyes. "I don't want to waste another moment. Brylee, I—"

"Kiss me, Lachlan."

I opened my eyes, meeting her amber ones.

She was smiling. "I've waited a year for this too."

"But your father—"

She growled, pulling my lips to hers as she kissed me hard. Her hand on my waist pulled me closer, and all I sensed was Brylee. She smelled like lavender still, despite her run through the forest and the fight in the castle. I let my hands settle on her waist, gingerly holding her away from my ribs but wanting nothing more than to crush her to me in reckless abandon.

"Brylee!"

She stepped back slowly, smiling at me before turning to face the voice that had haunted my nightmares for an entire year.

"Hello, Papa."

14

BRYLEE

Papa was turning an unusual shade of red as he stalked toward us. Knights from Findley milled about, and I noticed Uncle Benjamin still sitting on his horse, a bemused smirk on his face as he leaned against the pommel. I turned to face my father, tugging Lachlan behind me.

"What is the meaning of this?" A vein I didn't know he had bulged from his forehead.

"It's all right, Papa."

"No!" He jabbed his finger at Lachlan. "He hurt you once. He will not do it again."

"I don't intend to hurt Brylee, your highness." Lachlan's voice was soft, and I felt his breath on my neck. "I never meant to hurt her the first time."

"Then why did you?" Papa's voice was low, dangerous.

I turned to look at Lachlan. The color had drained from his face, and he was running his hand through his hair. "I… It's not only my story to tell, sir."

"You better tell it now, Lachlan, or I'm taking Brylee somewhere you'll never hurt her again." Papa grabbed my wrist, but I yanked it away.

"No." I turned, glaring at him. "Mama told me."

"Told you what?" Papa raised his brow at me.

"That the fairy story was about you and her. How she forgave you and how God changed you." I reached back, grabbing Lachlan's hand again. "I forgive him, Papa. I see how repentant he is, and I want to give him a second chance. I love him."

Lachlan stiffened behind me. "Brylee, you do need to know the full truth of what happened before you say that."

"No. I don't." I turned to face him. "You made a mistake. You were so regretful when we arrived, and I was angry. It would have been simple to hate you if you weren't sorry about what you had done. But you were. *Are*. And I… I cared for you the day you broke my heart. I don't think it was love then, but it is now."

Lachlan's mouth opened and closed a number of times before he glanced at my father. "I think we need to go clean up and then talk about this more."

It wasn't the answer I'd been hoping for, but something sparkled in Lachlan's eyes, a desire for something more. It gave me hope as he led me into the castle. His hand squeezed mine before we parted to our rooms.

A bath was waiting, a maid ready to help. I let her. Exhaustion had started to set in, every muscle weighing ten times what it should. She scrubbed my head, pulling out all the twigs and leaves that clung to my brown waves. My scalp burned by the time she was done. She dabbed some ointment on my cuts. The scabs had softened in the warm water, and the cool ointment soothed them. Plopping me on a stool, she silently brushed my hair and braided it before pulling a light pink gown onto me.

"There," she stated, with one final tug on my dress. "You're ready."

I nodded my thanks, deciding to forgo slippers as I padded into the hall. I thought over everything that had happened in the last twenty-four hours and sucked in a breath at the tears that wanted to trail down my cheeks. I would not cry. Everyone was fine; Lachlan would heal; we would make it past today. I wouldn't let it break me.

"I wondered how you were truly doing." I jumped slightly as Papa stepped up to me. His smile was soft, his eyes sad. "You always were one to hide your emotions, Bry."

He didn't wait for me to respond before he pulled me into his arms. I sank against him. Papa smelled like home, like cedarwood and lavender. A few tears slid down my cheeks as I grabbed a fistful of his soft linen shirt. Papa felt safe and resilient and far more confident than I had ever been.

"How do you do it?" I whispered, choking a little on my tears.

"Do what?" He leaned back to gaze at me.

"Be so brave and self-assured?" I hiccupped.

"I'm not." Papa chuckled softly, pressing a kiss onto my forehead. His beard tickled my skin, but it was a comforting feeling. He clasped my hand in his as he guided me down the hall to the dining room. "But I've learned to carry myself differently after forty-five years on this earth, Brylee. You're already better at it than I was at your age."

"But I don't want to hide, Papa. I want to truly be brave."

"Well, I haven't mastered it yet, daughter. It will probably take me another forty years to do that."

We walked in silence down to the dining room. Before we entered, I pulled Papa to a stop.

"I do care about Lachlan, Papa. More than I ever thought I would. He defended me, stood up to me, he even sparred with me. He's not afraid to treat me as an equal. He's… he's so good, Papa. One mistake shouldn't define him."

"Yes. It shouldn't." Papa winced, running a hand through his hair. "But I still want to hear his story."

"I do as well." I stood on my tiptoes, planting a kiss on my father's cheek. "That still won't change my decision. I love him. If he wants to marry me, I will accept."

"Silas was supposed to watch out for this." Papa shook his head, but a small smile danced over his lips.

"He tried." I laughed, stepping into the dining room. "You can't blame my cousin for my pigheadedness!"

"You heard her, Uncle Collins! No blaming the cousin!" Silas cried from his seat at the long table. It was fuller than before. To King Benedict's left sat Uncle Benjamin, Silas at his father's other side. Lachlan sat on King Benedict's right, an empty seat between them.

Lachlan stood as I entered, pulling a chair out on his right for me to sit in. Papa glared at Lachlan but sat down beside King Benedict without a word.

A heavy silence settled over us; none of us sure where to start.

"Well." Uncle Benjamin leaned his elbows against the table, glancing first at his son, then me, then Lachlan. "Will someone please tell us what happened?"

"A year ago, or today?" Papa asked, glancing around the table.

"Let's start with a year ago." Uncle Benjamin steepled his fingers, eyes zeroing in on Lachlan.

Lachlan laid his hands flat against the table. His black curls, still damp from his bath, fell into his eyes. Every muscle went taut as he stared at the table.

"Are you sure you want the truth?" he whispered, and I wasn't sure who he was directing the question to.

"Yes." Papa glanced at me from behind Lachlan's back. "We both want to know what really happened that day."

"Are you certain this is the right thing to do?" Silas cleared his throat, and Lachlan looked up at him.

"I have to, Silas," he said. "For Brylee and me. For this thing to finally be behind us."

"But it's not just *your* story."

"Avyanna made her choice that night, Silas. I—I can't protect her any more."

My cousin glanced at me, clearly unhappy with what was unfolding. But he crossed his arms over his chest and didn't say another word.

"All right, then." Lachlan cleared his throat. "Here is what happened."

15

LACHLAN

I told them everything. From the conversation with my father, to the kiss, to my heated words toward Avyanna after Brylee caught us.

"I was scared," I admitted, eyes flitting toward Brylee. "Scared to cart you away to a home that's never been a real home. It's only ever been Father and me here. You had family, love, and laughter in Findley. How could I ask you to give all that up? And then when you caught Avyanna and me…" I swallowed the lump lodged in my throat. "I truly didn't deserve you, Brylee. And I still don't."

The room had grown silent. So silent that we could hear the servants in the kitchen preparing the meal. I sank back onto the chair, what little energy I'd had left now gone. I roughed my hand over my face, daring to turn to the woman at my side. Her eyes were glassy with unshed tears, but she didn't try to hide them as she gazed at me.

"You—you were afraid to take me away from my family?" she asked.

"Yes, because you had—have—such a wonderful one. With parents and siblings and cousins. What do I have to offer you?"

"You!" She threw up her hands in exasperation. "You are enough, Lachlan. To leave Allura, my family and my friends, to come here for *you*." She reached out, clasping my hands in her own.

"What are you saying?"

"The same thing I've been saying since we escaped." She shook her head. "I love you."

"I still don't think I fully understand." A smile twisted my lips as Brylee frowned at me. "You love me?"

She squeezed my hands. "I love you."

"All right then." Silas raised his hand, making a gagging sound. "You love each other. Now can we get on to dealing with the lunatic in the prison?"

I chuckled as Brylee rolled her eyes at her cousin.

"One moment," Prince Collins interrupted, and I flinched as he clasped my shoulder. "I owe this young man an apology."

"Pardon?" I blinked, unsure if I had heard him right.

"Lachlan, I apologize for what I said in the courtyard. My daughter was right to show you mercy and grace. I, of all people, should have known better. Please, son, forgive me for the way I treated you."

I blinked again, looking over at Brylee, who simply shrugged her shoulders, and then back to Prince Collins. "Yes, your highness," I said. "I do accept it. And please know I will never do anything like that ever again."

"You better not." Prince Collins laughed, but raised a brow at me. "Especially if you do intend to marry my daughter."

"Marriage can wait for the moment." King Benjamin motioned toward my father. "Your majesty, if you would perhaps bring in the prisoner?"

Brylee's face paled and she leaned toward me, her voice dropping to a whisper. "I don't trust Willoughby, Lachlan. He was too easy to catch."

"What do you want me to do?" I asked.

Before she could respond, the dining room doors opened. Brylee stiffened as both Terrin and Everett led in Willoughby, five knights following behind. His hands were bound in front of him, but his stride was sure, his face etched with arrogance. He did not appear like someone imprisoned. He looked like he was in complete control.

"Watch him," Brylee whispered, her hand slipping into mine as her eyes followed Willoughby to his seat at the very end of the table.

Terrin strode to stand behind my chair. "I think Brylee's right," he said, leaning forward so only Brylee and I could hear. "He's planned something. I have all the men on alert."

"What do you think it is?" I asked.

"I don't know." Terrin glanced at Brylee, who had her eyes narrowed. "But it's something he thinks will ruin you."

I scratched the back of my neck as Father stood.

"Willoughby of Dothe," he began, face twisting in disgust. "You have betryesd this country and the king you swore to serve. What is your plea?"

Willoughby stared at Father for a long moment, a demeaning smile on his lips. Then the insufferable man began to laugh.

"You think you've won. That you have me right where you want me. And true. You have captured me." His gaze landed on each one of us in turn. "But I also have all of you right where I want."

The doors of the room burst inward, five knights charging in and retaining us men. Everett and Terrin charged Silas' and my father's captors, leaving Willoughby alone at the end of the table. The man was fast, his hands slipping between the bonds like fish. He bent, pulling a knife out of his boot before dashing down the table toward Brylee, a gleam in his eyes.

Brylee stood, the chair clattering against the ground as she dodged the blow that Willoughby had thrust at her. If she had not been watching for it, he would have killed her.

Willoughby turned, a feral sneer curling his lips as he gnashed his teeth in frustration. "I will win," he snarled.

"You will have to catch me first," Brylee shot back as Willoughby launched himself at her once more.

I struggled against the knight holding me, but every move sent shooting pain through my side. I turned, trying to see what was happening with Willoughby and Brylee's fight.

"I wouldn't try that, highness," the knight warned, reaching to pull my knife out of my sheath. With him off balance I grabbed his wrist, pushing my chair backward as I twisted beneath the man's arm and knocked his legs out from under him.

A cry echoed around the room, pulling me up short. My eyes locked with the horrible scene unfolding a few feet away. Brylee was weaponless on her back, trying to inch away from Willoughby. A trail of blood oozed from her leg, and tears were streaming down her cheeks.

Red clouded my vision as I leapt over the man I had sent to his knees. I strode up to Willoughby, yanking him toward me. He slashed at my chest, but if he cut me, I felt nothing. I pressed the point of my blade against his throat, backing him up until he bumped into the wall.

"Do not touch her!" I seethed, wanting nothing more than to plunge my blade into the sadistic man's heart.

"Make me," he hissed, his eyes gleaming with madness. "Kill me for hurting her. For when you do that, you'll become like me."

"I will never be like you." I shook my head. "Revenge is a poison I won't indulge in."

"Lachlan," Brylee gasped. "It's over."

A hand landed on my shoulder, but I could not seem to pull my focus away from the man in front of me. He betrayed me, hurt me, would have killed me all because of hate. I swallowed the bile in my throat as Terrin and Everett once again restrained him, pulling him back to the chair he had been in mere moments before, and securing him tightly.

I turned and dropped beside Brylee. The blood on her gown had not grown much, and I was hopeful it was a shallow wound. "He stabbed you?"

Brylee nodded, looking pale, but she managed a grin. "I don't think it's all that deep. A scratch. I suppose voluminous gowns are good for something."

"You're a wonder." I shook my head, laughing softly.

She cringed as I pulled her to her feet, her leg giving out as she tried to put weight on it.

"Is it worse than you thought?" I asked. When she ignored my question, I wrapped an arm around her waist. "Let me help you."

Brylee looked about ready to argue, but I pulled her closer to help bear some of her weight. Her arms snaked around my neck, and she laid her head on my shoulder as we hobbled over to the table, steering clear of the glaring Willoughby.

"Lachlan, see Brylee to her chambers. I'll send for the healer once more." Father stepped up to us, along with Prince Collins, who eyed his daughter worriedly.

"Please get her off her feet." Collins smoothed Brylee's hair away from her face, and she did not argue with him.

"Yes, Prince Collins." I tightened my arm around her waist. My ribs throbbed, but I ignored them as I guided Brylee toward the door.

"I'll make sure we take care of this mess." Everett clasped my shoulder as I walked by. "Take care of her."

"I plan to."

We practically stumbled up the stairs, me half-carrying her toward the end. My heart hammered hard, worry about Brylee's lethargic mood spurring me on. I scooped her up in my arms, sucking in a sharp breath at the pain raking down my side.

"Stop. You're hurting yourself." She leaned her head against my shoulder, no fight in her at all. As I laid her onto the bed, I ran my hand across her cheek.

"What's wrong?" I glanced at her leg. It was bleeding heavier, but still not enough to make her as tired as she was.

"I'm fine." Tears sprung into her eyes and she rolled to her side, hugging a pillow to her chest.

"Liar." I eased onto the side of the bed, laying a hand on her arm. "Talk to me."

"These past few days have just been—And I…I don't know what to do."

She burst into sobs and I froze, not accustomed to seeing this side of Brylee. I reached out to her and she sat up. Tugging her toward me, I enfolded her in my arms. She didn't battle me, burying her nose into my shoulder as she wrapped her arms around my neck.

"Why did this happen?" She hiccupped once and I chuckled.

"Maybe to draw us back together," I said into her hair. "Maybe to strengthen us in ways we can't see. Maybe both. But all I know is, I'm glad that I get to face this hard time together."

She sniffed, tightening her hold on my neck as a knock sounded and the healer came waddling in, clucking her tongue. I was promptly shooed out into the hall as she began to check Brylee over.

I want to marry that woman, I thought, not for the first time. *And I'm going to ask her as soon as I am able.*

16

BRYLEE

It hurt. Oh, how it hurt as the healer stitched up the hole in my leg. It had been deeper than I had first thought. He hummed soothingly as he handed me a warm mug of tea, promising that it would take the edge off the pain. I took a sip, hating the dirt flavor the moment it touched my tongue.

Is the pain worse or the tea? I laughed and wondered if I was losing my mind.

"Brylee?" Lachlan had slipped into the room once more and I sighed as a smile pulled on my lips.

"I think I'm going insane," I said.

"Oh?" Lachlan sank onto the edge of the bed, taking my hand in his.

"Yes." Tears filled my eyes again. "But I feel better with you here."

I'm turning into a sap.

I groaned, flopping back against the pillows.

"May I ask you something?" Lachlan's voice sounded higher than normal, and I cracked open one eye to peek at him. His cheeks were flushed, standing out against his black hair and he tugged on his collar, not quite looking me in the eye.

"What's wrong?" I asked.

"I'm not good with words, Brylee. I'm not flowery or elegant or—"

"I don't want you to be. Speak plainly to me, Lachlan. Please?"

"Marry me?"

I set the mug on the stand beside my bed, wiggling down to wrap my arms around his waist. "Why did that make you nervous, my prince? Surely you knew I'd say yes. A thousand times, yes!"

"But you're a most peculiar lady." He smiled, leaning his forehead against mine. "I'm never sure what to expect from you."

"A lifetime of surprises, m'lord?"

"Always." He brushed my hair behind my shoulder, leaning in to steal a small peck from my lips. "I want you to keep on surprising me, Brylee. Astound and amaze me like never before."

I sighed as he kissed me again, longer and more urgently. I had wanted this. That day I'd followed him out into the hallway in Findley Castle, I was hoping that he would propose.

Then, after catching him with Avyanna, I had despised him and prayed against falling in love with him. I had never wanted to care about a man again; yet God in his wisdom had blessed me beyond my wildest dreams. And it was good.

So very good.

EPILOGUE

ONE WEEK LATER...

Silas leaned against the wall, arms crossed, as he watched Brylee swing by on Lachlan's arm. She was beaming, larger than he had seen her smile in a very long time. It warmed him through.

"Are you ready?" Everett sauntered over and Silas bit the inside of his cheek. Everett grinned a smile that had made Silas' sixteen-year-old sister, Nettie, practically swoon earlier.

"To spend weeks in the woods with you?" Silas glared at the man. "No. I'm not."

Everett raised his brows, his smile never wavering. "Is that any way to speak to the man who saved your life?" When Silas scoffed in reply, Everett shrugged, his eyes hardening slightly. "Well, it will be an adventure for sure."

"An adventure?" King Benjamin stepped over to them, his wife by his side. "Are you talking about tracking down those thieves?"

"Yes." Everett bowed to Silas' mother. "May I have this dance, Queen Aurora?"

Aurora laughed, curtsying and taking Everett's hand.

"Well, he is something." Benjamin leaned against the wall beside his son, watching his wife laughing and swinging around the room with Everett. "I am surprised he volunteered to go with you."

"I wish he hadn't." Silas sighed. "You know I work better alone."

"Yes. But maybe you'll learn something by working with him."

Silas snorted, but did not reply.

"Come dance with me!" Avyanna ran up, grabbing Silas' arm and practically dragging him away in excitement. She had apologized to Brylee, and Brylee to her. The two were talking once more, though trust would be slow in coming.

Benjamin smiled, watching his family mingling around the hall in Hillingsfarth. From his daughter, Nettie—the youngest at sixteen—to Nicholas' eldest, Louis, it was good to see everyone together. It had been far too long.

"Well, I never believed that both my children would be married within a year's time." Collins stepped up to his older brother, grinning like a fool. "But I can't say that I'm unhappy."

"You'll have your wife all to yourself again." Benjamin smirked. "Whatever shall you do?"

Collins wagged his eyebrows. "I intend to fully enjoy every minute."

"Well, you only have a month until the wedding." Benjamin chuckled. "Then you'll be able to do just that."

The brothers laughed as they watched Lachlan lean down and softly kiss his bride-to-be. There was no doubt of the love in his eyes nor the gentleness of his touch. Brylee looked every bit as captured by him. They had been through a terrible ordeal, faced challenges that should have rent them in two. Yet they had come out stronger.

Benjamin sighed contentedly, stepping up to claim his wife from Everett.

"What has you smiling this evening, my king?" Aurora asked with a smile of her own as Benjamin swirled her in a circle.

"God's goodness, my love." Benjamin brushed his lips against Aurora's temple before leaning his forehead against hers. "He has blessed our family very much."

"Yes, love. He has." Aurora sighed, settling into his embrace. "And I know He will continue to do so for the rest of our lives."

THE END

ANNA AUGUSTINE

BEFORE *You* GO

SILAS AND BRIDGET'S STORY

"There is no fear in love, but perfect love casts out fear. For fear has to do with punishment, and whoever fears has not been perfected in love."

1 John 4:18 ESV

1

BRIDGET

HILLINGSFARTH FOREST—1435

The birds twittered merrily as I crouched in the underbrush, watching as Ronan signaled his men from the tree branches. He did not see me, had chosen not to see me for years. I shook off the sadness that wanted to cling to me, eyeing the wagon that was rumbling toward me. Toward Ronan.

"Let's go. They'll be busy for a few hours," Kara whispered.

I glanced at my sister who practically floated over the forest floor and into the underbrush. Her felt mask was securely around her face, her brown eyes sparkling in the warm afternoon sun. I took one more glance at

Ronan, who had leapt out of the tree and onto the back of the wagon, before following after Kara.

"It should be easier this time," Kara said softly, dancing over the top of a fallen tree trunk. "They're all there today."

"You're certain?" I asked, the thought of getting caught tying my stomach into knots.

"Yes." Kara nodded, tugging down her mask to smile at me. "We should be able to get some of their coin for the western village. They need it this month."

I nodded, adjusting my own mask as I followed her. The leaves rustled against each other, joining the chorus of birds as we glided deeper into the thick foliage. I was at home in the woods, having lived there all my life. The birds and forest creatures were my companions, the leaves and the trees my comfort. I was more comfortable talking to the owl that lived in the tree outside my cave than talking to my flesh and blood sister.

"Get ready," Kara hissed, intensity tightening her shoulders as she crouched behind a tree. Ahead of us, the clearing loomed. We waited for a long moment, watching for any sign of movement. Satisfied that the clearing was indeed empty, Kara motioned for me to ready my bow. I fitted an arrow against the string, following a few paces behind her as we crept into the opening.

It was always strange, walking into the camp again. A tightness clutched my chest, and I swallowed it down as Kara slid between the flaps of the leader's tent.

The faint rattle of coins reached me, but I kept scanning the forest edge, listening for the telltale signs of Ronan and his men returning.

I was so intently watching for a threat, that I startled when the flap opened, and Kara sailed out.

"Your turn." She pulled a knife out of her belt, weighing it in her palm as she slung her sack over her shoulder.

I unstrung my bow, slipping into the tent and to the chests that lined the far side. It was always the same, no matter where Ronan moved his men. His tent never varied, and without fail, Kara and I would rob the self-proclaimed Prince of Thieves every time.

I knelt, easing the chest open. Hundreds of gold florins sparkled up at me, making my stomach clench in disgust. I let my hand trail over them for a moment, a war waging in me. Shaking away the questions, I opened a sack of my own and scooped a few handfuls of the sparkling coins into it.

"Hurry!" Kara whispered from the doorway. "We have to go!"

I stood, glancing once more around the tent. A lump lodged in my throat as I let myself remember.

"Bridget!"

"Coming."

Throwing my bag over my shoulder, I eased out the flap. Nodding at Kara, we dashed into the woods like deer evading a hunter.

We paused at the road edge, looking up and down it as our hearts raced like runaway stallions.

"How much did you get?" Kara asked, pulling my bag from my shoulder. She opened it, her mouth turning down into a frown. "This isn't much."

"I was rushed," I said, glancing back at the road. "Are you ready?"

Kara pressed her lips into a thin line but nodded as she dashed across the road and into the woods on the other side, where our home was. I hesitated, forcing a breath into my lungs. I had to keep going, I couldn't give up.

This is your life, Bridget. There's no going back to the way things were.

With a sigh of resignation, I sprinted across the road and into the woods, my bag of coins bouncing against my back and weighing on my mind.

~   ~   ~

Kara threw her bag into a chest of our own once we had reached the cave, tugging off her cloak and mask and throwing them onto her bed roll. She crossed her arms, watching me critically as I dumped my bag in with hers.

"What?" I finally asked, hating her glare and condescending attitude, but not brave enough to tell her to leave me be.

"Why did you hesitate?" she pushed as I tugged down my mask and threw back my hood.

"I didn't."

"Then why do you have half of what I gathered in that bag?"

"I don't want to talk about this, Kara."

"Which is proof that you should!" Kara threw her hands up in the air with a frustrated growl. "Bridget, I need you to work with me."

"I am going for a walk." I slammed the trunk lid closed, stalking toward the cave door.

"Bridget!"

I ignored my sister, slipping out the narrow door of the cave and into the woods. The sun was slowly sinking behind the horizon, the cool wind whipping through the trees as I stalked further into the woods. Elms, oaks, and spruces were clumped around, leaving strange open places among them. The squirrels chattered to the birds, who sang their goodnights to creation.

I breathed a little easier as I scrambled up into my favorite oak tree. Its ancient branches stretched out, strong and sturdy. I settled against the trunk, breathing in the pine sap that was wafting over the breeze. The forest understood. No matter the chaos in my life, I could retreat here and find solace.

Tears pressed against my eyes. Every day we stole from Ronan, another little part of me died. Kara and I were living a lie. We weren't the good guys, no matter how hard we justified it.

We were thieves.

Like our parents had been.

Like our brother was.

And there was nothing I could do to change it.

2

SILAS

THE ALLURA/HILLINGSFARTH BORDER

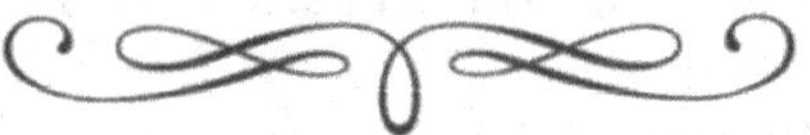

"Those thar' woods, they be spooked, I tell ya! Spooked!"

I barely resisted the urge to roll my eyes at the old border patrol guard. His quivering chin and glassy rimmed eyes were…telling.

"Just how much brandy have you consumed this morning, Sir Derek?" a voice behind me asked.

I allowed myself the luxury of an eye roll now as I turned to face my unwanted, yet constant companion, Sir Everett. Standing a good four inches taller than me, he dwarfed most men I knew. Broad shouldered and strong as an ox, he was mostly brawn although he did contain a small amount of wit which was in constant odds with my own.

"That's what you decided to ask?" I questioned.

Everett raised a brow. "What was I supposed to ask?"

"Anything but what you did." I sighed. "Let me do this, please."

"Fine!" He held up his hands in surrender before crossing his arms over his chest. His blue-grey eyes laughed at me as I turned back to the half-drunk guard.

"Why do you say the woods are spooked?" I asked.

"Wagons cross the border, sire, and then"—he snapped his shaking, weathered fingers together—"they vanish!"

Everett snorted but kept his opinions to himself.

"Surely you don't believe that?" I asked. "Wagons do not simply vanish."

"But they do! They come by 'ere and never make it to Hillingsfarth. The woods thar' be haunted, my prince. Mark my words!"

The man groaned, shaking worse as he poured himself another glass of strong drink. Some sloshed onto the tabletop. The offensive odor made me crinkle up my nose and clear my throat.

"Well, thank you, Sir Derek," I said, "for your help."

Everett snorted again, striding out the door ahead of me as the drunk man bowed toward me.

"That was a waste." Everett swore, patting his dappled mare's neck as he double-checked her girth.

"No, it wasn't." I swung up into the saddle, studying the rocky crags that the waystation sat in. "We know the wagons make it at least this far. They vanish somewhere between here and Dothe."

"Well, that just marvelously lowers our search radius, Prince Silas." He said my title mockingly, and I glared at him again. "Where do you suggest we start?"

I bit the inside of my cheek, wanting nothing more than to throttle the man. He had been insufferable since the moment we had left Dothe, needling me into glares and snaps—reactions I was usually able to keep fairly well controlled. I could not for the life of me understand why he enjoyed tormenting me. Yes, I had not wanted him with me on the hunt for the silk smugglers. He had volunteered. But that was no reason to continually annoy me.

"Let's go," I muttered to my horse, letting Everett spur his mount into motion behind me. He swore at me but I ignored him, studying the tree lined path as we moved forward.

We rode in silence, both of us scanning the woods for any sign of disruption. The steady beat of our horses' hooves against the well-packed earth helped the tension in my shoulders to unwind, and my mind began to wander as I studied the trees.

Brylee and Lachlan had been enthusiastic when I had told them I would hunt for the smugglers or thieves in the forests of Hillingsfarth. It was the least I could do. Brylee was busy planning her wedding; Lachlan was still recovering from a cracked rib that had been given to him by a traitor, and I…well, I was bored. This was the exact adventure I needed.

I glanced at Everett. *If only my new shadow had not volunteered to come along.*

"Why do you hate me?" Everett asked, raising his brows as he caught me glaring.

"I don't hate you," I lied, swinging off my horse and into the underbrush. Something shiny had caught my eye. A gold florin.

"What is that?" Everett asked, following behind me.

"Coin," I said. "From the coffers of Allura. See the crown?"

Everett's brows lowered. "What is an Alluran coin doing here?"

I scratched my chin, studying it. "It's not uncommon for Allura to trade coin for items from Hillingsfarth, and the fact that the silks have gone missing could mean my father was sending more than just silks this time around."

"So it's been taken again? Blast!" Everett kicked at a tuft of dying grass. "We're too late?"

I shook my head. "No, look." I pointed to a single overturned leaf. The ground was still moist beneath it. Someone had been here not too long ago.

"Truly?" Everett looked at me with his mouth parted slightly, brow raised. "You can follow such a faint trail?"

"Yes, and I'm going to catch these thieves once and for all." I tugged down my vest as I straightened. "If it's too much for you, Sir Everett, you're welcome to return to Dothe."

"No." He smirked, his eyes sparkling in the afternoon sun. "I would like to see you do the impossible, Prince Silas."

"Have you lost the trail?" Everett asked, leaning over my shoulder as I followed the scant path of disturbed underbrush. A breeze that still carried hints of summer ruffled my cloak. The leaves on the trees clattered together, the birds twittering in eager anticipation for their flight to warmer climates.

All of this I took in even with my attention transfixed onto the trail left by our unknown quarry. They were good, whoever they were. Their footfalls were light and swift, and it took a good ten minutes to catch the trail at times.

"Are you planning on ignoring me for the foreseeable future?" Everett asked. He had been silent for the most part, asking the occasional question which I only answered when necessary.

"I didn't want you here to begin with." I glared at him. "As I seem to recall, you volunteered."

"Yes, it was either me or Lachlan. Since my prince wanted to stay with his lady-love—"

"Don't call Brylee that," I said.

"—I volunteered," Everett continued, ignoring my interruption. "I did this to help both Brylee and Lachlan, so I would appreciate a small amount of civility."

I scoffed, but begrudgingly admired his tenacity. Not that I was planning on telling him that anytime soon.

I turned back to the leaves, my brows lowering in confusion when they abruptly ended at the base of a large elm tree. I turned, backtracking and following the trail once more up to the base of the tree.

"What the blazes?" I muttered, straightening and glancing around the small clearing once more. "It ends."

Everett ran a hand through his thatch-colored hair. "Where do you think they went?"

"I'm guessing up." I tipped my head back, searching the large branches of the tree.

"In the tree?" Everett snorted. "Are they monkeys from Taletha now?"

"This is why I work alone." I rolled my eyes, turning to hoist myself into the tree.

"Lonely life, working alone," Everett commented, leaning his back and propping his foot up against the trunk.

"Easier." I grunted, panting slightly as I managed to swing my leg around the bough. "Don't have to worry about anyone having anyone else's back."

Everett hummed an acknowledgement as I continued up the tree limbs, looking for any sign that someone had been there. A muddied footprint on one branch confirmed my suspicions: someone had indeed been here. And recently. The mud was still wet.

A small surge of uneasiness snaked its way down my spine as I began to descend to the forest floor. It was too quiet.

My leather boots groaned as I dropped to the forest floor. Remaining crouched, I scanned the tree line. Everett was nowhere to be seen.

If he's wandered off, I may very well leave him here, I thought sourly as I straightened.

A sound came from behind me, causing me to spin around, a dagger clutched in my fist. But I wasn't quick enough. Something solid landed against my temple, making my head spin. I stumbled, crashing to my knees as I was struck a second time. My vision began to tunnel as a small form knelt beside me, their face blurring as I slipped into unconsciousness.

3

BRIDGET

I gasped, staring at the men at my feet that I had just knocked senseless. I glanced at the heavy stick in my hand, tossing it to the side as I began to pace.

"Blast, this isn't what I meant to do!" I scratched at my chin, glancing at the snare that lay a few feet away. With shaking hands, I untied it, then sliced it in two. I quickly lashed the wrists of the men. They were both attractive, with the scruff of travel on both of their faces. I wondered where they had come from.

Shaking away my swirling thoughts, I bound the smaller man. His blond hair was falling across his forehead—a forehead that was sporting a lump on the side of it.

"Sorry," I whispered, gripping his underarms and hauling him up and onto my shoulders. I was strong, the result of hauling deer and bear carcasses through the woods as well as scaling trees, but this man was still heavy, all muscles and deadweight.

I stifled a groan at the noise I was making, brushing against leaves and branches. I reached our clearing with a huff, dumping the man to the ground and stretching my back as I returned to the tree. I glanced up at it, wanting to scramble up into it once more. But they had come too close to catching me, and I could not have that. Kara would murder me.

The second man was heavier than the first, and taller. I stumbled, swearing under my breath.

"You are heavier than the bear Kara and I took down last year," I muttered, "and not nearly so fuzzy."

I dumped him into the clearing, binding them both together before stepping back. My hands started to shake as reality struck. I had captured two men.

Two *men*.

Two men I knew nothing about, who could turn my sister and me in to the king of Dothe. I felt my chest tighten, but I turned toward the cave.

"Kara?" I called weakly, hoping she was out hunting.

"What?"

I swallowed a groan and laughed instead. It was a nervous giggle, high pitched and scratchy.

"What did you do now?" Kara appeared, brows lowering as she studied me. I bit the inside of my cheek as I stepped to the side.

"Who is that?" she asked.

"They're—" I cleared my throat. "I captured them?"

"Daggers!" Kara swore, glaring at the two men. "Why are they here, Bridget?"

"What was I supposed to do, Kara?" I snapped, sudden irritation flaring in me. "They were nosing around our woods. If I had left them, they could have wandered right into our home and known our exact location."

Kara's jaw flexed, her fists planted on her hips as she stared at our prisoners. "You hid your trail?"

"Yes." I jutted my chin out at her. "I know the rules."

Kara closed her eyes, rubbing her temple and muttering under her breath. One of the men stirred, his eyes fluttering open for a heartbeat. They landed on me, widening slightly before sliding closed again, a little moan rumbling in the back of his throat.

"Blast," I muttered. "Why do they have to be so handsome?"

"You find them attractive?" Kara glanced at me, her eyes narrowing.

A blush stole onto my cheeks, and it was my turn to clamp my lips into a tight line.

"Daggers and arrowheads, Bridget!" Kara huffed. "What are we going to do?"

"You claim to be the all-wise one!" I retorted, stomping to a tree and pulling myself up onto a limb. "You figure it out."

Kara started muttering again, turning on her heel and storming into our cave.

I settled against the tree trunk, crossing my arms over my chest to ward off the autumn chill. I stared down at our captives. Was anyone missing them? I could not help but appraise their features. They were both broad shouldered, muscular yet lean. Forest green cloaks hid their stash of weapons.

As I studied the men, the one who had looked at me earlier opened his blue eyes once more. He blinked several times as he glanced around the clearing for Kara and me. Satisfied that he was alone, he strained against the cords binding him, but I knew how to tie a knot. It was one of the only useful things that Ronan had taught me.

"Everett." He elbowed the taller man behind him the best he could, swearing when his friend groaned.

"Where are we?" Everett's accent was thick, definitely not from Allura.

He's from Hillingsfarth, I thought with a raised brow. But the first man was undoubtedly Alluran. From what I had heard, Allura rarely had dealings with Hillingsfarth. Though they were far from enemies and traded goods, they kept their respective political dealings to themselves.

So what has them working together now?

"I don't know." The first man swore again. "Do you remember what happened?"

"I remember you looking at the disappearing tracks and then climbing up the tree. But after that I don't know. I believe someone may have caught us unawares." Humor lit Everett's voice. "How does that feel, Silas?"

The first man—Silas—snorted but did not respond, tugging on the cords again even as he scanned the woods. What was he looking for?

"Do you feel someone watching us?" Everett asked after a long stretch of silence.

I froze, holding my breath as both men scanned the trees. Silas' eyes were intense, cataloging everything as they roved across the forest.

"I don't see anyone." Everett shifted against Silas' back.

"I do."

I gasped, my eyes meeting Silas' as he stared directly at me.

4

SILAS

The figure would have been hard for a normal scout to spot. They were even hard for me to see, pressed up against the tree like an owl. A large brown hood shrouded their face in shadows.

The figure gasped, gliding nimbly along the bough of the great oak before leaping to the ground. A mask hugged the lower part of their face, the only distinguishable feature being a pair of brilliantly blue eyes.

"Why did you capture us?" Everett called out, pulling at the cords in a futile effort to break free.

The person did not respond, staring fixedly at me. They were tall, only a few inches under my six-foot height. Yet the way the brown clothes hung on them, the way they moved…

"Yes. Why did you capture us? And how on earth did a young lady manage to drag two full grown men to…wherever we are?"

The girl startled back like I had slapped her, her eyes narrowing.

"Blast, you're good," she muttered, planting her fists on her hips as she stared me down once more.

"I've been trained to see more than most." I smirked at her, liking how uncomfortable my observations were making her.

A voice spoke off to our left, "Well, that poses an even greater threat to us then, does it not?"

The speaker stepped out of a shadowed rock formation, moving silently to stand by the first. Her brown hair fell past her shoulders and was tied back with a leather band. Her brown eyes studied first me, then Everett, who was being uncharacteristically silent.

"Why should we threaten you?" I asked calmly. "If you're simply living in the woods, then you should have nothing to be afraid of."

The girl with the blue eyes reached up, unhooking her mask from her ears. Freckles dotted her cheeks, and she lowered her hood to reveal brown hair a shade lighter than the bark of the oak tree.

"What are you doing?" the dark-haired girl hissed.

"We're already in trouble, Kara. Them knowing what we look like isn't going to change that."

"What do you mean, 'we're in trouble?' Why should we even let them go?"

I raised my brows, wondering if Kara's threat was in earnest.

"You want to keep them? Like pets?" The blue-eyed girl laughed grimly. "Or are you suggesting we kill them?"

Kara's eyes flicked to us, worry creasing her forehead. "I—I don't know."

"I would be willing to help you," I said, surprising myself. Everett must have been shocked as well, his elbow stabbing me in the ribs. "But I would appreciate you sparing my life. I'm sure my father would be most disgruntled if I turned up dead."

"Why should I care two florins what your father thinks?" Kara snapped.

I laughed. "You're obviously from Allura. Your accents are not of Hillingsfarth like Everett here."

"So?" Kara crossed her arms.

"So, your king—King Benjamin—happens to be my father."

"Daggers and arrowheads!" Kara turned to glare at the other girl. "Look what you've done, Bridget!"

"I didn't do anything," Bridget snapped back. "I'm sorry that you think that."

Kara glared as she turned on her heel and stormed off once again.

Bridget's eyes met mine once more and I swallowed, not understanding the sensation that sent tingles rippling across my chest.

"I need to go talk to her." Bridget sighed. "I'm sorry I brought this on you." She slipped into the shadows after Kara.

"Well." For a moment, Everett seemed to be at a loss for words. "This was not something I was expecting on this trip."

I grunted in agreement.

"Do you think they are going to kill us?"

"No." While Bridget's gaze had seemed curious, and Kara's angry, murder was not in either of them. "No, I don't think we have to worry about that."

Everett sighed. "I hope you're correct."

I hope I am, too.

The sun had disappeared before the girls returned. They quickly confiscated all our weapons, throwing them into a trunk and locking them with a key that Kara hung around her neck. Her brown eyes flashed at us, anger in the set of her mouth.

Strips of cloth were pulled from their pockets.

"Blindfolds?" I raised my brow, my mouth quirking up into a small smile. "You don't trust us?"

"There's few people I trust anymore, my prince," Bridget said.

Kara shot her sister a look at the use of my title but stomped over to Everett to tie his blindfold into place as Bridget tied mine. The cloth smelled good, like apples and vanilla.

Bridget hauled me to my feet, her grip firm as she led me forward.

"Duck," she commanded, a second too late. My forehead crashed into something hard and cold. Pain split behind my eyes.

"Blazes!" I hissed, shaking my head to rid the stars from the blackness.

"I'm sorry!"

A cold hand brushed back my hair, and I felt my breath catch. The blindfold was not the only thing that smelled good. Bridget did too. The sweet apple smell swirled around the cool space we were in—a cave, most likely. Her fingers probed at the spot I had hit, producing a hiss from me when she pressed a little too hard.

"Sorry," she repeated. She stepped back, taking the apple smell with her before tugging me forward once more.

"Where are we?" I asked.

"Telling you that would defeat the purpose of the blindfold, your highness."

I grunted in response to her as she pushed on my shoulders, forcing me to lower myself to the ground. A chill from the stones soaked through my pants and I had to force myself to not shiver.

Everett's voice echoed around the cave as his shuffling footsteps sounded in the entry. "Where are you taking us?"

A growl followed his question and I sensed Bridget stepping over to the entrance.

"You are somewhere safe." Bridget's promise sounded hollow, dead, as if she had told herself the same things before but did not truly believe it.

Who are these strange women? I shifted. *And why do I feel as though they are in very grave danger?*

5

BRIDGET

I could not tear my eyes away from Silas, who sat straight and unflinching as Kara stomped around the cave. The ceiling had brushed the top of Everett's head when he had been standing. He sat now, his mouth pulling downward.

"Kara, what are we doing for dinner?" I asked.

My sister glared at me in the firelight and I stifled a sigh, raising my brows at her questioningly.

She stared at our captives before grabbing me by the arm. "Can I trust you to watch them?"

"I caught them," I said, pulling away from her. "I'll be fine."

A huff slipped between her lips and she glanced one more time over her shoulder before slipping out the door.

"Where is your sister going?" Silas asked, and I swiped my sweaty hands across my shirt.

"To get something for dinner," I said.

"You're going to feed us?" His companion chuckled humorlessly. "I'm fairly certain your sister would rather *eat* me than feed me."

The comment was so ridiculous that a small laugh escaped my lips. Both men turned toward me. I wished I could see their eyes once more.

"My name is Bridget," I supplied, edging slightly closer to them as I sank down beside the fire. "Although, I suppose you gathered that."

"Yes." Silas smiled slightly. "Just as I suppose you gathered that my name is Silas."

"Yes." I marveled that a man could put me at such ease. No man had done that in years.

"I'm Everett, in case you cared to know," the other man said. "Charmed to meet you." The sarcasm was thick in his tone, and he leaned his head against the wall. "Why did you attack us?"

I glanced down at my fingerless leather gloves, tugging on a loose string. "I thought you were someone else."

"Who?" Silas asked, tipping his head to one side. His blond hair brushed against the blindfold, his nose scrunched up in confusion.

"That is for me to worry about." I stood again, glancing at the door before stepping over and pulling off both his and Everett's blindfolds.

They blinked in the firelight, glancing around at the cave—my home. I tried to see it through their eyes. The firepit was large and sat in the very center of the circular shaped room. Kara and my bedrolls were laid out on either side of the fire. Our two trunks, one with the stolen coins and the other with our cache of weapons, sat along the far wall. Shelves to the right of that held our provisions—spices, flour, corn, and the like—and our extra clothes.

I shifted from one foot to the other. I could feel their eyes on me, and I wondered why I had thought taking their blindfolds off was a good idea.

"You live here?" Everett asked, his tone unfeeling.

"Yes." I turned, sinking back down beside the fire. I tugged my legs up to my chest, staring into the orange flames. "This cave has been home for the last three years."

"How old are you?" I watched Everett's gaze sweep over me out of the corner of my eye.

"Twenty." I swallowed. "The woods have been my home all my life."

I clamped my lips shut, standing to fetch the stew pot from its shelf. I sensed their eyes on me the whole time. Especially the pair of bright blue ones that seemed to be able to read so much more than I was saying.

I chopped some wild onions and carrots, adding them to the pot while I waited for Kara to return. The men said no more, and I was not eager to share more of my life with them.

The sound of tromping boots at the door signaled Kara's return. I hurried over to the men, tugging the strips of cloth back over their eyes before my sister stepped into the room.

She raised her brows at me as I moved away from our prisoners but did not comment as she held up a sack. "Caught two hares. Should make a nice stew. I'll skin. Go fetch some water."

"All right." I bristled at her commanding attitude, but did not wish to be stuck in the cave a moment longer.

Grabbing one of our buckets, I walked along the deer path to the river. It babbled, gurgling over the pebbles and rocks. So happy and carefree, traveling far into the woods, into freedom.

"Oh, little river." I sank onto a rock, propping my chin in my hand. "When was I last like you?"

A snap of a twig had my eyes darting around wildly even as I held my body still. A figure eased to the edge of the water, his eyes trained on me. A cool smile twisted his lips.

"Hello, Bridget."

My stomach tightened. "Ronan."

"I knew you and Kara had not stryesd too far. But I didn't realize you lived across the road from me." His blue eyes narrowed even as he chuckled. "You wouldn't happen to know another band of thieves in the area, would you?"

"Thieves?" I snorted. "Who would be foolish enough to face you and your men? You're Ronan of Merryington."

"Yes." He hummed in agreement. "But I have been wondering if perhaps my baby sisters might be causing trouble for me."

Ronan had taken up our father's mantle the day a guard had shot him in the back. But unlike Father, Ronan had a cruel streak. There was a reason no one knew what happened to the shipments of silks and coin. No one faced Ronan and his thieves and lived. My insides quivered even as I jutted my chin out at the man.

"You haven't noticed us in years, Ronan." I stood, bristling as I stomped to the water's edge. Fetching the cold water, I quickly stepped back, glaring at the man on the opposite bank. "Why the sudden interest?"

"Because you were spotted today." His smile fell away, leaving cold indifference as the only expression on his face. "If you come near us again, Bridget, I will find you and Kara and kill you."

I swallowed, my hands clamped firmly around the bucket handle to keep them from trembling.

Ronan sneered. "Good day, Bridget." He rose, flicking his green hood over his head and then disappearing into the trees.

I gasped, doubling over as the reality of what had just happened hit me. I had come face to face with my brother after three years. For all that my father had stolen, he had never threatened anyone, and he had never stolen from the crown. Ronan had always been cold and cruel. He killed without thought, and his greed had led him to stealing from not only Allura, but Hillingsfarth as well. But to threaten his flesh and blood?

I sucked a breath through my nose. What was Kara going to say? If she knew Ronan was threatening us, she would never let me out of her sight again. Rubbing my jaw, I closed my eyes to collect myself as I eased back down the path. A pair of bright, icy blue eyes sprang to mind, and with it a plan sprouted. There was only a slim chance my sister would agree with it.

But it was the only chance I had.

6

SILAS

I hated the blasted blindfold. The fabric scratched at my face and I cursed under my breath as I shifted. I could hear Kara skinning the rabbits outside, Everett's heavy breathing, and the whistling of the wind across the cave door.

"What's the plan?" Everett asked, his words echoing softly around the stone room.

"There is no plan," I hissed. "There's something strange going on with these girls. I want to help them."

"That wasn't the mission." Everett strained against the bonds. "Blast it, Silas! I want to get back to Hillingsfarth! Staying here could endanger our lives, make no mistake."

"And hunting for smugglers or thieves doesn't?" I huffed. "Honestly, Everett. Are you scared of these girls?"

"No, I'm scared of Lachlan and Brylee." He groaned, his head thumping dully against the stone wall. "I want to capture the thieves and get back for their wedding. Or have you forgotten that it is in three weeks?"

"I haven't forgotten," I snapped. "I just have a feeling that these girls may be a link to the thieves."

Everett snorted. "I think you are infatuated with Bridget."

I did not dignify that statement with a response.

Murmuring voices outside the cave drew my attention, and I leaned forward trying to catch what was being said.

"He showed up at the river." Bridget's voice carried through the door.

Kara cursed. "How did he find us?"

I was unable to hear Bridget's response, but the shuffling sound told me they had entered the cave.

"I have an idea, Kara."

"What?" The splashing of water followed the terse response.

"They could protect us."

I stiffened as a hand landed on my shoulder. How had I not heard Bridget step over to me?

"Protect you from what?" Everett growled. "All I want is to leave you ladies and return to my home."

"They have seen too much." Kara's voice sounded tired as it moved closer to us. "We either have to kill them or—"

"Or trust us," I supplied. "I swear we will not harm you, miss. We only have one task—to find the thieves that have been robbing from Hillingsfarth and Allura."

A tension electrified the air around us and I wondered what had caused it. Were these girls the thieves? I shook my head.

"If you can promise me that you are not the ones stealing from the kingdoms," I said, "then you can trust us to do whatever we can to help you."

"You can trust Silas." Everett sighed begrudgingly. "I have known him only a short time and yet I cannot fault his loyalty."

"Why should you be loyal to us?" Kara questioned hotly. "You know nothing about us."

"Yet I sense trouble is dogging your step." I shifted, wondering why I wanted to assist these women so badly. "Please, let us help you."

"Kara." Bridget's tone was pleading. "It will benefit both us and them."

"Us?" Everett asked. "How can you possibly aid us?"

"We can—"

"Bridget!"

"Kara, honestly. Let them help us!"

A long, heavy silence descended over us. I refused to move, even as the cold stones bit into my backside. I felt the tension radiating off of Everett, and I wondered how much he would hate me if they agreed to this plan.

"Fine." Kara growled, yanking off the blindfold and a bit of my hair before turning to Everett and repeating the process. "But if you betray Bridget and me, or do anything I don't like, I won't hesitate to kill you both."

"Noted." Everett blinked, smiling at Kara like he was seeing her for the first time. "Now, may we be untied?"

Kara sized up Everett, her eyes scanning his face before snapping over to glare at me. "I still don't trust you."

"I can tell." I felt a smirk spring to my lips. "In all honesty, I don't trust you all that much either."

"Good. We have an understanding then."

"Yes." I pushed myself to my feet, nearly tumbling over as pins and needles stabbed my legs. A hand landed on my shoulder, steadying me. I turned, meeting Bridget's gaze. She quickly stepped away, clasping her hands behind her back.

"Did you happen to see our horses when you captured us?" I asked.

Bridget shook her head. "I can go look for them."

"Absolutely not!" Kara, who had been bending over the soup pot, straightened and glared at her sister. "I'll go. You tend the fire and the stew."

"You cannot keep me locked up forever, Kara."

"I can until I know there is no more danger."

"That's why we asked them for help."

Kara barely glanced in our direction. "They can keep you safe from here."

"Kara—"

"Enough, Bridget!" Her voice echoed around the cave and I faced Everett, who had a brow raised in curiosity.

"How about if I go with you?" Everett cleared his throat when Kara glared at him. "I know where we last had our mounts."

"It's a way to find your way back to the road, as well." Kara crossed her arms but nodded toward the door. "Come on."

Bridget undid Everett's bonds, and he rubbed his raw wrists as he followed Kara to the door. He hesitated by the entrance, glancing my way before stepping outside.

"Here." Bridget stepped behind me, untying my own restraints. She started to move away, but hesitated as I turned to face her. "I apologize for the trouble you are in because of me."

"I sense that you are in more trouble than I am."

She snorted but did not respond as she moved back over to the fire.

"What *is* the danger?" I asked.

Bridget stirred the stew, her eyes flicking to me. They danced in the firelight, making heat bloom across my chest again.

"The thief you are after," she said. "He lives in these woods."

"Oh?" I questioned. "Are you sure you're not the thief?"

"I am many things, my prince." Her stirring paused, and she seemed to shudder slightly. "I do not wish for *'thief'* to be one of them."

I cocked my head to the side but kept silent as she continued.

"Ronan of Merryington." Her voice tightened, her eyes getting a faraway look to them. "He and his men—most of them from Merryington—live in these woods. He hates Kara and me, for we left his little band. But up until today, I thought he had forgotten we even existed."

Bridget shook her head, turning back to the stew. "Anyhow, he is who you want, and who we need protection from."

"Why did he threaten you? If he hasn't cared about you in the last three years, why care now?"

She stiffened, glancing at the door then me. Her mouth opened in response but a whinny from outside the cave interrupted whatever she had been about to say.

A furious looking Kara stepped through the door, a laughing Everett at her heels.

"What happened to you?" Bridget asked, her mouth falling open.

I could not restrain my own laugh when I caught sight of her hair. It was slicked up on one side, the obvious result of getting too close to my mount.

"Draco got you, didn't he?" I winked at Bridget. "My horse has a nasty habit of trying to restyle hair. He is not well-versed in the matter and has horrible manners."

Bridget laughed softly, even as her sister glared at her.

"Is the stew ready?" Kara asked shortly.

Bridget swallowed and nodded, moving to the shelf to grab wooden bowls and spoons. My eyes followed her slight frame of their own accord. Her fear of Ronan was palpable, and I hoped I would be able to help protect her and Kara.

Please, Lord. Help me to keep Bridget safe, make it back for Lachlan and Brylee's wedding, and bring Ronan and all his thieves to justice.

7

BRIDGET

Silas a bowl of stew and his fingers brushed mine. I blushed, ducking my head as I settled onto my bedroll with my own food.

"What protection are you expecting from us?" Everett asked, staring hard at my sister.

Kara swallowed a bite of food, glaring at the tall man with her brow furrowed.

"I don't want any protection." She tossed her head toward me. "She's the one who needs it."

"I do not," I muttered. It was soft enough that Kara could not hear, but Silas flashed a smile toward me.

"I think it is foolish for two women to live in the woods *alone*." Everett glared at my sister, and she matched it with an equally terrifying expression. "You *are* aware that there are thieves in this area, are you not?"

"Are there?" Kara's tone oozed sarcasm. "I hadn't heard. And what do you think you can do about them, *Sir* Everett?"

Everett narrowed his eyes further, but Silas cut in with, "That's enough, Everett."

Everett snapped his mouth shut, turning his frosty glare toward his companion.

"It's been a long day." Silas yawned. "Let's all get some rest."

"If we're going to protect you, we will need weapons," Everett stated crossly.

Both men looked at me. Kara shook her head behind them, lips pressed into a thin line.

"We will consider that in the morning," I hedged.

The set of Kara's jaw meant I had said the wrong thing. I rubbed a hand across my face and stifled a sigh as I stretched out on my bedroll.

All I wanted was for this nightmare to be over.

I was the first to awaken the next morning. Light was barely slipping through the doorway and the overwhelming desire to escape my invisible confines had me easing out into the morning light.

I spun, arms outstretched, as I gazed up into the leafy canopy of the great oak that sat in front of our cave.

The tree Silas had spotted me in.

The thought of Silas brought unwanted heat to my cheeks and I shook my head. I was being a fool. The moment they had Ronan, they would leave again. We were merely a means to an end, much like we had been for Ronan all our lives.

I sighed, pulling myself up into the tree. Stretching out onto my back, I stared up at the colorful canopy of leaves. The cool dawn air rustled them, and I breathed deeply. Wet earth, crisp leaves, that barely noticeable sting that meant winter was on the heels of autumn, it all enveloped me like a hug. Like home.

The crunch of rocks under boots sounded from the direction of the cave, and I rolled into a crouch, watching as Silas stepped out. He gazed around slowly, until his eyes landed on me. He nodded, as if he expected me to be here, before striding over to the tree and pulling himself up to sit on a branch across from me.

"Had to escape while you could, hm?" He propped his foot up, resting his forearms on his knee and looking out at the rising sun.

"Kara is stifling." I bit my lip, shame twisting my stomach. "I know she means well, but I—"

"You crave freedom." Silas tipped his head to the side, studying me out of the corner of his eye. "You want to be your own person."

"Yes." I sighed, leaning my head back against the tree. "But that's a challenge when your sister wants to protect you."

"Hm."

We both lapsed into silence.

As the sun peaked above the trees, the purples, pinks, and oranges morphing into morning light, I turned to him and smiled.

"So tell me, what is Allura like?"

He shrugged. "It's much like Hillingsfarth, but with more forests, less hills, and more cities."

"That does not paint a very clear picture, my prince." I laughed, shaking my head. "I've never really left Hillingsfarth Forest."

"Truly?" Silas raised a brow. "Well, we will just have to remedy that someday, won't we?"

I blushed and turned away.

"And please, call me Silas."

"All—all right." I swallowed past the large lump of discomfort that had lodged itself in my throat. "But only if you will call me Bridget."

"I was already planning on doing that."

The teasing lilt to Silas' voice startled me and I turned back to face him. His blue eyes twinkled, a smirk tugging up on a corner of his mouth. But there was a look in his eyes, a scrutiny that made me squirm like a worm on a hook, as if he knew there was something we were not telling him.

I heard a shout and the crunching of stones before Kara, her hair a frizzy mess, stormed out of the cave door. She was mumbling under her breath as she stalked into the forest. A bleary-eyed Everett stumbled out after her.

"I think she realizes you're missing." Silas smirked at me again. "How unfortunate."

"Your compassion is overwhelming." I glared at him. "Are you normally this—?" I could not think of the right word and ended my sentence with a growl of frustration and a wave of my hand.

Silas laughed, a low rumble that sent butterflies zipping around my stomach again. "I am usually this much of a pest, yes."

A smirk tugged on the corners of my mouth and I swallowed it as I turned to scramble down the tree to the ground. "We better head back before I really upset my sister."

"I think it's a little late for that, Bridget."

My name. He had said my name. It sounded special coming from his lips. A shiver shook my frame as his boots crunched across the dead leaves toward me. The wind whistled through the trees, wafting the scent of cloves and musk over to me as Silas stepped closer still. It caused my heart to triple in speed.

What is wrong with me?

Panic clawed at my throat. Why was I acutely aware of every move Silas made, every breath, every word? I had met him—no, I had captured the man a mere day ago. Why did he have such a powerful grip on me already?

"Bridget?"

I shook my head as I turned toward Silas, his brow arched in question.

"I'm fine," I squeaked, clearing my throat as I rubbed the back of my neck.

"Good."

Blast it all. I had to get my emotions checked and quickly. If Kara knew how much power Silas had over me, she would not hesitate to kill him.

8

EVERETT

I tried to rub the sleep from my eyes as I stumbled after the enraged female in front of me. Kara was muttering under her breath, her shoulders thrown back and her spine ramrod straight.

"Kara." I smacked my lips to moisten them before continuing. "Slow down."

"I don't want you here, *Sir* Everett." She whirled on me, brown eyes blazing. "I never asked for babysitters."

"No, your sister did." I jutted my chin in the direction of the cave. "I think she may be the smartest one in our little group at the moment."

A scoff of disbelief slipped past Kara's lips as she stomped up to jab me in the ribs. "I don't know who you think you are, but I don't have to stand here and listen to this rubbish spewing from your mouth."

"What do you want to do then?" I asked, cradling her elbow in my hand. That brought her up short. Her eyes flicked from my hand to my eyes twice before she yanked her arm back. The motion wafted her scent over to me and I smiled. She smelled like apples and crisp, sunshine dried clothes.

Kara smoothed a hand over her tunic and sent another withering look my way. "I'm going to find my sister, Sir Everett. Are you going to help me or not?"

"Of course." I mocked a deep bow. "My duty is to you, *Lady* Kara."

She rolled her eyes, turning and stomping into the underbrush. I smirked. Infuriating our captor may not be the smartest thing in the world, but it was certainly entertaining.

We traipsed through the woods for a handful of minutes before Kara growled in frustration. She whirled on me again, eyes blazing.

"If something had happened to my sister," she stated, "or if your friend has touched her, so help me, I'll—"

"Silas is not my friend." I shook my head. "He's my companion. Although, I would still say that's too generous a term."

"Whichever he is"—Kara gritted her teeth, her jaw tense as color stained her tan cheeks—"if anything has happened to her, I'll kill you both."

"Why are you so terrified?" I found the words hanging between us before I even fully thought them. "What are you so scared of, Kara?"

"That is none of your business." Her eyes narrowed. "I have it under control."

"Of course." I shook my head. "How foolish of me to want to *help*."

"Help is for the weak. Only those who can take care of themselves survive in this world."

"That's a pretty bleak view of the world."

"Well, it's the only one I've been shown." Her chin jutted back toward the cave. "Let's go back."

I grabbed her arm as she stalked past. "Don't close yourself off from help. Silas and I do want to help you."

"You? Help?" Kara shook her head. "You didn't want to earlier. What has changed now?"

"I want you to see the world in a new light."

Kara scoffed. "Of course you do."

Yanking her arm free, she stomped back toward her cave, leaving me to pull my emotionless mask back into place and follow.

9

SILAS

Bridget had a stricken look on her face as she motioned me toward the cave. Her shoulders had tensed after I said her name and I wondered, not for the first time, how much trouble the girls were in with Ronan. Was he the thief we were looking for? Or were the girls the ones stealing?

A weight settled in my gut. If they were the thieves, I would have no choice but to turn them over to King Benedict. Duty dictated nothing less.

Yet did I owe allegiance to Benedict? He was not my king. My king was my father and he had instilled in my siblings and me a sense of right and wrong. But he and Mother also stressed mercy and grace. Often it was hard to know which was the right course of action—mercy or justice.

"Are you coming?" Bridget asked, her hand braced against the cave door.

I shook my head. "I believe it would be better for both of us if I am outside the cave when Kara returns."

"I think you may be right on that." Bridget's brows lowered, her lips curving down before she threw back her shoulders. "I'll go prepare our morning meal."

She disappeared inside and the ache lessened in my chest. I rubbed at it, hating it and loving it all at once.

My thoughts came to an abrupt halt as a crashing form emerged from the underbrush. With her hair streaming down her back and her brown eyes blazing, Kara stomped right up to me. Toe to toe, she was a good six inches shorter than me, but she seemed to tower over me in her rage. I backed up a step as she poked me in the chest.

"Where is she?" she asked.

"To whom are you referring?"

The glare she sent me could have melted stone.

I swallowed and pointed over my shoulder. "Bridget is in the cave, making the meal."

Kara huffed a breath through her nose, storming through the door.

Everett stepped up, shaking his head. He looked more alert than when he had followed Kara into the woods, but his lips were still turned downward. "That woman is something else, that's sure and certain."

I rubbed my jaw. "There is something going on here, Everett."

"You mean beside the fact that they clearly know who is taking the shipments? Or that they very well could be the thieves in question?"

Blazes, why does he have to be so good at this?

"Well, they're clearly terrified of something." Everett kicked at a tuft of grass. "I have a feeling neither of us are willing to leave them."

"You don't want to rush back to Hillingsfarth then?" I asked in surprise.

"Not before we sort out this mess." Everett shook his head again. "Do you have a plan?"

"That Ronan character." I paused. "Do you think there's any chance we can get some of our weapons back from the girls?"

"Possibly." Everett crossed his arms over his chest. "What are you planning?"

"I think we should go pay Ronan a visit."

~   ~   ~

"Are you completely insane?" Kara's jaw ticked in and out. "Or are you trying to get yourselves killed?"

"Probably both," Everett muttered as I smirked at Kara.

"Neither." I shrugged. "We want to help."

"And you think that by flaming off Ronan of Merryington, you're helping us?" Kara asked, her eyes flashing in the firelight.

"I think there is more to you two than meets the eye." I glanced at Bridget. "I also know that this Ronan, whoever he is, has you terrified. Neither of you strike me as the type of girls to be easily intimidated by anyone. So, this fellow obviously has some control over you. Or did. And that bothers you."

"Where did you get all that?" Everett asked.

I turned to him. "Observation."

Everett grunted, arms crossed over his chest as he turned to the girls. "As foolhardy as my companion is, I think this is our best course of action. Let us scope him out, see his weakness. If he is the one that is stealing from our two nations, then stopping him will benefit us both."

I watched the girls' reactions. Bridget paled slightly, swallowing hard as she glanced toward Kara. Kara's eyes were flicking back and forth between Everett and myself.

Kara finally spoke. "If we tell you, I need your word that you'll help to keep Bridget safe."

"What about you? Don't you need protection?" Everett's eyes dared Kara as he smirked.

"I don't need anyone besides my sister." Kara turned to me. "If she gets hurt…" She let the threat hang, and I noticed Everett's brows lower at her comment.

"We will protect her," I vowed, "but we will need our weapons."

Kara hesitated, and Bridget shoved her shoulder. "I think they have proven themselves," Bridget said.

"They haven't proven anything," Kara hissed, and Bridget took a small step back. The older sister turned back to Everett and me. "How about this: One week. One week you will stay with us, and if I think I can trust you, then you will get your weapons back."

"And if we refuse?" Everett challenged, a strange gleam in his eye.

"Then you are obviously the threat I thought you were."

Everett growled in the back of his throat. "Then there really isn't much of a choice, is there?"

"No, there isn't." Kara stuck her chin out. "Now, I would appreciate it if you would go get some kindling for us."

"No ax, I assume?" I questioned.

"I said kindling, not firewood. *Kindling* is the loose sticks on the forest floor." Kara smirked, and it sparked a wild look in her eyes. "Get going."

Everett growled again before stalking out the cave door. I felt Bridget's eyes on me as I turned to follow, and I paused before exiting.

"Kara." I waited to continue until she met my gaze. "I will protect you and Bridget. I swear it. And I don't break my promises."

Her mouth opened but no words spilled out. A small smile played on my lips as I duck out the door. I nearly collided into Everett, who stood with his arms crossed, a glare in his eyes.

"I don't like gambling my life, Silas."

"I am not fond of it either." I ran a hand through my hair. "But my sense of honor won't let me do anything else."

Everett snorted, but turned to stalk into the woods. I hesitated for a half second, the image of Bridget sparking a heat in my gut. I rubbed at my chest, frustration tightening my jaw.

It is simply because they are out here alone. I shook my head, moving to follow my companion. *That's the only reason I want to help them.*

I dumped a pile of kindling into the basket Kara directed me to as she bent over the pot of stew, stirring slowly. I could feel her eyes boring into my back as I straightened and brushed my hands together. Bridget was nowhere to be seen.

"Why?"

I started as Kara's voice echoed around the cave. I met her gaze. Her eyes were glowing in the firelight as she studied me.

"Why what?" I asked.

"Why are you so determined to help us?" Kara straightened as well, planting her hands on her hips and cocking her head at me. "You could just return to Hillingsfarth, tell the king about us, have us brought in for questioning. Why are you here, helping us at all?"

A battle played in Kara's eyes, telling a story of fear and loss, of broken faith and ruined relationships. These women had been hurt; they were cautious and slow to trust. I wanted to help, but would I be able to?

"I see a need in you, Kara." I shrugged. "I am a mender. A fixer. I have always been the one to see a need and meet it."

"I am not broken." Her jaw tensed.

"I did not imply that you were." A small smile inched onto my face. "But you cannot deny that you have a need."

"If you and your friend can get rid of Ronan, then my need is met." Kara turned back to the pot of stew. "It would solve many problems."

"I hope we can reach a place of trust so that Everett and I can do just that."

Voices at the cave door halted our conversation and I sighed as Everett, carrying a bucket of water, stepped through with Bridget on his heels.

"You sent Bridget to the stream?" My muscles tensed as I turned on Kara. "After yesterday?"

She raised a brow at me. "Ronan will not follow through on the threat today. He has just issued it. He will wait until we violate one of his conditions."

Bridget leaned against the wall, watching our argument. I swallowed the retort on my tongue. The girls did know Ronan better than Everett and me. But something still did not sit right within me. Like a pesky fly I could not shoo away, an idea kept buzzing in the back of my mind.

Something with these girls didn't seem quite right.

10

BRIDGET

Silas and Everett soon fell into a rhythm with Kara and me. In the mornings, they would go collect firewood for us. After the first day of collecting kindling, they realized that fallen limbs were easy enough to bring back for Kara and me to chop into manageable logs for the fast-approaching winter.

After they finished that, Everett would escort me to the stream to haul buckets of water up to the cave. Kara would glare at us as we came inside, but I decided that I liked Everett. He would tease and laugh with me while we walked, and we quickly fell into a friendship that I had often longed for with Ronan, but never had.

Silas, however, kept his distance. Sometimes I felt his stare as we sat to eat, or as we worked outside gathering berries and nuts. But he had not spoken to me since our talk in the tree on that first morning.

I sighed as I scrambled up that same tree, basking in the early evening sun and breathing the crisp fall air. A cool breeze rustled against my clothes and I sighed. A week. The boys had been here a week and yet it felt like they had been here forever. I could not imagine life without them. They were a comforting presence, lending a quiet strength that Kara and I lacked.

Those thoughts swirled around my mind as I leaned against the trunk of my oak tree, my foot propped against the branch. I closed my eyes, a tiny smile sprouting on my lips as the sounds of boots against tree bark reached me. I cracked open one eye to watch as Silas' head popped into sight. He pulled himself up to stand on the branch below mine, his hip braced against my bough. A deep sigh passed through my lips as I turned away from his face to stare up into the waning autumn sun.

"Can I ask you something?" I said, breaking the silence.

"Anything."

"How do you know if what you're doing is making a difference?" I turned to watch him out of the corner of my eye.

Silas cocked his head. "What are you referring to?"

"I—Kara and I—" I squeezed my eyes closed. "We steal, Silas."

I felt him stiffen beside me. "From whom?"

"Ronan." It was whispered, barely a breath, but I knew he heard it. "We steal from him and give to the poor around Hillingsfarth. Is that wrong?"

He took his time in answering, and I finally pried my eyes open to meet his gaze. The wind rustled his blond hair as he studied my face.

"I cannot answer that, Bridget," he said finally. "That's a decision only you can make in your heart."

"I can't, Silas." A tear leaked down my cheek. "If I listen to my heart, I'll lose my sister. It's an impossible decision. I'll lose everything I care about. I'll—"

"What about me?" He grabbed my hand, his eyes never leaving my face. "What if I …"

I dragged my gaze up to meet his once more. His words died on his lips as he tucked a strand of hair behind my ear. Silas' hand moved to cradling my cheek in his palm before he pressed his lips against mine. They tasted like the stew from dinner, of spices and meat. Yet, there was a sweetness lingering on them, a taste of a future not spent alone.

He leaned back and I gasped, feeling winded from that extraordinary kiss.

"Was that the end of the question, sir?" I managed to ask, smiling as he squeezed my hand.

Before he could answer, a commotion from the ground had us glancing at each other. We quietly scrambled down a few branches to see what was disturbing the evening.

The first person to break into the clearing below us was Kara. Her dark brown braid slapped against her back with each stride she took. Her lips were pursed, and her arms crossed. Another figure was only a few steps behind her, his thatch-colored hair standing on end.

"This is what I was afraid of! I knew we should have dumped you on the side of the road the moment Bridget dragged your sorry hides back here." Kara stopped, whirling on Everett in a furry. "This is all your fault!"

"My fault?" Everett scoffed. "All Silas and I have done has been to help you!"

"*Help*? You've gathered kindling and firewood, Everett! How is that helping anyone?"

"You may not like us. Saints, I don't even like Silas all that much." Everett stepped closer, the toes of his boots brushing Kara's. "But you cannot deny that we *have* helped you. You wouldn't have been able to gather nearly the amount of wood we have. We've also kept that Ronan character from coming back, haven't we?"

"He doesn't even know you're here." Kara scoffed and pushed the tall man back. Her eyes flamed, as they stopped right below the tree where Silas and I sat. "He's busy stealing from the people of Hillingsfarth, Everett."

"And you? You're stealing from him, aren't you?"

Kara's face paled, Everett hitting the truth on the head. But Kara didn't answer him. Instead, she clenched her fingers into fists and glared at Everett. He needed to tread carefully.

"Bridget and I are helping people!" she said. "Silas and you are simply endangering us."

Everett snorted. "You've done a pretty good job of endangering yourself, Kara."

"Why, I ought to—"

"Ought to what?" Everett leaned down, his hands on his knees as if he were talking to a child and not a twenty-two-year-old woman. I stiffened, certain that my sister was about to soundly bash the man's nose in.

But to my utter surprise, Kara grabbed Everett's vest and pulled his face to hers, kissing him soundly on the lips.

I gasped and felt Silas' gaze turn to me. My hand slapped itself over my mouth, my eyes twice as wide as normal. I couldn't turn my gaze from the ground, where a spluttering Everett was stepping away from a rosy-cheeked Kara.

"That…was not fair," he gasped, running a hand through his hair.

"Wasn't it?" Kara smirked. "It certainly shut you up for a moment."

Everett scoffed, but it seemed half-hearted. "So what was that for?"

"A thank you." Kara crossed her arms over her chest. "And a goodbye."

I narrowed my eyes, wondering what *that* meant.

"Goodbye?"

"Yes. You and Silas are leaving for Ronan's camp tonight, Everett." Kara gripped her braid in her hands, tugging on the end. "It's been a week, and I won't have you endangering my sister and me any longer. Each day, the odds are higher that King Benedict will send men out looking for you."

"Why don't you return with us after we apprehend Ronan? We can protect you."

"From the king?" Kara snorted. "Highly unlikely. Even with Silas' cousin betrothed to Prince Lachlan, there's no guarantee that he can protect us from the law. The *law*, Everett. You know, those written commands we are supposed to obey?"

Everett reached out, gripping Kara's elbows. "But we would do our best, Kara."

"Daggers, Everett, please! Don't make this any harder, all right? I never planned on this. On falling—" Her words cut out for a moment before she tugged out of his grip. "Help me find Silas and my sister. Then I need you to leave."

"Kara—"

"No!" she snapped, turning to march into the woods. "No, Everett, I can't do this."

He followed after her silently. I swallowed back tears as Silas leaned back against the tree trunk. Now we would both be nursing broken hearts after the boys left.

"Do you think she's right?" I managed to whisper after a long moment.

"About King Benedict? Or about us endangering you?" Silas asked.

"Both."

"I think she's right about the king," he started slowly. "But if you were to come with us to Allura, you wouldn't be in trouble for breaking the law. The king would never have to know."

"But we would." I swung my legs around, sitting cross-legged on the wide bough.

"Yes, you would," Silas conceded. "But I don't think your sister is planning on leaving anytime soon."

"What about the second part?"

"I don't know. I like to think you capturing us helped us protect you a bit. But I also believe Kara is right, and that Ronan doesn't know we're here."

"I think the second part is more likely."

Silas reached up and gripped my hands in his. I could not tear my eyes away from them. They were so right. So perfect grasping mine, sending shivers through my fingers all the way down to my toes. It took every ounce of willpower to pull away and climb toward the forest floor.

"She's going to be so mad, Silas."

"Blast it, Bridget!" Silas leapt to the ground beside me. "Why do you care so much about what she thinks? I know she's your sister, but you are your own woman."

"Am I?" I crossed my arms across my chest, turning away from him. I could see the frustration and hurt in his eyes, and it was almost enough to undo me. "You have no idea what I have faced, Silas, what I am. You know what we've shown you. You've yet to see the broken."

"Then show me." He laid a hand against my shoulder, swallowing a sigh when I flinched away. "Let me help you, Bridget."

11

SILAS

Bridget refused to look at me. I wanted to see her cerulean blue eyes, to read what she was thinking. But she had walled herself off like she did whenever I got close. She didn't do this with Everett. It was one reason I had stayed back over the week. Because I could see *her*—the happy, unashamedly brilliant woman Bridget was when she thought I was not looking.

But now she knew. She knew that I wanted her, her perfectly broken self. Something had sprung to life inside me the day I had met her, and it had only grown in the week I'd spent around her and Kara. Brylee once told me I would fall hard and fast when I met the right woman, and she was correct.

"Bridget," I said.

She kept her eyes down but turned to face me.

"I am going to catch Ronan," I continued. "And then I'm going to come back and take you with me to Allura."

"I am not skilled at being a lady, m'lord." Her voice trembled. "And I won't leave my sister."

"Then we'll take her stubborn self with us." I tipped her chin up to face me. "But I know there is something special about you, Bridget. We're two sides of the same coin." I reached out and cupped her cheek again, loving the softness of it as I leaned my forehead against hers. "Troubles can come calling, but if I have you by my side, there's nothing I cannot do."

"Silas. You have only known me for a week."

"And a brilliant week it has been." I smirked as she chuckled. "Truly, Bridget. A week is all I need to know that you're different from any other woman I have had the pleasure of meeting."

"Because I bashed you over the head?"

"Yes, there's that." I felt my breath hitch as she bit her lip. "But also your determination, your sharp mind, your strength to survive out here. And you are quite beautiful."

A small gasp caught in her throat, tears edging in the corners of her eyes.

"I want to learn to fall in love with you, Bridget," I said. "Please? Give me that chance?"

"Silas." She wound her arms around my neck, pressing her lips to mine. The scent of apple blossoms swirled around me, melding with the crisp fall leaves to create the most intoxicating scent. I wrapped my arms around her waist, meeting her kiss with burst of passion that left me breathless.

"What is going on?" Kara's voice shattered our blissful high.

Bridget jerked back, and it was only my secure hold on her waist that kept her from stepping completely out of my embrace.

"I knew it!" Bridget's sister stomped up, trying to yank her away from me.

I glared down at her. "Knew what, exactly?"

Kara's eyes were blazing. "That you wanted her! That you were using her!"

"I care a great deal about Bridget, Kara," I snapped, causing the older girl to step back. "I would never hurt her."

"You're leaving," Kara spat the words. "How is that not going to hurt her?"

"Because I'm coming back!" I released Bridget, stomping up to get in Kara's face, like she had done with Everett earlier. "I am not abandoning you both here in these woods."

"I want to be here," Kara retorted.

I raised my brow at Kara. "Does Bridget? Have you ever stopped for one minute to ask your sister what *she* wants? Or are you so busy thinking that you know best that you won't listen to her?"

Kara's mouth opened and closed as she glanced from Bridget to me, then back again. "I thought she was happy here."

"I am." Bridget's voice sounded thick with emotion. "But I'm tired of stealing, Kara."

Her sister stiffened, eyes flicking to me.

"She already told me," I said.

It did not make the consequences any easier to bear. For there would be consequences. Part of me wondered if I would be able to convince King Benedict to give a lenient punishment to the girls, for they were stopping Ronan from lining his own pockets with gold that belonged to Hillingsfarth and helping their people in the process.

"Daggers. I don't know what to say." Kara rubbed her hands on the side of her pants. She looked young, standing there with a bewildered look on her face as her eyes nervously danced between the two of us. For a moment I thought I caught a glimpse of the scared young lady that lay right below the surface of Kara's façade.

"Say you will come with us." I extended my hand to her. "Everett and I will capture Ronan and then—"

Kara laughed, harsh and cold as her steely mask slipped back into place. "There's your plan's first flaw. No one simply *catches* Ronan. We should know."

"How do you know?" I asked, my hand lowering a half inch.

"Oh, baby sister didn't tell you that?" She smirked, her eyes going cold. "Ronan is—"

"There you are!" Everett broke from the forest, flying up to grip Kara by the shoulders and shaking her slightly. "Don't ever do that again." A wild look was in his eyes as he studied Kara, one that I had never seen before. After reassuring himself that she was fine, he cleared his throat and stepped back.

"Silas." Bridget's small hand landed on my arm. When I looked down at her, her head and shoulders sagged, as if the weight of my stare was too heavy a burden. "Silas, Ronan isn't merely the thief of Hillingsfarth Forest."

"Oh?" Everett's annoying voice broke in.

"No." Bridget's hand shook, and I laid mine over it. "He's also—"

"He is related to us," Kara finished. "Ronan of Merryington is our brother."

It felt like a punch to the stomach. The air whooshed out of me and I turned, stepping away from the little group in the glen to brace myself against the oak tree.

This was bad. If they were related to Ronan, the king might be less inclined to show mercy. My father would, but I didn't know enough about Lachlan's father to risk Bridget's and Kara's life on it.

But I did know that they had been part of Ronan's band. That information might be useful. If they helped catch Ronan, then maybe Benedict would be more likely to pardon them.

"How much do you know about the way things work in Ronan's camp?" I asked, my voice gruff from the emotion resting there.

"A bit. Why?" Kara had her arms crossed when I turned back to face them. Bridget's were crossed as well, but her head was still bowed, her whole posture caving over her stomach like it pained her.

"Tell us everything you know. It will help us to catch him, and when you return to Hillingsfarth with us, it will go better for you."

"Is that a threat?"

"Blast it all!" I shouted, my temper all but spent with her stubbornness. "We want to help you! Trust, Kara! When did you forget that it is good to have people around you?"

"Silas?" Everett asked, smirking when I glared at him. "Do you hear yourself?"

"What?" I growled before the realization hit.

Everett had said the same thing to me right before we went and got ourselves captured. He had told me what a lonely life it was, working alone. I had said it was easier.

But now, staring at these two women, something fierce raced through my veins. Protection, loyalty, tenderness. I wanted to help them. Keep them safe. Be by their sides, no matter what. It was a weight that was both light and heavy, comforting and suffocating.

I glanced at Everett, my mouth hanging halfway between open and closed before I snapped it fully shut. I turned back to Kara.

"Please," I said, my voice quieter now, "let us help you."

"You can capture Ronan." She latched onto Brylee's arm and yanked her behind herself. "But once you apprehend him, you will stay away from us, *Prince* Silas. We don't need anyone."

I watched, heart shattering, as she pushed Bridget into the cave. I tugged on a look of indifference as Kara turned back to face us, glaring first at me then Everett.

"It's time for you to go."

12

BRIDGET

I bit the inside of my cheeks, glaring at my sister. "You are just going to let them walk into Ronan's camp?"

I could feel Silas' eyes burning into my back as he and Everett stepped into the cave, but chose to ignore him, training my eyes on Kara instead.

"What if I am?" Kara asked coldly. "Why do you care?"

I balled my hands into fists. "This is wrong. You know what he's capable of. What if he kills Everett and Silas? Do you want that on your conscience?"

Mentioning the men by name made Kara stiffen even further, but she did not answer. Stalking over to the trunk, she flung it open. Grabbing out the swords, she stared at them for a long moment. I caught the tremble that shook her arms as she tightened her grip on them.

"I am giving you these and your bows. I trust you will not harm us." Tension crackled through the air as my sister met Everett's gaze. A pained look crossed Kara's face but as soon as she blinked it vanished. "Here, take them and go meet with Ronan. Do not come back here."

She threw Silas his sword first and he nimbly caught it, settling it around his waist as a small sigh slipped past his lips. His hand gripped the pommel comfortably. He looked more natural that way, but his icy blue eyes remained sad as he glanced at me, his lips pressed flat.

I wanted him to smile. Needed him to. Somehow this felt too final, like another goodbye I had to face, even though I did not want to. I had said enough goodbyes to last a lifetime.

My breath caught in my throat, sudden and sharp. I choked on it, rushing out to cough and cool my burning cheeks.

"Are you all right, Bridget?" It was Everett, a concerned look on his face.

I cursed as I sucked in a slow drought of air to ease the tickle in my throat. I wanted to lie. But tears clouded my eyes, confusing me. I had not truly cried in years.

"Everett, I—" A sob slipped out and I found myself in his embrace, crying as I leaned against his chest. He was what Ronan never was, an older brother who wanted to protect me.

"It's all right, Bridget." His accent was thicker, and he cleared his throat. "I promise I'll keep the dunderhead safe."

I laughed weakly. "Keep both of you safe. Kara may say she doesn't care but, she does."

"It's our dashing good looks and winning personalities, yes?" Everett smirked as I laughed. He wiped at my tears with his thumb. "We will be careful, Bridget. I have to come back and protect my sister."

"Sister?" The word was barely audible as I gasped. "Truly, Everett?"

"Yes." He leaned his forehead against mine. "I haven't had a family in a very long time, Bridget, and I would be honored to call you part of mine."

"I would like that."

He smiled, stepping back and motioning someone forward. Silas appeared, a divot in his forehead as studied me.

"Are you sure you and Kara will be all right alone?" he asked.

"We have been alone for three years, Silas. Another few weeks will not make a difference. Besides"—I swallowed, crossing my arms over my chest as Kara stepped out of the cave—"Kara wants you to stay away."

Silas growled under his breath as he stepped up to me. "I would like to see her try to keep me from you."

Despite my grief, a small smile tugged at my lips. "Are you claiming me as yours, Prince Silas?"

"Would you have me if I did?" His whisper brought the butterflies back to life in my stomach.

"Yes," I said. "But you need to come back from facing Ronan."

A chill raced down my arms at that thought. Ronan had killed hundreds of people. Silas and Everett could very well be walking into a trap.

"Silas, be—"

He pressed his lips against mine, silencing any fear I was planning on voicing. I could hear an argument behind us, but I ignored it. Silas was all I wanted to focus on. This last goodbye. I poured all my desires into it, for it was possible that it may be my last chance to do so.

"Bridget." Silas' voice was husky as he pulled away. "I love you."

I shook my head. "You barely know me."

"A fellow can know his own heart." He pressed a kiss to my forehead. "My heart is in your hands, m'lady."

"Much can happen."

"Yes, and it can either be for good or bad. But I am choosing to trust that God's plan for us is not over. Because neither Ronan, nor your sister, nor a stubborn Hillingsfarth knight can change what I know is from Him. Don't you feel it, Bridget?"

I nodded, words failing me.

"Good." He pressed another kiss to my forehead. "I'll return for you soon."

"Please, be careful."

"Always." Silas smirked, winked, and then motioned for Everett to follow him into the foliage.

Everett stepped up to me. "Take care of Kara. She needs you more than you realize." He hugged me quickly then disappeared after Silas.

"You have them both wrapped around your finger." Kara glared at me. "Too bad we won't see them again."

"They will return soon," I whispered, hugging my stomach as I followed my sister into the cave.

"Yes, and we shall be gone."

"What?" I stared at her, not believing what I was hearing. "What do you mean? This is our home."

"*Was* our home."

"Kara—"

"Stop, Bridget!" Kara wheeled on me, her eyes flaming in the firelight. "You may think they care about us. Daggers, maybe they really do. But Ronan will kill them, and then he will come after us. He will know that the only way Silas and Everett could have known about him was because of us. And I will not—cannot—stand by and watch as he tortures you before killing us both. I won't do it, Bridget. Don't ask that of me."

"But what if Silas and Everett capture or kill our brother?" I stared at her, refusing to back down to her this time. "If we leave, we'll never know. What if this is our chance at love, Kara?"

"Bridget—"

"No, Kara! Shut up for once and listen!" Her eyes grew round at my outburst, but I kept going. "Silas is right. We cannot live from day to day. This isn't living. I want to dare to dream of more beyond hiding and stealing. Silas gives me hope that I can find that. Don't you want more than this? This cannot be all you want out of life. I want love, Kara. A family. A real *life*."

A sob choked off the rest of my words. Clearing my throat, I snapped my gaze back to my sister. "I saw you kiss him, you know."

Kara's red cheeks gave away her discomfort.

"You would not have kissed Everett if you didn't care for him a bit."

"Now it's your turn to shut up, little sister. Come on; time to fix our dinner."

A small smile ticked up the corners of my mouth as I moved to help prepare our meal, though it died as quickly as it appeared. My stomach clenched as I thought about the man I loved and the man I considered a brother out in the woods, facing down the infamous Thieves of Hillingsfarth Forest alone.

13

SILAS

"Brother and sister, eh?" I whispered as Everett and I crept through the underbrush.

Everett shrugged. "I think I make a rather good big brother."

"You cannot be that much older than me."

"I am a score and four."

"You are twenty-four years old?" I studied the man. "Then why do you act so…"

I could not think of the word. It wasn't that I hated the man. He was nice enough, as companions went. But I had always worked alone. Preferred it. It was safer, easier than trying to watch someone else's back. The fact that I was stuck with Everett made him unbearable, even if the man himself was rather likable.

Everett smirked at me. "Life is joy, Silas. Going through the life God has given us expecting the worst or being discontented makes us unbearable. You are proof of that."

"Well, thank you for that," I said dryly. "But why does Bridget think of you as a brother?"

"Anyway, I am claiming her as a sister because"—Everett lowered his voice even further, motioning to the clearing ahead of us, where voices murmured in the growing dusk—"I'm assuming that he was never much of a brother to her."

I didn't need to assume; I knew. A flash of righteous indignation surged through me and I wanted nothing more than to wallop Ronan between the eyes. I started forward, but Everett grabbed me by the arm, gesturing to a group of men walking toward us. I hunched back over, glaring at them and then at my companion before pointing to a large tent across the way.

Everett shook his head, motioning over his shoulder. He pulled me after him as he slunk into the shadows.

"I vowed to Bridget I would keep us alive," he hissed once we were out of earshot from the camp. "And you pulling a fool stunt like that *will* kill us."

"That man deserves every form of pain and more for what he did to Bridget and Kara. Do you not want that for the girls? Justice?"

"Yes. I want justice." Everett pointed over my shoulder, his other hand raking through his hair. "But that isn't justice; that's vengeance. Vengeance hurts no one but you. We will catch Ronan, but we have to be wise in our planning. Rushing headlong into a camp of at least twenty men is far from wise, my friend."

My friend. It was the first time Everett had ever referred to me as such, and I was a bit taken aback. My shock must have registered on my face for Everett smiled, shrugging a shoulder. "I've grown rather fond of you. Although you are still a stubborn pain in the—"

"Ronan! I come bearing news, sir!"

We crept back to the edge of the camp, peering through the tall grass toward Ronan's camp. A tall man with broad shoulders exited the tent. A dour expression pulled taunt the hard lines of his face. His dark brown hair was pulled back from his face in a que. From the distance we crouched at, I could not tell the color of his eyes, but I felt that they were cold.

The man who called out to his commander knelt, fist over his heart. Ronan waved him back to his feet with an agitated motion.

"Report!" Ronan bellowed, and I swore I could feel the vibration of it in the ground.

"Sir, there is rumor that King Benedict has sent men out looking for us. They left one week ago and have not been heard from since."

"What is this to me?" Ronan grunted, glaring at the man, who had begun to tremble. "Rumor is all it is."

"What if they found your sisters, sir?"

So they are keeping an eye on the girls. I mulled the information over in my mind, unsure of what I would do with it.

"If they found the girls, they found them. They are no concern to me, Daniel, and they should be no concern to you either."

His barking tone grated, and it was only Everett's steady hand on my arm that kept me in my place.

"They were dead to me the day they abandoned us." Ronan waved his forefinger in a circle. "They are no more my family than the king himself. You best forget about them, Daniel. They are no longer part of us."

Daniel dropped his head in submission as Ronan stalked past him and into the tent.

Everett tugged on my arm, and I followed him back into the now dark woods.

"What do you think?" I muttered.

"That Ronan is scum."

"That we already knew." I earned a snort of agreement from Everett. "But what about Daniel?"

"I am not willing to bet my life on it, nor the lives of the women I love."

"Love?" I smirked as Everett's cheeks began to redden.

He slapped his hand over my mouth before I could say anything. "Not a word."

I pulled his hand away. "You kissed Kara."

"Spy," he accused. "And she kissed me."

I shook my head. "This is great fun, however we do have to try to form a plan."

"Yes. Although, any plan will put the girls in danger." His face twisted as if he had tasted something unpleasant

"What if we took them away?" I raised a brow. "Back to Dothe where they would be safe?"

Everett rubbed the back of his neck. "But what if we lose Ronan's trail?"

"I don't believe he will stray too far from here. Not if he believes there will be another shipment of supplies coming."

"Why on earth would he think that was going to happen?"

"Because one will be coming." My grin bloomed. I had once been told that whenever a truly brilliant scheme was born in my mind, my smile was terrifying. Judging by the widening of Everett's eyes, it was true. "And with it, a trap to catch Ronan once and for all."

14

BRIDGET

"I'm not going." I glared at my sister as she flung a pack over her shoulder. "I'm waiting here for Silas and Everett to return."

"You're going to die, then, Bridget." Kara began to shake, whether from anger or fear, I did not know. "You're all I have."

"Why are you so certain that Ronan is going to kill me?"

"We left." Kara's jaw tensed. "That's reason enough. Ronan doesn't tolerate desertion."

"What does he call ignoring us for the last three years?" I snorted, jutting my jaw out in defiance. "Silas and Everett care, Kara."

"Caring is the worst thing they can do!" Kara stomped up to me, eyes flashing. "Stop thinking with your heart and start thinking with your head."

"I have thought with my head long enough." My body shook, and I relished the anger coursing through me. For too long, I had kept silent, meekly caving to whatever Kara said. This time, however, I knew what I had to do. "I love them, Kara. There is something different about them. Can't you feel it?"

Tears—something that I had never seen in my sister's eyes before—turned Kara's gaze glassy. "Bridget, you cannot mean that."

I nodded. "I do. I don't know what is going to become of it, if it's a passing infatuation or if it will stand against this test. But what I do know is I am done running and hiding. I do not want to run from this."

"You are willing to throw all of this away for them?" she whispered, gesturing around the cave. "You're willing to give up on your sister for two men you met a week ago?"

"They are good people, Kara."

A lump formed in my throat as a look I could not identify whispered across my sister's features. Then, like a door slamming closed by a sudden breeze, all emotion flew from her face. Her jaw tensed and she nodded.

"Fine. If it is them you want, it's them you will get." She flung her bag over her shoulder, nodding once more before walking out the door.

My legs shook and I crumpled into a heap by the door, tears making their way down my face. I had been strong for so long. I had held my emotions in check the day that we had run from Ronan. All through the last three years I had hidden my anger, fear, loneliness, and sadness from Kara, pretending to be all right. And I had even stayed strong when Silas and Everett had left.

But now it was as if my insides had been torn out. Raw, gaping, throbbing. Pulsing in the air for the world to trample and mutilate even more.

If Kara could walk away from me, who would choose to stay?

It was late at night when another bout of pity struck me. I crept from the cave into the cold evening as the stars blinked happily in the black sky, blissfully unaware of my loneliness. I hugged my cloak around me, gliding over to my tree before scrambling high into its naked boughs. I leaned against the trunk, letting my gritty eyes slide closed.

But my tree was no longer a sanctuary.

My traitorous memory showed me Silas, his lips pressed against mine. The warmth, the heat, the strength that exuded from him. Another tear trailed lazily down my flushed cheek. How could being alone for less than a day hurt so much?

A crunch of a twig jerked me up. A shadowed figure eased out of the underbrush. A hood covered his head, and the obscured moon gave off too little light for me to identify who they were. I pressed against the tree as another shadow followed at the heels of the first.

"Should we wake them?" The whisper carried up to me and I nearly cried out in relief. I recognized that voice.

"Do you think that is wise?" asked the second voice as I scrambled back down the tree faster than was safe. My foot hit a mossy spot, and a tiny shriek slipped out as I felt myself falling. I grasped wildly for a limb to latch onto, and my palms scraped against the branch as my hands found purchase.

"Bridget!" Hands gripped my waist, lowering me the rest of the way to the ground. I flung my arms around Silas' neck, a sob slipping out.

"You came back," I gasped.

"Are you hurt?"

I blinked up at Everett. The clouds sailed away, revealing the creamy moonlight once more. I could see the concern on his face and Silas studying me as I sucked in a shaky breath.

"I'm as well as can be expected," I said.

"Why are you out here in the middle of the night?" Silas had not moved his hands from my waist and I leaned back into him, a tremor raking across my body. "Bridget, what happened?"

"Kara left," I whispered.

"What?" Everett hissed. "Why?"

"She said you were going to die, and that if we styesd we were as good as dead." I swallowed. "But I knew you would come back. I knew you would be all right."

"You don't know where Kara is?" Everett asked slowly, his eyes rising to meet Silas'.

"No." I glanced between them. "Is that a problem?"

"Possibly." Silas shifted, his arms tightening around me. "We have a plan. But for it to work, we have to know that you two will be safe."

"What is your plan?" My eyes widened at their expressions, a wild smile forming on Silas' lips.

"We're going to use bait." Silas let his grin grow a fraction. "Lure Ronan out and catch him."

I shook my head. "That will never work. Ronan can sense a trap a mile away."

"That's why we are going to use you and Kara as bait," Everett said, glaring at Silas. "I think it's risky, but we are going to make sure Ronan knows Kara and you have been taken to Dothe."

"Why do you think that would matter to him?" Bitterness laced my words. "He has never cared before."

"You're a liability." Silas let his nose brush the side of my head. "We will make sure nothing happens to you. This is our best hope to catch him."

"But we need both of you. We cannot have this band of his"—Everett waved his hand in the air—"roaming about looking for the sister who is missing."

"I am unsure of where she went." I sagged against Silas, tears threatening me even as I tried to level my breathing. "She was so angry at me."

I buried my face against Silas' shirt, hoping to settle my thundering heart and screaming mind. I wanted to cry, laugh, shout, all at once. I shook, the hopelessness of our situation pressing against me like a bag of rocks.

I felt my legs give out and then I was floating. The pounding beat of a heart vibrated against my ear. The smell of smoke and wood nipped the edges of my senses, and I sighed as the coarseness of a blanket scraped the back of my hand. Strong arms tightened, holding me close.

"You are safe," a voice whispered, sounding for all the world like an angel sent to protect me. To be my companion and friend. To show me how to hope again.

15

EVERETT

Silas cradled the trembling Bridget in his arms, his brows pinched in worry as he draped a blanket around her shoulders. I added a log to the fire, watching the embers spark up to the cave ceiling. I had seen the terror in Bridget's eyes as she had flung herself at Silas. Her trembling and sobbing stabbed at me like a knife to the heart.

I fisted my hand, resting it against my lips. Kara had better hope I was not the one who went looking for her because if I found her—

I straightened. If I located her, I could speak my piece before hauling her sorry hide back to Dothe. She needed to know that what she was doing to Bridget was killing her.

I nodded, turning to Silas. "I'm going to go find Kara," I whispered. I could feel my forehead wrinkle and forced myself to unwind the tension that was crawling up my neck. "She needs to know how she is hurting Bridget."

Silas nodded. "But do you think it is wise to separate? Ronan knows we're out here. What if he has men out looking?"

"I can be discreet." I smirked as Silas rolled his eyes. "Besides, Bridget is in no shape to traipse through the woods with us. We have to be quick, in and out, before Ronan knows that the rumor is true."

Silas sighed, his eyes flicking down to Bridget. He ran a hand through his hair and, after a moment of contemplation, nodded. "Yes, I think it is what we must do. But I still don't like it."

"Silas." I wiggled my brows at him. "Have you some fondness for me after all?"

"Yes, I do." He smirked. "Like one loves his favorite hunting hound."

"Wounded." I clutched my heart, thankful that we were past the tense resentment that had been simmering since the beginning of our mission.

But perhaps that was due to the fact that our objective had changed. It was no longer about the glory of catching the Hillingsfarth Thieves. No, it was more about saving two vulnerable ladies who were a little too stubborn for their own good. About loving the orphans of our world and caring for them.

One of those orphans was like the sister I had lost.

The other…

I shook my head. Those were thoughts best saved for another time.

I grabbed extra supplies from the girls' cache, threw my hood up over my head, and tightened my belt around my cloak to keep it from snagging on the underbrush.

"Will you be all right?" I asked, adding another log to the fire.

"We will be fine. Just find her and hurry back." Silas clenched his jaw. "We have to keep them safe, Everett."

"We will. God led us here. He won't abandon us nor them."

Not waiting for a response, I slipped out into the ominous night.

I had too much time to think as I followed Kara's trail deep into the forest. It had taken some time to locate the exact direction she took from the cave, but once I'd located it, it was almost too easy to find her light prints in the wet earth. Now I subconsciously tracked her as my anger flamed at her treatment of her sister.

After nearly an hour, my eye caught the faint glow of a dying fire in a small clearing. A small form laid curled on its side. A blanket covered Kara, her hood drawn over her head to ward off the coolness of the night. A set of knives lay beside her.

Now to figure out how to approach her without getting stabbed.

That thought caused a smile to tug on my lips as I crept, silent as a falling snow, to Kara. I leaned over, clamping my hand over her mouth and pinning her arms to the ground.

She flailed, her eyes widening in shock for only a few seconds before she caught sight of my face.

"No stabbing now, eh, love?" I smirked, yanking her knives away as I released her and stepped back.

"What are you doing here?" she snapped, her eyes flashing in the moonlight.

"I followed you."

"Why?"

"Bridget."

"What's wrong with Bridget?" The panic in her voice made me even angrier.

"Did you not think about what your *leaving* would do to her?"

Kara grunted. "She was waiting for you two. She was fine."

It was my turn to scoff. "No, she fell apart. She was up in that blooming oak in the middle of the night and nearly fell out of it when we came into the clearing."

"Is she all right?"

"She's fine," I snapped. "No thanks to you. Saints, Kara, do you ever think of anyone besides yourself?"

"What?" She looked shocked at my outburst, but I couldn't seem to stop.

"You heard me," I stated as I began to pace, agitation fueling every step. "You never seem to listen to Bridget. You order her around like a soldier. She's your sister, Kara! She loves you. You should have seen her tonight, shivering and trembling in Silas' arms. She was broken, more so than anyone I have ever seen, that's sure and certain."

"Broken?" Kara wrapped her arms around herself, her shoulders shaking ever so slightly.

"Yes. Broken. Shattered. Gutted." I took a step toward her with each word. "And you did that to her."

"You don't think I know that?" A sob slipped past her lips. "But I was hurting her worse by being there."

"How?" I stopped in front of her, wanting to see her dark brown eyes, to read the truth in them.

"I was…I was stifling her." Ever so slowly, she raised her head. Tears glistened in her eyes, making them shine in the light of the moon. "I am controlling. I know that. But I cannot help it. She's all I have left."

"And you left her for Ronan." I could not keep the venom out of my tone. "If I had my sister with me still, I would die before I would let *anyone* touch her."

"Sister?"

"She died. Ten years ago, when the plague spread through Hillingsfarth. My parents followed soon after from starvation. I was on my own. King Benedict took me in as a knight in training. So, forgive me, m'lady, if I cannot stand the way you are treating your *family*."

Kara swallowed, her mouth opening and closing before she fell to her knees and sobbed. A small fissure formed in my heart, releasing the anger and letting pity fill in the crack. I knelt beside her, resting a hand on her shoulder.

"It's not too late to trust us," I whispered, after her tears had lessened.

"Ronan is on our heels. If you try to capture him—"

"We have a plan. But it will require that you rely on us, Kara. Can you do that?"

Her lashes were wet from her tears, and as she blinked up at me, the gleaming droplet splashed onto her cheek, trailing down it. An overwhelming urge to wipe it away hit me and I gave in, letting my thumb graze her cheek. A gasp shuddered through her chest and she pressed her lips together. Lips that I wanted very much to kiss.

"Can you trust us?" I whispered even softer, leaning toward her.

"I think—" She reached up, her hand resting against the back of my neck in order for her to push my lips down to hers.

It was slower than her heated kiss in the woods that afternoon. It was searching, as if she wondered if I was being honest with her. I returned her kiss, pressing one hand against her cheek and the other I wrapped around her waist.

Slowly we parted, my breath feeling ragged as I leaned my forehead against hers. "I swore to Bridget that I would protect Silas. And now I vow to you, Kara. I will protect you and your sister. You need only to see that Silas and I want to help you. We want to be there for you. Do you believe that?"

"I want to." She hiccupped. "But I am not good at it."

"You are simply out of practice." I smiled, gently tucking a loose strand of her hair behind her ear. "Let me help with that, too."

A smile—something I had only seen in mockery from her—bloomed slowly, as if it had forgotten how to exist at all. It made her seem younger, easing lines around her eyes and mouth from worry.

"You are beautiful." I had not meant to say that out loud, but the blush that infused Kara's cheek made it worth it. "Kara, that kiss—"

"Everett." She laid her hand against my cheek. "I don't know what this is. I don't know if it is born of desperation, or fear, or—"

"I know that I care about you." I cleared my throat, pulling her to her feet as I stood. "I was furious because you ran away, away from a sister who could help protect you and from us when we promised to return. Kara, I am not perfect, but if you will give me the chance, I want to show you how much I care about you. And Bridget is already my sister."

She smiled wider at that, another layer of hardness fading as the sun began to lighten the horizon. "I would like that, Everett. But please, be careful with my heart."

"With God as my witness"—I wrapped my arms around her waist—"I vow to treat it like the precious jewel it is."

I leaned down, claiming her lips once more. Her fingers played with the hair at the nape of my neck, a sensation I quite enjoyed. We lingered long before leaning back.

"Time to catch a thief." I smiled, pressing a kiss to her forehead.

For once, Kara did not argue with me. Instead, she laced her fingers with mine and let me lead her back to the cave without a murmur.

16

SILAS

I jerked and moaned, forcing my eyes open as Bridget stirred in my arms. Had I fallen asleep? I glanced at the cave opening, seeing the sunlight pouring through. Everett sat along the far wall, Kara's head resting in his lap as she stretched out on her bedroll. He pushed her hair away from her forehead, smiling down at her in a lovesick way. Did I look like that when I stared at Bridget?

"Silas?"

I smiled slightly as Bridget reached up and laid a hand against my cheek.

"What are you doing…?" she began before her brows lowered and her eyes closed again.

"You remember?" I asked, my eyes flicking to Kara and Everett. Pins and needles began to shoot through my arm and up into my shoulder. I had been holding Bridget for hours, refusing to lay her aside for even a moment.

"Yes." Bridget buried her nose into my neck, whimpering ever so slightly. "I was hoping it was all a horrid dream."

I hummed sympathetically. "But look who is back."

Helping her sit up, I winced as the blood began to circulate back into my arm.

Bridget blinked, then a small smile tugged on her lips when she saw her sister.

"So, Everett dragged her back here." She leaned into me, resting her head against my chest. "How much kicking and screaming did that entail?"

"Not much." I could not resist nuzzling my nose into her hair. "She came back hand in hand with Everett and then they sat down right there."

Bridget stiffened. "Of course, she would come back with him."

I was confused by the harshness in her tone as she pushed to her feet. She swayed, bracing a hand against the wall. After a moment, she staggered out of the door. I followed her, halting when she stepped behind a tree.

A crow cawed. The leaves rustled in the breeze. A strange foreboding encompassed the camp and I shivered.

"Bridget?"

"What?"

I angled my head back, seeing her up in the tree. I smiled, though it felt strained after the night we had been through.

"Please come down."

"Why? So you can make me trust you, only to have you leave again?"

I furrowed my brows. "Where is this coming from? I want to help."

"Everyone I care about leaves. So just abandon me now and get it over with." Her voice sounded strangled, like she was working hard to push the words out.

"Bridget—"

"I'm done being hurt, Silas."

"Bridget, come down and talk with us." I startled around to see Kara standing beside me, her arms crossed in frustration.

"Oh, yes. So you can tell me exactly what to do? I don't think so." She pulled herself up another branch, glaring down at us. "Even you left, Everett!"

I turned to see Everett standing at my other side. He shrugged as if he did not understand the girl in the tree any better than I did. I huffed a sigh, tipping my head back up to spot Bridget climbing even higher. I squinted against the sun as it shone through the skeletal limbs.

"Bridget, we want to help you!" I said.

"Go help yourself!" she hollered back, but it was drowned out by a sickening crack. A scream split the air, followed by the crashing of body and boughs plummeting to earth. It filled my senses before I heard another crack, this one of bone, that made my stomach curdle.

It took a moment for my head to catch up to my body, and by the time I was aware of what I was doing, I was already rushing to Bridget. She gasped a breath between screams as tears of pain raced down her cheeks.

"Bridget." I felt my stomach churn at the sight that met my gaze. Her ankle was twisted at a grotesque angle. Blood oozed down her leg from a deep cut, and I swallowed the bile that was pushing its way up my throat.

"Oh, help."

I turned. Kara stood over my shoulder, her face paler than a new linen sheet. Her eyes glanced at Bridget's ankle. Her face turned from white to a sickly shade of green before she turned and rushed into the underbrush.

"I'll go see if she's all right." Everett swallowed, looking a little green himself before following Kara.

Bridget screamed again, the ragged sound grating on my already frayed nerves.

"It will be all right," I tried to soothe, but I knew it would not be. With an injury like that, it was highly unlikely she would ever walk without a limp.

"It hurts," she whimpered, her scream tapering off into pure sobs. I pushed her hair back from her forehead, and my hand came back sticky with blood.

Footsteps behind me had me steeling my nerves and I took a deep breath. I could not panic. Right now, Bridget needed me. Kara and Everett too, whether they wanted it or not.

"I need bandages and water," I ordered. "Everett, we need to saddle the horses. We can no longer play it safe. Bridget needs a doctor. The safest place we can get help is Dothe."

"Yes," Everett agreed without argument, tugging Kara after him. "Let's go. The sooner we can get everything together, the sooner we can help your sister."

As they retreated into the cave, I assessed Bridget for further injuries. Besides her ankle, leg, and forehead, she had a nasty bump on the back of her head. She was still crying, though not as hard as she had been.

"I am a fool." She whimpered again, shifting and sucking in a sharp breath. "Why can I never make the right choice?"

Pain speared my heart. "Am I a wrong choice, Bridget?"

She pried her eyes open. "No, that's not what I meant."

"Then what did you mean?" I cocked my head to the side, taking the bowl of water Kara thrust at me, along with a clean rag. After wetting it, I dabbed at the gash along Bridget's forehead while Kara hastily tended to Bridget's leg.

"I have always been a follower." She closed her eyes, moaning as I dabbed at her head again. "I had a dream last night and it was horrible." She hissed as Kara wrapped a bandage around the cut on her leg. "So I decided to take the reins, make my own choice. I ruined it. I fell from that blasted tree and broke myself. All I do is break. Over and over again."

"Breaking isn't the same as broken, love," I whispered. "Broken can be beautiful too. Both of my uncles tell stories of their greatest failures. Yet they say that they can look at them as blessings now. Though their choices hurt people, they say that God used their failures to show them the power of forgiveness and mercy."

She shuddered, a shiver rippling across her shoulders. "I don't know if this can be redeemed."

"It will be, someday." I clumsily wrapped her head in one of the bandages before glancing at her ankle. While Kara had tended to the gouge, the ankle itself was now about three sizes larger. Taking the bandage, I wrapped it the best I could. Bridget flinched, subconsciously trying to yank her leg out of my grasp.

After I finished, I scooped her into my arms. She sucked in a sharp breath, one arm wrapping around her middle and the other around my neck as I carried her to the clearing where Everett had the horses waiting. Kara handed up a satchel to Everett before he grabbed her hand, hauling her into the seat behind him. She scooted as close to him as she was able, her arms snugly around Everett's waist.

I glanced down at Bridget. A sheen of sweat dotted her forehead, and I could feel the tension in her body as I stepped up to the horse.

"Everett, give me a hand."

He blinked, detangling himself from Kara before swinging off his mount and hurrying to take Bridget from me. I leapt into the saddle, hating every moment I did not have Bridget cradled against my chest. It felt as if part of me was missing.

Everett handed Bridget to me and I settled her as comfortably as I could in the saddle. She wrapped her arms around my middle, her nose buried into my chest.

"It hurts," she muttered as tears leaked out of her eyes.

"We'll get to Dothe soon." I glanced at Everett. His brows were pinched with worry.

With a deep breath, I urged the horse through the underbrush. If Bridget's ankle was not treated soon, she could lose it. And that would kill her faster than a fall from any tree.

17

BRIDGET

The pounding of the horses' hoof beat an agonizing rhythm into my already sore body. I tried to focus on Silas to distract from the pain, but it did nothing to help. My ribs felt like they had been lit on fire, my ankle was so sore it was numb, and the ever-present throbbing in the back of my head made me want to vomit.

We broke out of the trees, and Silas encouraged the pace. We flew down the road, for we had to beat Ronan. Somehow, despite the haze my mind was in, I knew that much.

"We will be there soon, Bridget." Silas' voice rumbled in my ear, and I let my tired body sag against him as we thundered down the hard packed road.

I forced my eyes open. Had I fallen asleep or passed out? I groaned, tightening my grip around Silas' waist as the horses slowed to a walk.

"Do you think he saw us leave?" Everett's voice seemed to hover over me, but I could not force my eyes to open any further than the slits they were.

"If he did, he's not following," Kara replied, and I felt her cool hand rest against my forehead. "How far until we reach Dothe?"

"A few hours yet." I noted the frustration in Silas' voice. "We have to get her to a healer soon. She could lose her foot otherwise."

Is that a bad thing? I was no longer sure. I was floating, sailing above Hillingsfarth, Allura, Ironwolf. I skimmed the ocean of the North Sea, seeing Taletha in all its sandy glory. Then, slowly, it all faded to black as I dropped back into the world of oblivion.

18

SILAS

Bridget's skin burned as I slipped off my horse in the courtyard of Dothe Castle. My heart caught in my throat as she moaned.

"You need to be fine," I whispered as I hurried up the castle steps. Brylee stood at the top. Her skin shone with sweat, her split skirt swishing as she turned to follow me with a determined stride.

"Are you all right?" She glanced from me to Bridget. "Who is this and what happened to her?"

I dropped my eyes to Bridget, wincing as I noticed the bright red splotch growing on the bandage around her forehead.

"This is Bridget of …" I shrugged. "Hillingsfarth Forest. She fell out of a tree."

"A tree?"

"Yes. She needs a healer. Her ankle is in blasted shape as well as her head."

"I will call for one. Take her to the rooms we stayed in when we first visited."

"Are my things—?"

"They are in the same room. I didn't allow anyone to touch your belongings." Brylee smiled. "In that way, you and Uncle Benjamin are exactly alike."

I smiled but it was painful, as if my facial muscles could tell that now was not the time for humor.

"Go," Brylee ordered, then she sailed down the hall like the future queen she was. It took me no time to find the room that had been mine only a few weeks before. I managed to open the door, jostling Bridget in the process. A moan slipped past her lips as I stepped into the room.

"Sorry, love," I mumbled as I laid her on the bed. Exhaustion pressed in on me, but I shook it away as I added a log to the fire and covered Bridget with a blanket that had been left on one of the chairs.

I paced the length of the room, my head shouting at me to go after Ronan while my heart wanted to stay at Bridget's side. I clenched my fists, forcing myself to sit in the chair by the bed. But my legs bounced, my nervous energy refusing to be tamed.

The door opened on silent hinges, and the quick steps of the Dothe healer came toward the bed. His round glasses, pursed lips, and wispy white hair helped the muscles in my neck uncoil. Bridget would be in good hands.

"Silas."

I glanced at the door, and Brylee motioned for me to leave. My eyes turned back to Bridget, and my chest tightened.

"She will be all right, your highness." The healer smiled at me from where he stood beside Bridget, the bandages in his hands.

"If anything…drastic needs to happen, please come get me?" I rubbed the back of my neck, my eyes glued to Bridget.

"Yes, sire." The healer nodded in agreement. "But I do believe she will be fine. You're fortunate the bone did not break skin. She may very well have died if that had happened."

I swallowed the bile rising up the back of my throat and nodded.

A long, exasperated huff sounded in the hall, interrupting our conversation. Stomping feet came closer, then Brylee's hand clamped around my bicep. I was all but dragged out of the room.

"Oh, you have that look." Brylee huffed again, her hand still firmly fastened around my arm.

I feigned innocence. "What look?"

Brylee glared at me. "The look I knew you would get when you eventually fell in love with a girl."

"You knew I would have a look?" I asked, ignoring the fact that Brylee had been completely correct in her assumptions so far.

"Yes. You would fall fast, hard, and be completely in love before your family could blink." She ticked her list off on her fingers as she motioned for one of the guards to open a door for us.

We stepped into a well-lit study. A large, round table was situated at the very center. Around it sat King Benedict, Lachlan, Everett, Kara, my father, Uncle Collins, and my cousin, Marcus. I blinked at the sheer number of my family members in one room.

"What are you doing here?" I asked, running a hand through my hair and feeling decidedly bedraggled as I flopped into a seat between Everett and Marcus. "The wedding is not for another two weeks."

"Couldn't let you have all the fun now, could we?" Marcus grinned, one side of his mouth turning up higher than the other. His strawberry blond hair was neatly combed out of his face. He had not inherited Uncle Nicholas' wild curls, something he was secretly thankful for, I knew. His hazel eyes sparkled in the light from the wall of windows across from us.

"*Fun* is not the word I would use to describe this last week." Everett yelped as Kara elbowed him in the ribs, saving me from smacking the back of his head.

"Everett filled us in on what happened, Silas." Lachlan crossed his arms, leaning them against the table as his eyes scanned a map in front of him. "The next shipment of silks is scheduled to arrive tomorrow afternoon."

"Making it in Ronan's territory by tomorrow morning." Everett stood, stepped around a few of the chairs, and leaned over Lachlan's shoulder. He pointed to the area where we knew Ronan was camping. "He has his camp here. There are probably around twenty men or so."

He glanced at me. "What was the name of the one who wanted to help the girls?"

"Daniel," I supplied, crossing my arms and tipping the chair back on two legs. I ignored the disapproving look Father sent my way. "He seemed quite peeved that Ronan was abandoning the girls."

"Enough to testify against him?" King Benedict asked, arms crossed over his chest, his fingers drumming on his bicep.

"Possibly." Everett shrugged. "It's hard to know with only one meeting. We were a little"—he smirked at Kara—"tied up for part of this mission."

"Yes, so you've said." King Benedict studied Kara now. For her part, Kara sat straight and tall, her brown eyes never wavering as she stared back at the king. They gazed at each other for so long that even my stoic father began to shift uncomfortably in his chair.

At last, Benedict broke the silence with a question, "Sir Everett, what do you think is a fitting punishment for stealing from the crown of Dothe?"

"Your majesty?" Everett glanced at me and I shrugged.

"What should Kara of..." He cocked his head. "Where are you from?"

"Originally from Merryington, sir. But my sister and I have lived nearly all our lives in Hillingsfarth Forest. I consider this land my home more than Allura."

No emotion showed on King Benedict as he turned to Father. "How would you punish them, King Benjamin?"

Father glanced at me, a question deep in his gaze. I was unsure of what he was looking for, but I prayed that he would have mercy on Bridget and Kara. Yes, they had stolen, but what choice did they have? They had given most of their goods to the people in and around Hillingsfarth Forest. I did believe there needed to be consequences for their wrong doings. Yet mercy over justice was not always a bad thing.

I shrugged as subtly as I could, hoping Father understood.

"I think these boys are in love with them. And I think their punishment, should they choose to accept, would be to marry them and live wherever their husbands choose to settle. Be it here or Allura."

King Benedict raised a brow, as if he were truly thinking over Father's suggestion. I could not drag my gaze away from my father. I could see the smile tugging at the corners of his mouth and I wondered if Everett had told him something. Or had he seen Brylee and me carting Bridget to my room?

"Yes. That shall be their punishment, if they should choose to accept it."

I jerked, shock causing my jaw to drop open. "Marry them?"

"What?" Everett squeaked, glancing at Kara who had stiffened.

"We captured them," Kara protested weakly.

"Are you saying you do not wish to marry one of the young men?" Father asked, his black brow raising.

"No!" Kara hid her face in her hands. "I am simply…concerned. We were—" She trailed off, refusing to raise her head.

"They were thieves themselves, Father." I swallowed the lump in my throat, picturing Bridget as she told me that very thing. "They stole with Ronan before leaving him."

"But we could not fully escape him." Kara's muffled voice was soft, but in the stillness of the study, it bounced around with surprising strength. "I know this will never atone for stealing from Hillingsfarth, but I would like to be there when you capture my brother."

"Brother?" King Benedict glanced at Everett, brow raised once more.

"Honestly, did you tell them anything of importance?" I huffed as I glared at Everett, exasperation coloring my words.

Everett shrugged. "I am not as good at reporting as I once thought, apparently."

"I never would have noticed."

"Silas." Uncle Collins had been surprisingly silent through the whole exchange and I turned to him now. He had trained me as a reconnaissance officer, and I valued his opinion on nearly everything I did.

"What are your feelings on Kara and Bridget?" he asked.

I had been dreading this question. I took a deep breath, trying to formulate my thoughts into a way that made sense.

"Ever since I became a reconnaissance officer, I have worked alone. I quickly learned that I did better that way. I could sneak in and out of the places easier when I did not have to worry about watching someone else's back. It meant that I did not have to feel the loss of a partner dying or getting captured.

"But then Everett and I met these two wonderful, strong, brave women. And I saw the way they protected each other, nearly to the point of driving each other insane. I saw the danger they were in and I wanted to help. But Kara wouldn't let me." I smiled at her and she ducked her head. "I saw what holding others at arm's length did. It hurt the people wanting to help. It hurt the one in need. And it hurt whatever relationships could have been. I'm tired of living this way." I sighed, running a hand through my hair. "If Bridget will have me, I would like to marry her."

A chair grated against the wooden floor as Everett dropped to one knee beside Kara's chair. "If you will have me, Kara of Hillingsfarth Forest, I would truly be honored to be your husband. To protect your body, heart, and mind until the day I die."

Tears trailed down Kara's cheeks as she nodded. Everett pulled her off of her feet, spinning her in a circle.

"But you know what we still need to do?" he asked as he stopped and set Kara back on her feet. His arm was still curled about her waist, and I felt the strange desire to bolt back upstairs to sit at Bridget's side.

"We need to catch a thief," Lachlan stated, jabbing at the map. "And I think I know how we can do it."

19

EVERETT

"I would be more comfortable with this whole plan if you were staying here with Bridget," I grumbled as Kara helped me lace my arm guard to my forearm. "I hate the thought of you being in harm's way."

She smirked up at me, her brown eyes flashing. "And to think, one week ago you wanted nothing more than for me to disappear."

Now the thought of Kara disappearing made my stomach clench. I turned and threw a quiver of arrows over my shoulder to hide the shaking in my hands.

Kara and Bridget.

Silas. Lachlan. Brylee.

All people who could get injured. My friends. My family.

I growled, tearing a hand through my hair. I could handle this. I had to handle this.

"Everett." Kara's hand landed between my shoulder blades. She let it run down the length of my spine before she wrapped her arms around me from behind. "What's wrong?"

"I—" A lump had lodged itself in my throat. "Nothing."

"You are a horrible liar. This happened in the woods earlier, too. What is it?"

I turned, but Kara did not release her hold on my waist. Her hands settled on my hips, her head tipped to one side as she studied me.

"I told you about my sister."

She nodded slowly, waiting for me to continue, to push out the words that seemed clogged in my throat.

"She was the last of my family. Over the past ten years, I have created a family for myself." I rubbed the back of my neck. "I know I pretend to be carefree and jovial. But I am terrified of losing what I have. Because I cannot—"

My voice choked out and I tipped my head back to keep Kara from seeing my tears. Her hand landed against my chest, right above my heart.

"I understand, Everett," she said. "It's the same fear I have lived with for the past three years."

I sighed, rubbing at my eyes with my forefinger and thumb as my other arm wrapped around Kara's shoulders.

"You asked me to trust you and I am trying. But I also need you to do this for me." She paused, waiting for me to lower my gaze to hers. "I need you to trust that while you have our backs, we also have yours. That nothing that happens is out of God's control."

"God's control." I huffed a small laugh. "I told Silas that."

"God has us." Kara shrugged, her eyes focused on the front of my leather vest. "I suppose I forgot that until recently."

I pressed a kiss to her forehead, some of the tension leaving my shoulders as she tightened her hug. We stood like that for a while, simply content to be together.

"Are you certain you want to marry me, Kara?" I asked, breaking the silence.

"I told you yes. I would not have said that if I didn't mean it." She stepped back, eyeing me. "You meant your proposal, yes?"

"Yes." I laughed as she released a pent-up breath. "Listen to us. Questioning everything. We both need to work on the trust thing, hm?"

"Yes." She smiled, glancing shyly at me through her long, dark lashes. "Although, a kiss might help."

I raised a brow. "A kiss?"

She stepped closer, smiling now. "A kiss like this."

She gripped the quiver strap and pulled my face towards her. Pausing a hair's breadth away from me, she hesitated, but I did not. Wrapping my arms around her waist, I pulled her the rest of the way to me.

She smelled like apples and sunshine, despite the relentless pace we had set to reach Dothe. She tasted like hopes and dreams coming true and it took every ounce of chivalry in me to pull back.

I leaned my forehead against hers. "When this is over, marry me?"

"I already said—"

"No." I shook my head, moving hers along with it. "No, not waiting for a large celebration like Lachlan and

Brylee. I mean a small gathering. A priest, our friends and family, our vows. Married."

She smiled, her brown eyes glowing. "Yes."

"Yes?" I blinked, not expecting that quick of a response.

"Who else do I care about but you, Bridget, and Silas?"

"Well, Silas is…" I shrugged and then laughed at the glare Kara sent.

"He is going to be your brother-in-law. You need to start treating him better."

"Ah." I sighed, but I couldn't hide my smile. "A sister, a brother, and a wife. What did I sign up for?"

"An adventure." Kara hugged me tightly. "You signed up for a lifetime of adventures."

20

SILAS

I sighed, running a hand through my hair as I rested my elbows against my knees. Bridget had passed out as the healer tended to her. Her head was wrapped tightly in a stark white bandage. Her ankle was propped on a pillow with several ice-wrapped bundles gently resting around it. The doctor had bound the wound on her calf with a bandage, but he said he had to wait for the swelling before he could fix her bone further. He was not sure if Bridget would be able to walk normally again.

Why, God? I blinked back tears. Bridget had not deserved this. What had she done, except being born into a family of thieves? She had foregone that lifestyle, had wanted to do better.

Now she would forever have a limp.

Cursing, I pushed to my feet and reached for Bridget's hand. With a sigh, I squeezed it. I couldn't wait for her to wake up. It was time to go capture her thieving brother.

Ronan is going to pay for pulling me away from you. I swear it.

"I will be back soon, love." I battled a moment longer, then I dropped her hand and stepped to the door. Hesitating only a second, I turned to face Bridget's still form. "And when I return, both you and Kara will be safe."

"Saints above, isn't this fun?" Everett growled sarcastically as we huddled under a tree in our damp cloaks. Raindrops pattered against the leaves still stubbornly clinging to the trees, and the sun was turning the horizon a brilliant red.

Lachlan laughed, but it sounded forced. His teeth clattered, his black curls plastered to his forehead. "We would certainly be bored if we were back at Dothe Castle."

Kara snorted, but that was it. She scooted closer to Everett, her eyes wide as she stared at Lachlan. It was halfway between awe and fear. I could not fault her for it.

"A few more hours and we'll have him." Uncle Collins nodded at Lachlan. The hardness he had had for the prince a few weeks ago had faded, replaced with respect. It was strange to see such a change. But Uncle Collins always extended forgiveness to others, no matter their fault. It was something I admired more and more as I grew older.

"Do you truly believe it will be this simple?" Kara whispered, her forehead pinched. "He's never been close to being captured and we think we can do it two days after you found his camp?"

"He will be cocky, then. He won't expect this, that's sure and certain." Everett's lips were pressed into a thin line, his shoulders thrown back. "We'll get him. One way or another."

His gaze met mine and I nodded. We had talked about this before we left the castle. If it came to it, Everett and I would make sure Ronan was taken care of. Captured or dead, it only mattered that the girls were safe.

"I hear the wagon." Marcus edged forward, crouching behind one of the large tree trunks. He peeked around, eyes up in the trees. A flash of green caught my gaze and I eased my bow off of my shoulder. I strung an arrow to it as I knelt behind my cousin.

"You ready?" I whispered, eyeing the bend that the wagon would come around at any moment. I shivered as a stray raindrop trailed down my back.

"Always." His cockeyed smirk made a small smile of my own form on my lips. "Are you ready to be the hero to your lady love?"

"Always. And don't call her that."

Father, King Benedict, and a handful of trusted knights from both kingdoms were in position on the other side of the road. I could see them from where I crouched. Father nodded and we all tensed.

"Why not? 'Lady love' fits," Marcus whispered as the wagon rolled into view. I watched the green cloaked figure walk nimbly down the branch, much like Bridget had that first day in the clearing. The wheels of the wagon splashed through a puddle as Ronan leapt onto the wagon bed.

That was our cue. All of us sprung out of the woods, intent on one thing.

Ronan.

Marcus grabbed at the horses, pulling them to a halt as I pointed my arrow at Ronan's chest. A shout sounded from both sides of the road, but I ignored it. I could feel Kara and Everett behind me, poised to take whatever challenge came.

Ronan's blue eyes studied me before flicking over my shoulder.

"Should've known you would be the one to betray me." He sneered. "Bridget never had the guts to stand up to me."

"She was the one who convinced me." Kara held her head high. "And they know it all, Ronan. You are finished stealing from the people of Hillingsfarth and Allura."

"Am I?"

He was fast. He reached for his belt, whipping a dagger toward me before I knew what he was doing. A hand grabbed my collar, yanking me back and to the ground. I gasped, the wind knocked out of me and my bow clattered away.

A scream tore through the air, but I was too busy trying to fill my lungs with a decent breath to notice where it came from. I pushed to my knees, coughing, before finding my feet. I turned to see Everett on his back. The knife that had been meant for me was lodged in his shoulder. Kara gripped his shirt, her chest heaving as she studied the wound.

"Too bad about your friend."

I whirled around to face Ronan as staggered toward me. A knife was embedded in his leg, the blood mixing with the rainwater in a bright red stream. His lips curled as he said, "This is what happens to anyone who gets close to my sisters."

If Ronan was trying to shock me, he failed. The girls had already told us the truth.

"Nothing you can say is going to change what is about to happen to you, Ronan." My hand slowly inched to my side, my eyes never leaving Ronan's cold gaze. "Your sisters want out, so let them go."

"Why? So that you can pretend to love them?" He snorted. "They deserve to be with their brother. But they refuse to abide by my rules. So they left. I have been protecting them for three years."

"Saints, he's deluded." Everett's voice was a mere gasp against the howling wind, but I smirked at the statement.

"You're going to pay for the crimes against Allura and Hillingsfarth, Ronan." My hand clamped around my knife and I eased it out of its sheath. "Now, are you going to come peacefully?"

"No." Ronan smiled, and it shook me to my core. Cold, hard, emotionless.

I struck, steel meeting steel as Ronan parried my thrust. He was still agile, despite Everett's knife stuck in his calf. It was like the man could not feel pain. He stabbed at me, nicking my shoulder before I knocked it away.

Around and around we went, each blow matched perfectly. My breath came in rasps and I stumbled over a rock, barely dodging Ronan as he dove for me. He was just pushing to his knees when a shout rang out over the howling wind.

"Move, Silas!"

I side-stepped as another knife cut through the air where I had been standing. A sickening *thunk* reverberated the air as the knife embedded itself into Ronan's chest.

Ronan stared down at it, shock etched on his face. He staggered a step, then two, before tipping forward, face first, onto the muddy road.

It's over.

I doubled over in relief, my hands on my knees trembling, but it was short lived. Everett moaned, and I hurried to his side.

"Blast it all, Everett! What were you thinking?" I asked, shaking my wet hair out of my eyes.

He smirked, but it was filled with more pain than mirth. "I was saving your sorry—"

Whatever he had been about to say was cut off as Kara pressed her cloak against his shoulder. He hissed and squeezed his eyes shut against the pain.

"Well, you're an idiot."

"And you're alive." He cracked one blue-gray eye open. "That's all I care about."

"Daggers!" Kara swore as she pushed against Everett's wound once more. "He needs a healer, Silas."

The squishing sound of boots in mud made us all look up. Father stood there, Lachlan at his side.

"Ronan's men have been apprehended." Lachlan's green eyes studied the still body of the thief. "I see he's been taken care of."

"Not how we hoped." I shrugged. "But yes."

Lachlan nodded, his face grim. He whistled, long and low, and two of his men stepped out of the woods, hauling one of Ronan's men between them.

"That's Daniel." I pushed to my feet, ignoring how shaky my legs felt now that the adrenaline rush was gone. "He wanted to help the girls."

"But he didn't. He stayed with Ronan." Lachlan glanced around my shoulder, his face going pale when he noticed Everett. "Why didn't you tell me we had an injured man?"

"Lachlan—"

He pushed past me, kneeling where I had been moments before. His jaw ticked, and he glared at Ronan's corpse on the ground. "You two, take the body," he ordered his men, "and you four, help me get Sir Everett in the wagon."

"I can ride back."

"No, you cannot!" Lachlan and Kara interjected at the same time.

I snorted and all three of them glared at me now. I held my hands up in surrender, but could not seem to stop smiling. We had stopped Ronan. The girls were safe. And Everett, stubborn mule that he was, was going to be fine.

"Are you all right?" Father asked as the knights hauled Everett into the wagon. Kara scrambled up next to him, ignoring the glances from the other men.

"I'm fine." I shrugged away the hand he had placed on my shoulder, moving through the woods to the far clearing where we had tethered the horses. "I want to return to Bridget."

"Silas," Father sighed, his words faltering. I turned to face him. He looked tired, but he stood straight and tall, the man I respected more than anyone else. He was a king, a husband, a father, a brother, and he wore all of them with a strength that dazzled me. He laid his hand on my shoulder once more, his eyes studying every nuance of my face. They were still the same icy blue that they had always been. They were the only features I had inherited from my parents.

"I am proud of you, son."

I swelled at those words. They had been what I had longed to hear for years. I had hungered for them, pursuing them like a starving wolf chasing down a deer. Willhelm had always received them, having had much of Father's attention over our growing up years. As I grew older, I had spent hours and hours training with Uncle Collins to be a reconnaissance officer and had only passed Father at mealtimes.

Now those words soothed a spot I had not known hurt. I smiled at Father, nodding my thanks as the words stuck in my throat.

He smiled, wrinkles crinkling the corners of his eyes. "Now, let's get you back to your lady love."

"Don't call her that," I moaned.

Father laughed, swinging into his saddle before urging the horse onto the road. Following the wagon, we all headed back to Dothe.

Back to warmth, food, and home.

21

BRIDGET

I heard voices buzzing around me. My head throbbed and my foot felt cold. My eyes refused to open, and I groaned.

"She's waking up!" Soft footsteps glided to my side of the bed. "Silas is going to be so mad at us for sending him away."

"He needed to sleep," a motherly voice chided gently. "He has been awake for nearly forty-eight hours. Although, your father would have been the same way with me."

A laugh floated about, twinkling sweetly. "Lachlan *was* that way with me, and my wounds weren't nearly as severe."

Wounds. I wanted to reach up and touch my head, but even moving my fingers sent pain spearing through my chest. I sucked in a sharp breath, regretting it when even more pain laced across my torso.

"Here, drink slowly." Gentle, callused fingers stroked my cheek as a cool glass was pressed to my lips. Water trickled down my throat and I wanted to gulp it. But no sooner had I begun to drink then the glass was pulled away. "We have to go slow, the healer said."

"I'm going to go get Silas and Kara, Mama," the higher voice stated.

"All right, Brylee."

Soft footsteps retreated as I finally managed to pry my eyes open. A kind face smiled down at me. The woman's amber colored eyes seemed to warm me down to my core. Her honey-colored hair was streaked with gray, and laugh lines creased her lips and eyes. Freckles sprinkled around her nose, bright against her skin.

"I am Princess Sage." She squeezed my hand through the blankets. "How are you feeling, Bridget?"

I swallowed. My tongue felt like a wool blanket, and it took all my willpower to whisper, "My chest hurts."

"The healer said you have a couple of bruised ribs." She winced. "I've had those before. It takes a while for the pain to ebb. I heard you fell from a tree. I did that before, too."

She began to tell me the story of her tumbling out of a large tree back before she had married Prince Collins. She was just finishing when the door flew open, banging against the wall. I startled, wincing at the pain that raced through my entire body.

"Silas!" Sage reprimanded, her eyes flashing as my knight rushed to the bedside.

"Sorry," he mumbled absentmindedly, kneeling beside me. His eyes devoured my every feature like he was a starving man, and I was a five-course meal. I smiled, wishing I had the strength to move my hand to his cheek.

"Are you all right?" he asked.

"Yes," I whispered. "I am simply sore."

"She needs rest," Sage stated, tapping her foot against the rug with her arms crossed. "I kept her awake only for you to see that she was fine. Now you can quit hovering and driving the rest of us to distraction."

The girl who had spoken earlier stepped into my line of sight. She looked so much like Sage that she had to be her daughter.

"Besides, I need you to rest for the wedding tomorrow." Brylee laid her hand on Silas' shoulder. "With Everett injured—"

"What?" I rasped, my throat sore from lack of use. "What happened?"

Silas slowly dragged his eyes up to meet mine. "We stopped Ronan, but Everett took a knife to the shoulder. He's fine, but he has to stay in bed and regain his strength. Lachlan asked me to be his best man."

I smiled at that title.

Yes, you are the best man, Silas of Findley. The very best man in the world.

Silas' eyes danced as his face scoured mine once more.

"The healer still needs to set her ankle, Silas." Sage laid her hand on Silas' shoulder. "I think you need to be here when that happens, to help hold her down. It will be painful, but it must be done."

The thought of more pain made me sick to my stomach, but I nodded along with Silas. Sage hurried to summon the healer. Silas climbed to the other side of the bed, gripping my hand in his as he smoothed his hand against the bandage wrapped around my head.

"There's much for us to talk about," he whispered, his voice husky. "I wish I could stop this pain for you."

"I'll be fine," I gasped, hating the weakness I felt.

Silas smiled, his eyes continuing to flick all across my face. I heard the healer enter the room but could not seem to tear my gaze from Silas.

"Bridget." He cupped my cheek with his hand. "I—"

"Good, the swelling has gone down."

I smiled as Silas scowled at the older man, a sigh slipping past his lips.

"Tell me later, hm?" I winced as the healer removed the bandage from my ankle, and squeezed Silas' hand tightly to keep from crying out.

"Hold her down, Prince Silas. You too, Princess Brylee."

Panic gripped my chest. How bad was my ankle? I glanced up at Silas, who smiled in reassurance. He glanced over his shoulder, his face paling slightly before he turned back to me.

"Be strong for me, love," he said. "It will be all right."

My fear did not subside. I felt the healer grip my foot and my calf in his rough hands, slowly tugging on it. I felt the bone shifting and a scream tore from my throat. I arched my back and Silas pushed against my shoulders, Brylee trying to help as best she could.

I screamed again as the healer began to poke and prod at my ankle. I tried to kick his hands away, but a steady pressure kept my leg down. I ground my teeth, tears burning my eyes.

"Make it stop!" I moaned, my head pounding and blackness edging my vision. My stomach heaved. I thanked God that Sage had kept my water intake to a sip.

"It's almost done." Silas soothed, but I shook my head.

"Don't—don't lie to me," I gasped as the healer slowly pulled on my ankle again. I closed my eyes, wanting unconsciousness to come. But I remained alert. More pain laced up my leg and I sat up, trying to yank my leg out of Sage's grip.

"Stop, please stop." My breathing turned rapid. I tried to slow it, but it grew quicker, running away with the frantic pounding of my heart. "Silas." I moaned, before turning and vomiting. There wasn't much in my stomach to lose, and the dry heaving was almost as painful as my throbbing head, ribs, and ankle. Once my stomach was emptied, I flopped back onto the pillows, groaning.

"It's going to be all right."

I looked up at Silas. Tears trailed down his cheeks. He looked exhausted. Dark circles marred the underside of his eyes. His blond hair was wild, as if he had run his fingers through it multiple times. He had the shadow of a beard and his shoulders slumped.

"I'm sorry," I croaked, cradling my arm across my stomach.

"For what?" He quickly wiped at his cheeks. "You did not do anything, love."

"I'm sorry for climbing that tree. For falling. For worrying you so." I closed my eyes as Silas picked up my hand, running his thumb across the back of it.

"You don't have to apologize for that, Bridget. It's because I love you that I worry."

"You shouldn't—"

"I should. I do. I love you."

I stared up at him, my mouth hanging open at the admiration and care shining out of his eyes. Tears clogged my throat and I turned away, unable to handle anything further in that moment.

"We are finished with her ankle." The healer smiled, sympathy lining his face. I hated it. Hated him.

That's not rational. Where's Kara when I need her? I groaned. I wanted to sleep, to escape my pain. But I couldn't. I was wide awake. *Will this nightmare ever end? And where is my sister?*

22

EVERETT

My shoulder hurts.

A groan rumbled in the back of my throat as I ran my tongue across my lips. A hand held mine tightly, and I pried my eyes open.

Kara sat beside me on the bed, tear stains marring her pale face. "Oh, thank God," she said. "I was worried you were going to die and leave me here all alone."

"God's…got us," I gasped, my free arm wrapping across my chest.

"Brylee came in a bit ago to say Bridget's awake."

"Good." I licked my lips again. "Water?"

Kara moved to pour me a cup and pressed it to my lips. I took two big gulps and then waved it away. "What happened?"

"Ronan's dead but you took his knife to the shoulder. It was meant for Silas. I think you care for him a little more than you want to admit."

Color climbed my neck, but I ignored her comment. "Have you gone to see Bridget?"

Kara winced, turning to set the cup of water on the end side table. "I was sitting with you."

"That's not an answer and you know it." I sighed, the stitches in my shoulder pulling taunt with the action. "You need to go talk to her, Kara."

"It's my fault she fell." Her voice sounded strangled. "I caused her to think everyone leaves, Everett."

"And you're proving her right by hiding in here with me." She glared at me and I smiled. "Not that I mind the company. But Bridget needs her sister."

Kara visibly swallowed, her hands shaking as she sank beside me on the bed. "What do I even say?"

"The truth, love. Tell her the truth." I picked up her hand, running my thumb across the back of it.

"I think I can do that."

"I know you can. And then we have a wedding to go to."

"You cannot go to Lachlan and Brylee's. Not with the stitches."

I raised my brow. "How long was I unconscious for? Their wedding is not for—"

"It's tomorrow."

"What?"

"They moved the date up for—" She tapered off, a blush blooming in her cheeks. "They gave us their wedding date. You, me, Silas, and Bridget are getting married in two weeks. If he ever asks her, that is."

My mind whirled with that information. "You need to talk to Bridget. Go. I'll be here when you return."

With slow steps, Kara eased out the door. Once she was gone, I gingerly reached up and poked at the bandage wrapped around my shoulder. Pain shot down my arm and I winced.

Not doing that again.

A knock sounded on the door before Silas stepped in. He smiled at me, though he looked horrible.

I raised my brow at him. "You look like death personified, make no mistake."

He smirked, slumping into the chair by my bed with a heavy sigh. "I feel like death. The healer finished setting Bridget's ankle."

"By the look on your face, I take it you didn't ask her yet."

"No. It was not the most romantic of settings. Blood, screaming, vomit."

I wrinkled my nose. "Best you waited."

"My thoughts exactly." Silas crossed his arms, studying me. "You look like death, too."

"But I am a more handsome version of death."

"That might be the daftest thing to ever come out of your mouth. And trust me, I have kept score."

I shrugged, forgetting about the stitches until pain lanced down my arm.

Silas rubbed at his face, leaning forward to rest his elbows on his knees. "What if she doesn't want to marry me, Everett?"

"Why wouldn't she?"

"I—" Silas' throat bobbed. "She ran away from me."

"She was confused, Silas. She was scared. Her sister had just walked out on her."

"I just don't want to hurt her." Silas stood and began to pace. "She's had enough of that. I love her. I do. And I will protect her with my last breath. But what if that's not enough?"

"Why are you asking *me* this and not your father or uncle?"

"Because I already asked them."

"I am the last resort, then?"

"Basically." Silas grinned but it quickly disappeared.

"The one who should be making this choice is Bridget. Talk to her." I shook my head. "I just gave the same advice to Kara. Talk to Bridget. It's the only way to know one way or the other."

Silas grunted, crossing his arms in a disgruntled manner. "You sound just like my father."

"High praise, that." I smiled. "Now go. I'm sure Kara is done. She doesn't hold back her words."

Silas steadied his breathing before turning and marching out the door like he was going into battle.

I chuckled, closing my eyes, and let myself fall back into the dreamless void of sleep.

23

BRIDGET

Warm arms held me, feeling very much like a mother's embrace. A hand brushed back strands of hair from my face and I sighed, wrapping my arm around the slim frame.

A knock sounded on my door and shattered my dream, but the figure remained beside me. They moved to stand, and my arm fell away. I forced my eyes open and smiled as I watched Princess Sage move toward the door. She had sat with me, held me, comforted me. Tears trailed down my cheeks and I hiccupped as she let whoever was at the door enter.

"Bridget?"

I blinked, staring up at Kara. Tears were in her eyes as she reached out and let her trembling fingers trail across the bandages on my head.

"I…I am so sorry Bridget."

"For what?" I shifted, pain spearing my ribs. "I ran out of the cave; I climbed the tree; I fell. You didn't do anything."

"I left," she whispered, so softly I thought I had imagined it. But the tortured look on my sister's face told me I had not misheard. "I left without thinking about you. I was mad that you weren't doing what I wanted. That I was not in control anymore. I…I failed you, Bridget. I'm sorry."

Her speech ended with a sob and I patted the spot on the bad next to me. With a nod, Kara crawled up beside me, gingerly wrapping her arm around me and laying her head lightly on my shoulder.

"Does this mean you forgive me?"

"Yes. I already had." I leaned my head on top of hers. "But why did you stay away?"

"I was scared of what you would say. We also went and stopped Ronan."

"You captured him?"

"No." Kara shuddered. "I killed him."

"What?"

Kara sat up, a small grimace on her face. "He stabbed Everett in the shoulder and was trying to kill Silas. So, I stopped him."

"Kara." I reached out to her and she curled back up beside me. Another sob shook her shoulders and I held her while she cried. This time, I had to be the strong one, and I liked it.

After a while, her cries lessened, and she sniffed. "I'm getting married."

"To Everett." It wasn't a question. I had seen the love in my sister's eyes for him.

"Yes. And—"

A knock sounded on the door and a head popped through. A beautiful blond head with icy blue eyes that found me immediately.

"Can I talk to her?" Silas asked. "Please?"

It sounded important, urgent, yet Kara smiled, glancing at me while nodding at Silas.

"I'll be back soon." She kissed my head. "I love you, Bridget."

"I love you too, Kara."

Kara glided out the door, letting the latch click closed. Silas stood in front of it, his gaze arresting mine. He demanded my full attention. I was acutely aware of every breath he took, every jerk of his fingers as they nervously tapped against his leg.

"Are you going to stand there," I asked, "or are you going to come talk to me?"

Silas' mouth twitched as he stepped closer, but he still did not speak. His fingers tapped faster as he stopped beside me.

"What's wrong?" I asked.

"I want to do this right." He swallowed, rubbing the back of his neck. "But I'm suddenly at a loss for words." He swallowed, rubbing the back of his neck.

"Words for what?"

Silas shoved his hand into his pocket, drawing out a simple gold ring. "Father said it would be Kara's and your punishment for stealing from Allura and Hillingsfarth. But what he did not know was you're still stealing. From the moment I saw you up in the blasted oak tree, I haven't been able to stop thinking about you, worrying about you, wanting to know more about you."

He sucked in a breath, his eyes meeting mine. They burned with intensity. "Bridget, you stole my heart. It's yours. And I want you to keep it for the rest of our lives, if only you will give me yours in return."

My chest ached, but not from the bruises. "Silas, what are you saying?"

He reached for my hand, staring at it as he pinched the golden band between his thumb and forefinger. "Bridget of Hillingsfarth Forest, I love you. And I would be honored if you would agree to be my wife." He dragged his gaze to mine again. I could barely breathe.

"Do you mean that?" I whispered. "You want me? You're not going to run out on me someday?"

"Bridget"—he waited to continue until I looked up at him—"you have my heart. It's yours. No one can take it away, save God above. And until He takes one of us, we will be one in His sight. I want to love, cherish, and protect you for the rest of my life. Please, marry me?"

A tear trailed down my cheek as I nodded, my voice gone. Silas smiled, as brilliant as the sun slipping out from behind a cloud. He pushed the band onto my hand before dropping to one knee. Gently, he turned my face to his, pressing his lips against mine. His thumb caressed my cheek as he pulled back, our noses brushing in the process.

"Thank you." His eyes sparkled. "You've made me the happiest man in the world."

"You are far too good for me, Silas."

"And you are far too wild. But that is the beauty in us. We balance each other."

"Yes, that we do." I grinned as his lips caught mine again.

I smiled at the sight that was my room. News had quickly spread that I had said yes to Silas, and soon all the friends and family had piled in to eat a meal with us. Everett, determined not to miss the fun, was sitting on the settee by the fire. Kara hovered around him, and I could tell by the smirk on Everett's face that he was thoroughly enjoying the attention.

Silas had pulled a chair to my side and entwined his hand with mine. His smile had not wavered since I had said yes. I found it hard to pull my gaze from him and the joy he was radiating around the warm room.

Brylee, with Prince's Lachlan at her side, glided up to me. "I am truly so happy for the both of you. I wish you could come to our wedding tomorrow."

"I'm sure it will be lovely. Silas will simply have to tell me about it," I said.

"Seeing as he is now the best man, he has no choice but to attend!" Everett called from the other side of the room, earning a light smack on his good shoulder from my sister.

Silas smirked. "It appears as though you're easily replaced, Everett!"

"Silas!" Brylee exclaimed, but she was laughing. "Honestly, considering the two of you are going to be brothers-in-law, you could at least attempt to get along."

"But this is more entertaining," Lachlan whispered loudly, and I couldn't help the giggle that slipped out.

"Don't tell them that!" Brylee huffed. "Come, let's go talk to Aunt Aurora before you fill my cousin's ego further."

"Ego, hm?" I asked after they had left and Silas shrugged, still smirking.

More faces walked past, more names to try and remember.

Nettie, Silas' sister.

Far too many cousins whose names I would never remember.

Prince Nicholas and Princess Della, Silas' uncle and aunt.

Prince Collins, who had helped stop my brother and his thieves.

King Benjamin and Queen Aurora, who were far less intimidating than I had expected. Queen Aurora had smiled kindly at me, while King Benjamin had welcomed me into the family. His eyes, the same shade as his son's, also held the same warmth and love that Silas had in his. They were going to be my family. My parents.

I sucked in a breath, realization dawning. Everyone in this room was going to become family in some way. Cousins, sisters, brothers, parents, uncles and aunts. I was never going to be alone again. I had found people who were ready to love me, and I them.

I squeezed Silas' hand, smiling up at him.

"Thank you," I whispered, as he leaned his head lightly against mine.

"What for?" he whispered back.

"For staying." I sighed contentedly, my smile growing at the thought. "Thank you for remaining with me through all of this."

"Always, Bridget. Until our dying day." He pressed a kiss against my temple. "You're stuck with me now."

"Yes. And there's no one better for me than you."

No one better at all.

EPILOGUE

TWO WEEKS LATER...

Collins wrapped an arm around Bridget's waist, Sage standing on her other side as they helped her down the aisle. It was slow going. Each step was agonizingly paced to put as little weight on Bridget's bad ankle as possible. Her face was pinched with concentration. She was determined, Collins would give her that.

"Almost there, sweetie." Sage's soft words of encouragement made Collins smile as he caught sight of his nephew waiting at the altar. His eyes were suspiciously glassy as he stared at his bride.

Everett stood on the other side of the altar, Kara already beside him. Her red gown shone in the sunlight that poured through the windows behind the priest who was waiting for Bridget to reach the end of the aisle.

"There we are." Collins sighed, letting Silas wrap his arm around his bride before stepping back and sinking onto the bench beside Sage.

It was a short ceremony. Everett and Silas both slipped the rings on the girls' fingers, speaking their vows with strong, loud voices. The girls were quieter with their vows, but strength and sincerity were in the words. Bridget's voice wobbled at the end when she added, "My heart has been captured by you, Silas. I vow to treasure it like the jewel it is."

A tear trailed down Silas' cheek, causing tears to fill Bridget's eyes. Collins sniffed, somewhat loudly, and Sage elbowed him in the ribs in dismay.

"I now pronounce you, Everett and Kara, husband and wife in the sight of God and these witnesses. Everett, you may kiss your bride."

Everett tugged Kara to himself and kissed her deeply. She was cautious, trying to avoid jostling his right shoulder. When she eased back, however, a large smile was on her face.

"And now I pronounce you, Silas and Bridget, husband and wife in the sight of God and these witnesses. You may now kiss your bride, Silas."

Silas grinned, swooping Bridget up into his arms before leaning in and kissing her. He picked her up off her feet and spun, causing Bridget to wrap her arms around his neck before he pulled back, grin still in place.

"I give you Sir Everett and Kara of Hillingsfarth!" A cheer rang through the chapel and Collins grinned out over his family, new and old, before turning back to the couples before him.

"And I give you Prince Silas and Princess Bridget, heirs of Allura!"

The family could be contained no longer. They stepped forward, slapping backs, shaking hands, and kissing cheeks. Sage's hand slipped into his, her head resting on his shoulder as they waited for some of the crowd to dissipate.

"Did you ever wonder?" Sage asked.

"Wonder what?"

"What the future was going to look like when we wed over twenty years ago?"

Collins cocked his head. "I was blissfully happy that day. I still am. Yet, we've both grown wiser. More aware."

"I know we've had our share of struggles, but here is something so wonderful. So beautiful. It's something

I never would have imagined experiencing when I met you."

"Yes. I promised you then that I would protect you." Collins pressed a kiss to the top of his wife's head.

"And you have. You have been by my side for all the highs and the lows."

"I'll always be there, love. Always."

As they moved to greet the happy new couples, Collins breathed a prayer of gratitude heavenward. God had blessed his family beyond measure. He might not know what was to come, yet Collins knew that God would be with them through it all. His love would hold them together.

No matter what.

THE END

ANNA AUGUSTINE

A *Love* LIKE *Ours*

A *Love* LIKE *Ours*

NOTE FROM THE AUTHOR

It seems crazy to think that these stories—and this book as a whole—have existed for nearly a year. I knew as soon as I wrote *It Came Upon a Midnight Clear* that I had a world I could explore. Benjamin, Nicholas, and Collins had kids, and oh what stories they had coming.

I finished Thad and Amirah's story almost directly after *It Came Upon a Midnight Clear*. I knew I wanted to do a Cinderella type story with them, and it just fit for it to be about being worthy of love and acceptance, no matter our differences. Writing Thad's hearing loss was a challenge, but was also what a lot of my beta readers loved most about it, which was super encouraging.

Then came Brylee and Lachlan. At first, I had a completely different opening chapter for them where we see the events of the fateful kiss from Brylee's point of view. But a beta reader pointed out that it built the suspense if we didn't know what happened between them right away, and so I cut out the entire thing. (Seriously, it's one of the hardest things to do). Halfway through their story, I got stuck. Brylee was left soaking in her tub for months, until God slowly revealed the story he had for them. Theirs is a story that wasn't based off any fairytale or bible story, but rather a Biblical truth. Forgiveness—something I've personally grappled with God about—was hard to write, but I know the freeing power of it, and I hope you see it in Brylee and Lachlan's story.

And lastly—Silas, Everett, Bridget, and Kara. This one was created thanks to my sister, Abby. She made note that a lot of my characters are pretty outspoken. "You don't have any passive aggressive characters," she said. Enter…Bridget. I based a lot of her personality after my sister, from her silence until she blows, to her willingness to keep the peace with Kara. This story was twist on Robin Hood, but what if he were a bad guy? Ronan of Merryington was that version of Robin Hood, with the girls playing at what Robin Hood was in the stories. It was fun, challenging, and the climax of this one changed a number of times as well.

I also want to make note of the dates. These stories are a non-magical fantasy, meaning that they have similar aspects to our world, but in a fictional land. Allura doesn't exist, therefore, I took some liberties in what they have/don't have, their manner of speech, and so on. The dates on the family tree are mainly so I don't mess up ages and times, but also for you to be able to keep up as well. Hopefully, it's a tool more than a hinderance.

ACKNOWLEDGEMENTS

There are so many people to thank for this project. Writing a book really does take a village, and I'm so thankful for all my people!

First off, to Jesus: the Giver of stories, the Author of the world, and the Creator of the creative. Thank you for helping me to bare Your heart on the page, for sloshing Your love into the words written, for giving me an imagination that longs to glorify You. Thank You so much. None of this would be possible without You.

Next, to my family. My cheerleaders and supporters in every sense of the word. Without them, half of the banter, relationships, and zest in these stories would be lacking. Thank you for putting up with my scribbles, rambles, and fangirling over this world. I love you all so, so much!

To my hype squad: Nathaniel, Anna, Eve, and Alexis. Thank you guys for being there to bounce ideas off of, dig myself out of plot holes, and for literally being the reason these characters exist on page. I'm so thankful that Instagram brought us together, and I'm so blessed to call you friends.

To my alpha/beta readers: Alejandra, Ashlee, Brigitte, Jenessa, Joelle, Lily, Lorelei, Maryam, Natalie, Rosalynn, Serena, Sofia Tejomai, Victoria, and Virginia. Thank you all so very much for your feedback. This story wouldn't be what it is without y'all and I'm very happy you were willing to take the time and effort to make this book beautiful!

To my editors: Anne, Isabella, and Kyrsten. Thank you, thank you, THANK YOU for all your edits. Seriously, this book would have been a whole lot worse for wear if it weren't for your helpful suggestions, typo catches, and punctuation flops. I'm thankful for all your hard work.

To my formatter: Victoria, you were such a trooper with me! I am so thankful you fit me into your schedule and made my book so beautiful! Thankful for your encouragement and joy for these stories!

And last, but not least, to YOU, the reader: thank you for taking a chance on this indie author. Thank you for picking up this book and diving into the world of Allura, and the characters that have lived in my head—rent free—for the last two years. Thank you for taking time to read these stories. I hope they bless you.

ABOUT THE AUTHOR

Anna Augustine is the author of the romantic fantasy novella collection *When You Found Me* and the companion short story *It Came Upon a Midnight Clear*. She has been a part of a number of anthologies, including *The Depths Will Go To* complied by Alex Silvis and *Aphotic Love* complied by Effie Jo Stock. Her a number of her flash fiction piece have also been featured on Havok—a website for speculative fiction stories under a thousand words. *A Love Like Ours* is her second novella collection.

Anna lives with her family of eight in a small, midwestern town with two dogs and a whole lot of crazy. When she's not writing, she is either working as a teacher's aide in her local elementary school, taking photos for her bookstagram, or trying to put a dent in her never ending to be read pile.

Follow her on Instagram! @anna_augustine_author

NEED SOME NEW TUNES?

Check out the A Love Like Ours Playlist on Spotify!

AESTHETIC LOVER?

Check out The Princes of Allura boards on Printerst!

9 781736 539149